A BODY? REALLY?

"You're sure he's dead?" she asked.

Six faces turned to look at her. The only one she recognized was Jon Avramson, not only because he wasn't wearing a balaclava but because he was easily a head taller than anyone else there.

"What the hell do you think?" he asked.

Kate took a deep breath to control a spike of anger and immediately regretted it as the cold air froze the inside of her nostrils.

One of the figures stirred and a stray beam of light caught the reflective fabric of his armband. There was a bright red cross on it.

"No pulse, no respiration and there's morbid lividity," said the paramedic, confirming her guess as to his gender.

"He's dead."

BOOKS BY THE AUTHOR

Mendenhall Mysteries series:

The Shoeless Kid
The Tuxedoed Man
The Weeping Woman

On Her Trail

THE TUXEDOED MAN

by

MARCELLE DUBÉ

FALCON RIDGE PUBLISHING

THE TUXEDOED MAN
Copyright © 2011 by Marcelle Dubé

All rights reserved, including the right of reproduction,
in whole or in part in any form.

Published in 2012 by Falcon Ridge Publishing
www.falconridgepublishing.com

Cover art copyright © 2011 AISPIX by Image Source/Shutterstock
Cover art copyright © 2011 pictureguy/depositphoto
Book and cover design copyright © 2012 Falcon Ridge Publishing

ISBN: 978-0-9918746-0-6

This book is licensed for your personal enjoyment only. All rights reserved. This is a work of fiction. All characters and events portrayed in this book are fictional, and any resemblance to real people or incidents is purely coincidental. This book, or parts thereof, may not be reproduced in any form without permission.

For Josée
Thanks for always being there.

Acknowledgments

My thanks to Dennis Berry, Fire Marshal with the Government of Yukon; Chris MacPherson, Emergency Management Planning Coordinator, also with the Government of Yukon; and Constable Andrew West, with the RCMP "M" Division, for their patience and willingness to answer all my questions. (And special thanks to Constable West for the ride along—too cool!) Any errors and infelicities rest at my door, not theirs.

www.marcellemdube.com

THETUXEDOED**MAN**

by

MARCELLE DUBÉ

*To Marilyn,
I hope you enjoy meeting Kate!
Marcelle Dubé
Christmas 2013*

CHAPTER 1

Kate Williams squinted at the two HazMat guys as they scurried around the derailed freight train, their headlamps bobbing like will-o'-the-wisps over the snow-packed, night-shrouded prairie. In their blue HazMat suits and helmets, they looked like astronauts exploring the remains of an abandoned civilization on a cold, long-dead world.

At least, that's what they would have looked like if it weren't for the half-dozen victims milling around them, tugging on their suits, crying out for their attention.

While the drama unfolded only a hundred yards from where Kate and the other emergency responders stood on the shoulder of the closed Trans-Canada Highway, she had to strain to hear what was happening at the crash site. Between the constant radio chatter, the shouted observations of the dozen men and women huddling with her on the wind-polished highway, and the constant background hum of vehicle engines all around her, she could barely make out the increasingly shrill shouting of the walking wounded.

There would be no help for those poor people until the HazMat guys determined that the scene was safe for the responders. She hoped no one would freeze to death while they waited.

Ice fog rolled in from the Assiniboine River, settling in low-lying areas, further obscuring visibility. Or maybe that was wood smoke from nearby Burndale.

Jon Avramson, Mendenhall's fire chief, had organized his men in teams to carry the equipment that would free the passengers trapped in the Blueline bus. It had been T-boned by the train and pushed hundreds of yards past the railroad crossing. Kate counted six still figures lying in the snow around the wreck, where they had been thrown by the impact. There was no telling how many more were on the other side, out of sight.

The paramedics were distributing backboards to any responder with free hands. There wouldn't be enough boards, but she could already hear sirens coming from the west. That would be Brandon's emergency responders coming to help. She hoped Winnipeg would show up soon—they were going to need the help.

She glanced down at the accident site. If she was cold, what was it like for the passengers trapped inside the bus? What about those still, still figures lying in the snow?

Next to her, a paramedic kept repeating into a megaphone, "If you can walk, please move to the flag. Move to the flag." His voice sounded tinny and barely cut through the din.

The HazMat guys had planted a post with a flag a hundred feet away from the wreck. It had a battery-operated repeating light at the top to attract attention, but the light kept stuttering in the brutal cold and Kate expected it to fail at any moment.

The wreck looked stable enough to her. The locomotive and an empty flatbed car were still upright but the other two railcars had had flipped over. It could have been worse. It could have been a passenger train. Kate's concern focused on the bus that the train had broadsided. The train had crushed the middle of the bus, wrapping both ends around the locomotive. The bus's headlights were still on, illuminating tendrils of ice fog and two dark shapes slumped and unmoving in the snow.

If anyone cried for help from the destroyed bus, she couldn't hear them. The crash site was down an embankment that flattened out to the railroad bed, about halfway between the highway and the forest beyond. Not that far. Not beyond help, if they could only *get* there.

Red lights flashed from fire trucks, ambulances, and squad

cars, reflecting off the snow and against the forest beyond the crash site, which could probably be seen from space. It was two-thirty on a frigidly cold Manitoba morning in February and ice fog had deposited a layer of black ice on the highway. Only a fool or a trucker would be out in these conditions.

"What the hell is taking so long?" muttered Avramson next to her. The fire chief was a burly man made even burlier by his insulated firefighter suit. His attention was fixed on his two men down at the crash site. The Brandon sirens were getting closer, but Kate couldn't hear anything coming from Winnipeg. What was taking Bert's crew so long?

Bert Langdon, Deputy Chief of the Winnipeg Police Department, was supposed to have been here fifteen minutes ago.

She sensed Avramson's gaze on her but ignored him. For tonight, she wasn't the chief of police. Constable Boychuk was acting chief of police. Once he determined that the crash wasn't actually a crime scene, Avramson could take over. But Dan Boychuk couldn't get down to the scene until the HazMat guys gave the all clear.

Although, frankly, the chances of any chemical going volatile at minus thirty Celsius were pretty damned slim.

At last one of the HazMat guys straightened from the equipment he had been studying and put one arm straight up in the air.

At once, a figure detached itself from the crowd on the highway and descended to the ditch, where an enterprising paramedic had set a backboard as a bridge. Boychuk hurried across and up the other side into the field. Various flashlights caught the reflective tape on the back of his parka that read POLICE in big white letters.

Behind her, car doors opened as her constables left their patrol cars.

Boychuk struggled through the snow, deliberately not matching the footprints already there. He was tamping down the trail. When he reached the wreck, the two HazMat guys fell in beside him as he began a circuit around the wreck to determine for himself that this wasn't a crime scene before he turned responsibility over to Avramson. Immediately, three walking wounded headed for him. Boychuk paused and spoke to one of the HazMat guys, who moved away from the other two and drew the walking wounded with him. He started herding them toward the flag. Boychuk and the remaining HazMat guy continued their circuit, disappearing behind the wreck.

Kate found herself holding her breath as she waited for them to reappear. The voices around her gradually faded into tense silence as the minutes ticked by. The cries of the victims rose on the air, thin, wretched, and impossible to shut out.

Finally, Boychuk and his shadow emerged from the far side of the wreck and made their way back to where they had started. A moment later, Boychuk's voice sounded on the common channel of the Emergency Measures Organization radio in her inside pocket.

"This is Police One. All clear. I repeat. All clear."

At once the paramedics plunged across the ditch, carrying backboards and heavy first aid kits. Someone had laid another backboard across the ditch in preparation for the go-ahead, and now the rest of the emergency responders swarmed across, led by Avramson, who called out, "Come on, ladies!"

While waiting her turn to cross, Kate turned clumsily to check EMO's Site Command tent that was still being erected in the flat, empty space between the eastbound and westbound lanes of the Trans Canada. EMO had arrived twenty minutes ago, and now a cluster of parka-clad figures moved purposefully in the harsh illumination of a portable flood light.

A movement in her peripheral vision caught her attention and she pushed her hood aside to see someone approaching from the left. Like Kate, the figure was bundled in a heavy red parka, with black snowpants and the ubiquitous white Sorels. A velcroed, reflective white armband read "EMO" in bright red letters.

Took you long enough, Kate thought. She had expected Alexandra Kowalski to show up much earlier, keeping her eagle eye on everybody.

At last Kowalski stopped next to her. "Forty-three minutes," she said.

Kate nodded. "Not bad." All things considered.

"Too long," Kowalski snapped. "We'll have lost some people

who could have been saved."

Kate wanted to point out that the HazMat guys had worked as fast as they could but that might set Kowalski off. Or she might shrug it off. Kate never knew how Kowalski would react to any given situation.

As an experiment, Kate said, "It *is* minus thirty."

Kowalski was also wearing her balaclava pulled up, although the hood of her parka extended far enough to protect her face from the worst of the wind. The hood created a kind of cave from which only the slash of a smile could be seen.

"Disasters don't wait for warm weather."

Really? That was the best she could do?

Kate stared at the shadowed face but couldn't see Kowalski's eyes. All she could think of were those poor people lying in the snow.

Without a word, she pulled down the balaclava to cover her face. Her constables would have to guess who she was by height. She was, after all, the shortest member of the Mendenhall Police Department. Immediately, her cheeks began to burn as circulation returned to her poor face.

"Have you seen any reporters?" asked Kowalski.

Kate shook her head. She doubted they would see any media. It was the middle of the night and it was bloody cold. Besides, EMO would submit pictures to the media in the next couple of days.

Below, dark figures swarmed over the white snow, headlamps bobbing, flashlights searching. She tucked the bottom of the balaclava into her scarf and sighed.

Show time.

* * *

"Don't try to move." The paramedic kept his hand firmly on the victim's shoulder. He didn't even look up as Kate crunched by. A yellow card rested on the victim's parka-covered chest, indicating this one's injuries were Priority Two. Not at immediate risk but needing attention.

She kept the recorder inside her right mitten to keep it warm. Every once in a while, she pulled her hand out of her mitten to say a few words into the tiny machine. She trusted her memory, but the recording would be turned over to EMO to form part of the official record of the exercise.

It was a nice change to be an adjudicator rather than a respondent in one of these exercises. Her job was to observe and take notes of what had worked well during the exercise and what hadn't, which was why she had made Boychuk acting chief for the duration of the exercise.

She didn't mind being an adjudicator. It sure beat having to haul "victims" around on a backboard. Although, frankly, she was getting too old for this crap. At fifty-three, she should be back at the station coordinating the Mendenhall Police Department's response from her warm office, not tromping through the snow in the middle of the night in the middle of a Manitoba cold snap. She *was* the chief of police, after all.

The snow was hard packed beneath the top six inches, which had the consistency of granulated sugar. It was hard hauling her heavy Sorels through it, but at least she wouldn't be getting soaked. And the work was warming her up.

This was her first Manitoba winter and she had yet to see a snowman anywhere. The snow was too dry. Like her skin.

Temperatures rarely dipped below minus twenty, they had all told her. And yet, here she was, at three o'clock in the morning, freezing her butt off for an exercise that was supposed to have been called off once the thermometer hit minus twenty.

Thank you, Alexandra Kowalski.

At minus thirty, the cold air hitting the warmer open water of the Assiniboine created ice fog in low-lying areas, according to her Deputy Chief, Rob McKell. She'd never heard of ice fog before moving here. Frankly, she could have lived another fifty-three years without experiencing it.

Dark figures, occasionally brightened by a beam of light, moved purposefully in and out of her field of vision. Men and women called to each other and the injured moaned or cursed, depending on their supposed injuries. Already half a dozen victims had been carried across the field and into the waiting ambulances. She suspected a few of the fake victims would end up with very real frostbite.

Her Blackberry rumbled against her flesh, startling her. She had tucked it in her bra, since both inside parka pockets were already occupied with her police radio and the EMO radio. She fumbled her down mitten off and unzipped the parka to fish through her shirt for the phone. She hissed as the cold air unerringly found her exposed flesh. Finally she pulled the phone out and stared at the lit touch screen, trying to find the right button. There. She touched the tiny icon and pressed the phone to her ear over the balaclava.

"Williams," she said.

"It's Bert."

"Hey," she said, staring at the activity by the train. "Where are you?" She had expected the Winnipeg crew much earlier.

"Still in Winnipeg," he replied. "Six-car pileup on Portage." His voice was clear and crisp in her ear and she could almost imagine that he was standing next to her. "And a suspicious fire on North Main, with injuries. It's going to be at least half an hour before we can spare anyone to attend."

Kate nodded. Bert should really be talking to Boychuk, but what the heck. So it would be at least an hour and a half until the Winnipeg Police Department showed up, since Winnipeg was almost an hour away. "Ambulances?"

"One's on the way now, and they'll send a couple more as soon as they can."

The EMO rep from Canadian Forces Base Shilo passed her, talking into his radio. He was the only one with a khaki parka. She had met him at the first tabletop exercise five months ago, when this mock accident had only been a gleam in Alexandra Kowalski's eye.

"Kowalski's going to be pissed," she warned.

"I know," said Bert equably. "But she's usually pissed about something. Gotta go. Call you later."

Kate found the disconnect button and stashed the icy phone back in her bra. Then she turned back to the scene.

As EMO director, Kowalski had done a good job of setting up the accident, much as Kate hated to admit it. The woman must be more persuasive than Kate had given her credit for. There was no federal money in this exercise, but Kowalski had managed to persuade Manitoba Rail to donate the use of a locomotive and a few decommissioned freight cars. And Manitoba Rail had donated the transport costs, too.

Now, the bus, that was pure genius. Kowalski had convinced the CEO of the Blueline Bus Company to let them use a bus that had been in an accident and was still in their Winnipeg compound.

Alex Kowalski was one determined woman. And young to be in charge of a full-blown exercise. Kate figured Kowalski to be in her mid-twenties, with an almost permanent scowl that made her look older.

A sharp cry pierced the air and everyone stopped to look in that direction before resuming their work. In spite of herself, Kate felt a laugh well to the surface. The Brandon University drama department had supplied most of the "victims" for the exercise. Base Shilo had supplied a few soldiers, too. And some off-duty Emergency Medical Services staff had volunteered.

She'd been through at least a dozen of these exercises over the years, in different parts of the country, and in every one, the EMS volunteers were the sneakiest ones. They knew better than anyone how a dangerous injury could masquerade as something minor, and they loved tripping up their colleagues.

She kept moving to convince her toes they were still needed. Emergency Measures had four other people doing exactly as she was, watching the emergency responders and taking notes about what was working well and what needed improvement. Flashes went off regularly as the other observers took photos. There were supposed to be a couple of volunteers filming, although she suspected the equipment wouldn't cooperate at these temperatures.

She didn't have a camera. She figured she would have enough problems with the recorder. Besides, she could always use her new Blackberry to take photos. If she could figure out how.

She studied the entire scene but paid particular attention to her constables. This was a golden opportunity to see them under pressure and identify any training that might be needed. She'd been in Mendenhall less than a year, and except for the incident last fall where they'd had to track down a missing boy and deal with his deranged mother, there hadn't been anything more exciting than fender-benders and the Saturday Night Drunk Parade.

So far, her constables were doing all right. She had assigned the exercise to the ones who had the least experience. Boychuk had already sent Parker to the roadblock to relieve Fallon so he could warm up. Good. Boychuk was paying attention to his men, in spite of everything that was going on around him.

That left Friesen and Trepalli. She hadn't seen them in a while.

A familiar voice rose above the din. "I have a bleeder here!"

Good lord, was that Ben Friesen? A *bleeder*? How dramatic.

Her Blackberry rumbled against her chest again, startling her. She scrambled to pull it out, almost dropping the recorder in the process.

"Williams," she finally managed.

"Avramson." The fire chief's voice sounded very close. Why was he calling her on the cell phone? Why was he calling her at all? "How many victims we supposed to have?"

"Twenty-four on the bus and two on the train," replied Kate promptly. She resumed walking before her feet could turn into blocks of ice.

There was a long silence before he said. "We count twenty-seven."

Kate passed four figures hauling a moaning victim out on a backboard. She grinned. "I wouldn't put it past EMO to slip in a ringer."

"Well, this one's dead."

Kate stopped walking. Dead?

"Repeat, please." She waited for what seemed like an eternity before he finally spoke again.

"I think you need to come here," said Avramson. "I don't think this guy's part of the exercise."

CHAPTER 2

THE DEAD man wasn't wearing a coat or boots. He didn't have mittens or gloves, or even a hat. He was, however, wearing black dress pants, a snowy white shirt with gold cuff links, a black silk bow tie, and an honest-to-God cummerbund. His shirt was rucked up beneath him.

A layer of frost covered the body, obscuring the features and turning the black pants white in spots.

A half dozen people stood looking down at the body in silence. Their flashlights barely cut through the ice fog swirling around them, first hiding, then revealing the body. Kate couldn't even tell if there was a paramedic among them.

"You're sure he's dead?" she asked.

Six faces turned to look at her. The only one she recognized was Jon Avramson, not only because he wasn't wearing a balaclava but because he was easily a head taller than anyone else there.

"What the hell do you think?" he asked.

Kate took a deep breath to control a spike of anger and immediately regretted it as the cold air froze the inside of her nostrils. She wore the best balaclava she could find and still the cold reached greedy fingers through it.

One of the figures stirred and a stray beam of light caught the reflective fabric of his armband. There was a bright red cross on it.

"No pulse, no respiration and there's morbid lividity," said the paramedic, confirming her guess as to his gender. "He's dead."

Kate looked around. The body was about a hundred feet from the derailed train cars and the bus, between the wreck and the forest. Nowhere near the rest of the victims. Not surprising that Boychuk hadn't seen it on his initial walk around.

"Did anyone touch the body, besides you?" she asked the paramedic.

"Yes," said Avramson before the medic could reply. "I checked for a pulse before I sent for a paramedic."

"Who found him?"

Avramson looked around at the masked faces and hesitated. "I'm not sure."

"Your HazMat guys didn't see him?"

He scowled. "If they did, they would have thought he was part of the exercise, wouldn't they?"

Really? In a tux with no shoes or coat? The HazMat guys clearly hadn't seen him, either.

Kate stepped away from the group and fished her EMO radio out of its warm pocket.

"This is Chief of Police Williams," she said. "No duff, no duff, no duff."

The radio crackled, then fell silent. In the obscuring fog, voices fell silent one by one as those who hadn't heard the code were told by those who had. Only the voices of the remaining "victims" could be heard.

Her radio beeped to signal an incoming message.

"This is EMO One," came Kowalski's voice. "Report."

Kate couldn't tell what the woman was thinking from the sound of her voice, but she could guess. Kowalski's beautiful exercise was now shot to hell.

"This is Chief Williams," said Kate crisply. "This exercise is now ended. I repeat: the exercise is now ended."

"Oh, for Christ's sake!" said Avramson over the murmurs of the others.

Kate ignored him and turned the volume down on the EMO radio as Kowalski demanded an explanation, although she could still hear the woman squawking on Avramson's radio. She stuck her EMO radio back in her pocket and pulled out the police radio.

"This is Chief Williams," she said. "All officers except those on the barricade report to me. I am located south of the wreck. Look for flashlights."

She turned back to the small group and found them all watching her. At least she thought they were watching her. It was hard to tell between the balaclavas and the hoods.

"I need you all to step away from the body," she said firmly. She pointed at a spot twenty feet from her but well away from the body. "Over there. We will need to take your statements before you can go."

There was still squawking coming from the EMO radio, so she pulled it out, turned up the volume and interrupted Kowalski.

"EMO One, you need to stand down," she said. "This is now a crime scene."

The figures around the body hadn't budged. Avramson hadn't budged. Jesus Murphy. She pulled up her balaclava to reveal her face and raised her voice.

"Move!"

Avramson scowled at her again but finally moved.

* * *

The first one to show up was Marco Trepalli. At least, she thought it was Trepalli. He rounded the end of the train wreck at a clumsy run. Kate suspected his Sorels were too big. She'd seen him back at the station pulling on two pairs of thick, hand-knit socks. She turned the flashlight on him to attract his attention and waited while he angled toward her and the body.

He slowed to a walk as he got nearer and finally stumbled to a halt a few feet away from her. He pulled up his balaclava.

"Chief," he said, not even breathing hard.

"We have a body," she said flatly. "Stand by."

He stared at her uncomprehendingly, his headlight blinding her, until she nodded toward the body. He turned his body and finally pushed off his hood so that he could see more clearly. Fog swirled around the body, first hiding, then revealing it.

She caught his sharp intake of breath and his start of surprise.

"Williams, are you there?" Alexandra Kowalski's voice almost shouted from Trepalli's radio. Trepalli looked up from the dead body, a question on his face.

"Williams!" Kowalski's voice was growing louder.

"Turn it down," Kate ordered. When he did, she put the police radio up to her mouth. "Boychuk?"

It took a moment, but Boychuk answered. "Chief?"

"Find EMO One and bring her with you."

"Yes, ma'am."

Not that she wanted Kowalski to join them, but it was better to bring her in early. Poor Boychuk. Not only was he going to be stuck with an angry Kowalski, but his moment to shine as the police lead for the exercise had been snatched away from him.

She glanced around again, to reassure herself that Boychuk wasn't at fault. There was no way he could have seen the body. Not with the distance, the lack of lights on this side of the wreck, and the ice fog.

Two more figures rounded the wreck and hurried toward the cluster of lights formed by Avramson and his crew. Kate flashed her light on and off to redirect them toward her. It wasn't until she saw their name tags that she knew they were Terry Fallon and Ben Friesen.

They glanced around until they saw the body, then they looked at her.

"Friesen, connect with EMO," she said without preamble. "They need to get the bus back to haul all these witnesses out."

One of them groaned and she would have frowned except that she understood the sentiment. This was now a crime scene, which meant they had to interview every single volunteer and emergency responder, including the organizers, but they couldn't do it on site. It was just too cold. So they would have to remove the witnesses from the scene and find a warm location for the interviews, while containing the scene and investigating it.

It was going to be a long night.

"Call Albertson on the duty desk," she continued, still looking at Friesen. "Tell him to get the principal of Henrietta Blum School to open up the gymnasium for us. We're going to need to keep these people warm while we get their statements." Friesen nodded before taking off.

Kate turned to Fallon. "I want you to start with this group," she said in a low voice. "They were first on scene. Get their names and particulars, then pull them out for the first interviews when the gym is set up." Fallon nodded and headed for the small group clustered around Avramson.

Next Kate turned to Marco Trepalli. She was pretty sure this was his first body, but rookie or not, she didn't have time to coddle him.

"Constable," she began. At that moment, a dark figure hurried around the east end of the wreck, flashlight bobbing wildly, and came to a stop next to her.

"What the hell are you doing?" panted Alexandra Kowalski. She had pushed back her hood and now she yanked off the balaclava as if it were strangling her. "Do you have any idea…" Her voice trailed off as she followed the beam of Trepalli's flashlight to the body. "Who the hell is that?"

"You don't recognize him?" asked Kate. She'd held out a faint hope—however unrealistic—that this was one of Kowalski's volunteers. She peered at the corpse, in case it was someone she had seen before, but between the ice fog and the frost, the body could have belonged to one of her constables and she wouldn't have been able to tell.

As the EMO director for the exercise, Kowalski was supposed to have a record of every volunteer, and a site map with the location of every victim. Someone on her staff would have one duty: identifying every victim who was loaded onto an ambulance.

"He's not one of mine," said Kowalski, shaking her head. "At least, I don't think so. Looks like the jackass got drunk and chose the wrong place to pass out."

Kate privately agreed, but she wasn't about to say so. "Trepalli, is there any ID on him?"

He started with surprise and swallowed hard, but he squatted by the body. He removed his mittens to search through the victim's pockets.

Good boy. Her first dead body had been a homeless man in Moncton, in the middle of winter. She could still remember the feel of his frozen flesh through the thin lining of his pockets.

Her Blackberry rumbled again and she pulled it out impatiently. "Williams."

"It's Boychuk," said the voice at the other end. "I can't find her."

What the hell was he talking about? Then she remembered. "She's here," she said. "We're going to need lighting here, good enough for pictures. See if you can borrow the floodlight at the Site Command tent." She tucked the phone back inside her bra and waited for Trepalli to finish. She could hear Avramson's deep voice answering Fallon's questions, but otherwise the scene was oddly silent. Even Kowalski couldn't seem to stop staring at the body.

After a moment, Trepalli stood up and replaced his mittens.

"Nothing." He cleared his throat. "No wallet, nothing."

"Look," said Kowalski suddenly. "I know you have to deal with this, but there's no reason the rest of the exercise can't go on. Can't we just cordon off this part?"

Kate took a breath, remembering just in time to keep it shallow. "I'm sorry, Alex. It's over."

"Damn it!" Kowalski's voice was tight with anger. Kate could understand the woman's frustration. She had spent months—and a lot of provincial money—organizing this exercise. Aborting it meant rescheduling it at a later time, at added expense. A *lot* of added expense.

Couldn't be helped.

Kowalski would just have to deal with it. Kate turned to Trepalli, who was back to staring at the body. Only this time, he was frowning.

"What?" asked Kate. "Do you know him?"

Trepalli shook his head. "I don't think so. But he does look familiar."

A person's face looked different in death. Trepalli might eventually remember, especially when the frost on the corpse's face had melted. No use forcing the issue now.

"Help Fallon with the interviews."

Her tone seemed to brace him. "Yes, chief." He turned toward the wreck and the small group stamping their feet to keep from freezing.

Dan Boychuk finally arrived. He pushed back his hood as he came up to her. "I've called it in to the station. The floodlight is too big to haul into the field, but they have a portable one they can let us use. Should do us until it gets light enough." His gaze fell on the dead man and he stopped.

"Good," said Kate briskly. The reactions of her men surprised her. Surely they'd all seen dead bodies before. Any cop had, if only traffic fatalities. The younger ones—Trepalli, Friesen—she could understand their shock, but Boychuk had been a cop for a while.

"Chief," he said uncertainly. "I'm sorry."

She glanced back at him in surprise. "No one saw him, Boychuk. Don't blame yourself. Now. We need to alert Doc Kijawa," she told him. "And get Albertson to pull Tourmeline in." Thank God Stan Albertson was on the duty desk tonight. He was a steady man in a crisis.

Boychuk shook himself. "Tourmeline's on days off."

She nodded. "Call him in. I want him here as soon as it gets light." John Tourmeline wasn't trained as a detective, but he had patience and attention to detail.

"Excuse me!" said Kowalski, stepping in front of Kate to get her attention. The woman loomed over Kate like an angry yeti. "We haven't finished discussing this."

It was now past three thirty and Kate was tired, cold, and hungry. She managed to swallow a sharp retort but couldn't keep the sting out of her tone.

"Yes, we have. I need you to leave the scene. And I need you to provide a list with all the volunteers' names and their locations on the exercise site." She looked up at Alexandra Kowalski's angry face and sighed. She was not going to win Miss Popularity any time soon.

"We need to interview all the volunteers, as well as your staff and the emergency responders." She wished her DC were here. Deputy Chief McKell would take over the interviews. As it was, her constables would have to handle the interviews on their own while she handled the scene. They would have to identify any of the volunteers and responders who had been near the corpse, anyone who might have seen or heard something that would tell her what had happened here.

And they would have to find out how Avramson's crew happened to stumble onto the body when Boychuk and the HazMat guys missed it.

Kowalski glared at her for a long moment, then turned and stomped away.

Boychuk raised his eyebrows and walked off to make his calls.

Kate sighed. Oh yes, it was going to be a long night. "Don't forget to find out where each of the victims was in relationship to the crash," she called. Boychuk didn't answer but raised his hand to indicate he'd heard. His other hand was hidden inside his hood. Kowalski might have a plan for where the victims were supposed to be, but Kate wanted confirmation of where they actually ended up.

That left her alone with the body. A movement in the sky caught her eye and she looked up to see green lights sheeting down in curtain-like folds. The northern lights.

Finally she looked back down at the body and studied the man's face. He had been good looking. His face was a little long, maybe, but he had a strong jaw and well-sculpted lips. He *did* look familiar, but she didn't know from where. Not surprising. Death stole the elasticity of a person's skin, changing the look of the features. Whoever he was, she didn't know him well. His hair was thick and dark, and cut short. It was a little tousled. He lay on his back with his legs straight out and his arms slightly splayed at his sides. His hands were curled into loose fists. His head was aimed at the train and was slightly bent, as if he'd fallen asleep listening. The frost hid any lines and she couldn't tell his age.

There wasn't a mark on him.

It could have been an accident that took his life, but she

couldn't think of any reason why he would have ended up here, in the middle of nowhere, in the middle of the night, wearing most of a tuxedo.

You poor bugger, she thought. *What the hell happened to you?*

CHAPTER 3

At ten-thirty in the morning, the sun glittered on fields covered in three feet of snow sculpted into gentle ripples by the wind. The sky was achingly blue, a blue so uplifting that it raised hope about the goodness of the human heart and the power of resolve. No doubt about it—February in Manitoba was beautiful.

It was also bloody cold.

Despite regular breaks inside the warm Site Command truck and frequent high-protein snacks of cheese and nuts to keep her going, Kate was slowing down. It was mind-numbingly cold on top of the flat car, the best vantage point from which to direct the operation.

All the "victims," firefighters, and paramedics were gone, the ambulance had taken the body back to Mendenhall and the medical examiner, Site Command had packed up, leaving only a skeleton crew to provide shelter and support, and the highway was open.

Both Bert Langdon and Jerry Wolsynuk, her old RCMP friend, had called to offer assistance, but she had turned them down. She didn't need help figuring out what had happened here. Only time.

Now she used binoculars to follow her constables' moves as they criss-crossed the open field, looking for evidence. Tourmeline paralleled the path that led in a straight line from the woods to where they had found the body. Kate could tell already that his search would be fruitless. She'd been studying the path through her binoculars and couldn't tell if the path was made by one man staggering through the snow to his death, or by someone dragging the already-dead man behind him and then walking back over the path.

"Boychuk," she said into her radio.

A crackle and a moment later he responded. "Chief."

She looked around and saw a figure waving at her by the tree line. She raised an arm to indicate she had seen him. "Time to go home," she said.

"All right," he replied, and she thought she detected a note of relief in his voice.

She didn't blame him. He'd been out here all night. Trepalli and Friesen had just about finished searching the woods, and she was going to send them home, too. She had pulled Nick Martins and Kyle Holmes from patrol and they had taken over the last of the interviews at the gym.

McKell was a pain in the ass, but he was also much better at keeping track of personnel than she was. She didn't want to end up calling in a constable who'd just gotten off shift. But her DC was in Ontario looking after his ailing father. No telling when he'd be back.

She ignored the sound of the traffic from the Trans Canada Highway, above and behind her, and looked around the exercise site. Sunlight bounced off the snow, forcing her to squint against the glare. The Burndale road was off to her right, where the EMO truck was parked along with one of her patrol cars. Straight ahead was the line of trees. It was a miniature forest that swept south to the Assiniboine River and east for about a half mile before petering out.

She was willing to bet there was more than one tree fort in there, built by the kids in Burndale.

The radio crackled again and she snapped back to the here and now.

"Found the car, chief."

That was Samantha Paterson, who never bothered to identify herself on the radio, seeing as she was the only other female in the Mendenhall Police Department. She and Russell Oppenheimer had been looking for a vehicle that would have transported their dead man.

"Good," replied Kate. "Call in the plate. Then tow it in. Don't forget pictures."

"Will do," said Paterson. The radio beeped as she broke the connection.

The tension Kate had been carrying in her shoulders eased. Finding the car helped confirm the theory everybody had been working from.

The dead man had probably been at a party. He had probably gotten behind the wheel of his car. Maybe the car had broken down and he'd stumbled out into the cold, looking for help. He could have been attracted by the lights and the activity at the derailment site. Dressed as he was, hypothermia could have gotten him before anyone noticed he was there. He hadn't been reported missing and he'd had no identification on him. Heck, he hadn't even had a handkerchief on him, let alone a wallet. Probably they would find his jacket and wallet in the car. Or in the woods.

All logical. But until she knew for sure, she had to treat this as a suspicious death and investigate. She hadn't smelled any alcohol on him, but she didn't trust her sense of smell at minus thirty. She'd have to wait for Dr. Kijawa to finish examining the body.

"Chief."

She looked down to find John Tourmeline staring up at her. She glanced up at the field, where she'd last seen him.

"Yes, constable?" She let the binoculars hang from the strap around her neck.

"You didn't hear me calling you?" She could tell he was frowning under the navy balaclava.

"What is it?"

"Chief, I think it's time for you to go home," said Tourmeline firmly.

He looked short from this angle. She opened her mouth—to say what, she didn't know—but he forestalled her.

"Ma'am, we're almost done here. There's nothing more you can do that I can't do for you."

Kate felt a grin forming. Who knew Tourmeline had it in him? For the first time, she could believe that he was the father of two young children.

Still.

"I appreciate your concern, constable," she said, "but I'll stay until we're done."

Tourmeline shook his head. As if to emphasize the seriousness of his concern, he pulled up the balaclava to show his face.

"Pardon me, ma'am, but that's wrong-headed, as the DC would say."

Well, yes, that did sound like something DC McKell would say, but DC McKell was precisely why she had to stay. There was no one else to take charge.

"You're not going to have a lot of time to rest," continued Tourmeline relentlessly, "once the doc is finished with the autopsy. There are all those interviews you're going to have to read. Not to mention the report you'll have to fill out after cancelling the exercise." He looked at her critically, as if she were an open book to him. Despite the fact that he couldn't be older than thirty-five and that she was almost twenty years his senior, he suddenly reminded her of her dad.

"And," he added, "frankly, you look like hell. You need a hot bath, some hot food, and sleep." His mouth set in an uncompromising line, he crossed his arms and waited for her to answer.

Well. Kate remembered to close her mouth finally. She blinked a few times.

Tourmeline wasn't a detective—Mendenhall couldn't afford a detective—but he was the closest thing she had to one. Despite his startled-deer look, he had a keen, observant mind. He wouldn't let anything get by him. Besides, the car was being towed to the station garage and they would be shutting down the scene here soon, having gathered all the information they could.

And her thinking had grown sluggish from the cold and exhaustion. Tourmeline was right.

"All right, constable," she said on a sigh. "You win."

His face relaxed and he nodded. He held his hands up to her and she hesitated a moment before accepting the help. Their hands made clumsy by down-filled mittens, they had trouble clasping each other, but she finally managed to jump down. The forgotten binoculars almost smacked her on the chin as his steadying hold kept her from losing her balance.

A wave of weariness washed over her. She'd been working on adrenalin and stubbornness. Definitely time to go home.

"The car's being towed in," she remembered to tell him. "Once it thaws out in the garage, I want you to dust it for prints."

"Yes, ma'am."

Boychuk got to the Burndale road at the same time as she did. She detoured to the Site Command truck and told the EMO officer there that they were shutting down the scene and thanked him for the support. He nodded politely and pulled out his cell phone. Unlike the fellow he had replaced a few hours ago, he didn't give her the fish-eye. She knew she wasn't the darling of the Emergency Measures crew, but honestly, was it her fault a real dead body landed in the middle of their exercise?

Then she radioed her constables and informed them that she was headed back and that they should report anything they found to Tourmeline. A spate of "Yes, ma'ams" followed and then she and Boychuk climbed into the warm squad car and let Constable Abrams drive them back to the station. She fell asleep slumped against the door and startled awake when Abrams stopped at the station.

As Gerald Abrams drove away, she and Boychuk headed for the door only to stop when they heard raised voices from inside. The glass door was iced over on the inside so they couldn't see anything but white.

Boychuk gave her the raised eyebrows and Kate wanted to shrug, but her parka was just too damned heavy. Instead, she pulled open the door and stepped inside.

"I need to talk to the chief!" insisted Alexandra Kowalski, standing in the hallway in front of the duty desk. She was so focused on whoever was at the duty desk that she didn't notice Kate's arrival. It gave Kate a moment to prepare. She never knew if she'd find Kowalski in a collegial mood, or in a berating mood. Judging by the woman's behavior last night—this morning—this wasn't going to be pleasant.

From behind the raised desk, Tattersall's low voice answered calmly.

"Ma'am, the chief is still at the scene. I'll be happy to take a message."

Boychuk entered behind Kate and allowed the heavy door to thud shut. Kowalski turned to face them, her eyes bloodshot. Her hood was back and her long, skinny braid was coming undone, with static electricity making the shorter, mousy strands rise above her head. She looked like an anemic Gorgon.

"About time you showed up," she said. In another person, it might have been a joke, but she pressed her thin lips together so tightly, they seemed to disappear.

"Kowalski." Kate stomped the snow off her Sorels and then wiped her boots off on the runner. Boychuk did the same next to her.

Ed Tattersall emerged from the duty room and stopped in the doorway, casually blocking it. He crossed his arms and nodded at Kate and Boychuk. There was a distinct chill in the air that had nothing to do with the temperature outside.

"What is it?" Kate asked Kowalski. She could have been a little more tactful, maybe. At least, she could have been more polite. But she was tired and there was a crap load of work to do. She really didn't want to deal with whatever was peeving Alexandra Kowalski right now.

Kowalski responded to Kate's tone by bristling. "What do you think it is?" she demanded. "You usurped my exercise! Do you have any idea how much it costs to set something like that up? How much *time*?"

Kate hung on to her patience with both hands.

"I'm sorry about the exercise." She realized at once that she didn't sound the least bit apologetic. "But you have to agree that finding out what happened to that man has to take precedence." Out of the corner of her eye, she saw Boychuk shrug out of his parka.

"First of all," said Kowalski, "he was already dead." She waved a hand in a plea for understanding. "And everyone knows what happened to him." Her expression changed from pleading to scornful. "He got drunk and passed out in the snow. Case closed." Her voice dropped. "For that, you cost me my exercise? Maybe my *job*?" She took a step toward Kate.

Boychuk stiffened and Tattersall took a step forward. Only then did Kate see that Charlotte Hrebien, the station's one and only support staff, had been standing behind him. Her eyes were wide with alarm.

Time to defuse this, thought Kate grimly. But before she could open her mouth, Kowalski spoke again, oblivious to everything but her own frustration.

"And then you treat my volunteers like criminals!" Her face flushed and she spread her arms wide, prompting Tattersall to take another step forward. Kate shook her head minutely. This was no time to escalate the situation.

She was growing uncomfortably hot in her parka. She unbuttoned the outer flap covering the zipper as she carefully considered her next words.

"Alex," she began calmly, looking the angry woman in the eye, "I wanted this exercise to go ahead, too. We've invested a lot of energy and resources in emergency preparedness." Not to mention time. If she had to sit through one more of Kowalski's tabletop exercises, she might have to throw a chair through the window and make her escape. "But," she continued, "it's my job to find out if that man's death was natural or not. And if not, we need to find who caused it."

Kowalski's face was a study in bunched muscles—along her jaw, her temples... even her neck was corded. "The damage is done," she said stiffly. "The exercise can still go ahead, even though it will be flawed."

Kate stared at her for a moment before her words sank in. "Not right away, it can't," she warned. "I haven't released the scene." Nor was she going to, not until she was satisfied she had learned everything there was to learn there. "I'm sorry," she said again.

All the rage seemed to flush out of Kowalski, leaving only bitterness behind. "You're not sorry at all," she said. "I'm laying a formal complaint against you. And we're going to bill Mendenhall for the costs of the exercise."

With that, she stomped out of the station, brushing past Boychuk when he didn't move fast enough.

Charlotte peered around Tattersall's wide back. "Holy cow." She had dark circles under her eyes. "Is she serious?"

Kate sighed. The adrenalin slowly receded to leave her even more exhausted than before. Mendenhall couldn't afford to foot the bill for the exercise. It was an empty threat. She hoped. As for the formal complaint, what the heck could she complain about? Kate was doing her job.

"Charlotte, how long have you been here?" she asked. Although she was twenty-five, right now Charlotte looked more like a little kid who'd been allowed up way past her bedtime.

"Since about four this morning," said Tattersall, edging around Charlotte to return to the duty room. He climbed the step to the platform of the duty desk and sat down.

Good grief. "It's Sunday. Go home," Kate ordered the young woman. "You don't need to be here."

As the detachment's sole administrative support, Charlotte Hrebien did everything from type up reports to minor research. She'd been at the station for five years and considered herself as much a part of the detachment as any one of Kate's constables. Kate couldn't imagine running the station without her.

"I'll be going soon," said Charlotte, eyeing Kate up and down. "There's hot chocolate in the lunch room, with sandwiches and cookies from Carter's Deli."

"Hot damn," muttered Boychuk. He clomped off toward the

lunch room, carrying his parka.

Kate finally took off the heavy parka and stuffed the mittens and balaclava into its cargo pockets. She shuddered to think what her own blonde-going-on-gray hair would look like after eight hours under a balaclava. She surreptitiously checked the bun at the back of her head. Not bad. Her eyes probably had more red than blue at this point.

Tattersall grinned. All the tension had left his shoulders with Kowalski's departure. He was a good cop. Not a natural leader, maybe, but dependable. He knew how to stay calm and consider a situation before acting. His green eyes were bloodshot, too, and his thinning brown hair could use a comb, but his uniform still looked fresh. How long had he been on duty?

Damnitall. She had to start keeping better track of these things.

"Report," she said, moving into the duty room.

Charlotte sighed in resignation and stepped out of the way. Tattersall glanced at the computer screen on the counter before answering her.

"Martins and Holmes are almost done with the interviews," he said, still scrolling down his screen. He rubbed one hand through his hair, adding to its messiness. "They've been sending each interview in as they finish inputting it."

"I've been plotting everyone's location," added Charlotte, pointing to a white board fastened to the wall between Kate's office and McKell's. Usually they used it to jot down reminders of needed supplies. Today, the white board showed a crude drawing of the train, the bus, the railroad, the Trans-Canada and the Burndale road. A squiggle near the top of the board indicated the woods. Throughout the drawing were numbers. The dead man was identified as a red X.

"Each number corresponds with a victim," said Charlotte, staring at the board. She was dressed in jeans and a navy wool shirt over a white turtleneck, and her thick brown curls were brushed away from her face. "They're the easy part because most of them stayed put. It's the emergency crew I'm having trouble keeping track of."

Kate set her parka on the chair at Charlotte's desk, ignoring the heavy clunk of the radios in the inside pockets. She took off her Sorels and set them in front of Charlotte's desk, where no one would trip over them. She rubbed her face and yawned. Sunlight streamed through the windows that gave onto the locked compound, leaving rectangles of light on the linoleum tile. Already the cold was seeping in through her wool socks.

The station was deserted except for the four of them. Everybody who could be spared was dealing with the scene and the interviews.

"Is anybody on patrol?"

Tattersall shook his head. "No."

Kate nodded. "Are you keeping track of who's been pulled in?"

Tattersall tapped a sheet of paper on the duty desk. "Yes, ma'am. It's not so bad. I haven't had to pull anyone who's on duty tonight, so we should be back to normal in a few days."

Kate nodded again, relieved beyond measure.

The outside door opened and they all automatically glanced at the convex mirror set in the corner of the hallway to see who had come in.

"It's the fire chief," murmured Tattersall over his shoulder.

Twenty years ago, the city had converted an old military police detachment into the police station. The building might have worked for the military when there was still an air base in Mendenhall, but it was far from ideal for a modern police department. This was the first place she had ever worked where the duty desk didn't have a direct line of sight to the door and where the lunch room was accessible to the public.

But if she couldn't get the mayor to sign off on replacing a seven-year-old Crown Vic, she doubted she'd get approval for a new building.

Jon Avramson stopped in front of the desk, exuding cold air like an open freezer. He grinned at the three of them and leaned his elbows on the duty desk. He was the only person Kate had seen who was tall enough to do it naturally. He removed his gloves and dropped them on the desk. Tattersall stiffened slightly but didn't say anything. Charlotte resumed her work at the white board without speaking to the man, either.

Huh.

"Interesting night," said the fire chief. His blue eyes were bloodshot and his cheeks chapped and red. "Any news on the dead guy?"

Kate shook her head. "No identification yet."

Avramson sighed heavily. "That's a shitty way to go," he said. "You're out having a good time and you have a few too many. Next thing you know, you're dead in the middle of a field."

Kate shrugged. "We don't know that he was drinking."

Avramson's eyebrows rose. "Really? How the hell else would he have gotten all the way out there?"

"That's what I plan to find out," said Kate with a smile. Why was the man here? She had work to do.

"Well, good luck," said Avramson. He started pulling his heavy gloves back on. "What was Kowalski so pissed about?" he asked. At her raised eyebrow, he explained, "She almost ran me over coming out of the parking lot."

The fire station was only a few blocks away from the station. Of course Avramson had walked over.

"Maybe she was in a hurry," murmured Tattersall.

The look Avramson shot him was unfriendly but then he pasted a smile on his face. "Anyway. Just thought I'd check if there was news," he said. "Drop by sometime for coffee." There was a glint of malice in his eye.

Kate ignored it. "Very neighborly of you, chief. I'll do that."

There followed an awkward silence until Avramson finally said, "Well, see you then," and left.

Once the door had closed behind him, Tattersall's shoulders relaxed.

"Jerk," muttered Charlotte under her breath.

"I take it neither one of you is too fond of the new fire chief?" asked Kate, trying not to smile.

"My cousin is gay," said Tattersall. "Avramson tried to get him banned from the gym."

Kate's eyebrows rose in surprise. "I would suspect that violates a number of human rights."

"Damned right," said Tattersall, stabbing the keyboard keys with his index finger.

"And you?" Kate asked Charlotte.

The girl turned away from the whiteboard. She was frowning. "I don't like him."

Kate waited but Charlotte returned to her project.

Well, that's that, thought Kate.

"I think it's the interview that set her off, you know," said Tattersall.

Kate stared up at him uncomprehendingly. "What?"

"Kowalski. Martins called to warn us she was coming. I guess she got pi— ticked off when he insisted she needed to be interviewed, too."

Kate shrugged. She didn't know Alexandra Kowalski very well, but the woman was wound tighter than a top. It wouldn't take much to set her off.

"It's not that," said Charlotte. "Her job is at stake."

They both turned to look at her blankly.

Charlotte shrugged. "She wasn't joking. I think she was counting on this exercise to save her job."

Tattersall pursed his lips but said nothing.

"They call her Screw-up Kowalski," said Charlotte sheepishly. Her cheeks turned pink and she avoided Kate's gaze.

Kate frowned. "She can't be fired for this," she said. "I cancelled the exercise. It wasn't anything she did."

Charlotte nodded in agreement. "I know, but there's more to it than that. She was off sick for a few months last summer. I think she was on stress leave. Things haven't been going well for her for a while."

Well, that would explain the woman's irritability.

Kate turned back to Tattersall, not wanting to stand there gossiping. "They found a car," she told him. "It's being towed in. Make sure it gets into the garage. Lay a tarp down to capture anything that might melt off." It was probably overkill, but heck, it was only a tarp. "Has Paterson called the plate in yet?"

"Not yet," said Tattersall.

"I want ownership determined as soon as possible. The car needs to be dusted for fingerprints and searched." She already knew that the missing tux jacket and wallet weren't in the car, but she didn't plan on missing anything. "Tourmeline's going to lift prints once it's warmed up."

Tattersall nodded as he jotted down notes. Kate grabbed her parka and boots and padded in stocking feet to her office. She dumped the heavy coat on top of the filing cabinet and set the boots down on the mat next to it before grabbing her indoor shoes. The tile floor was cold.

When she came out, Charlotte was back at the white board, adding more names to the legend in her neat print and Tattersall was busy filling out the log book. Part of her wanted to get rid of the physical log. It was redundant. After all, everything was also copied on the computer log file.

But she could read a lot into how a constable wrote information in. Were there exclamation marks? Did the pen go through the paper in the writer's excitement or anger? Were the letters cramped or big? She was just Old School enough to like standing at the end of the counter to peruse the book at the beginning of a shift. And she'd noticed quite a few of the constables liked it, too.

Besides, she didn't trust computers. They crashed.

She'd started her police career in New Brunswick thirty years earlier when cops relied on the written word, not computers. Sure, a notebook could get lost or destroyed, but it couldn't get hacked or corrupted and she could stuff it in her pocket.

Charlotte came up to her, took her arm and turned her toward the corridor. "Eat," she ordered. "Then go home."

Kate allowed herself to be led into the lunch room. Boychuk hadn't even bothered to sit down. He was probably afraid he wouldn't be able to get up again. He leaned against the counter where a big plastic container of sandwiches stood uncovered. He ate from a sandwich in one hand and drank from the mug in the other.

At the sight of the sandwiches, Kate's stomach growled. Cheese and nuts were fine, but she needed real food.

Boychuk indicated a second mug on the counter and Kate nodded her thanks. He'd poured her a mug of hot chocolate from a pump thermos. Kate grabbed the nearest sandwich and bit into it. Egg salad. Not usually her favorite but it was delicious. They stood drinking their hot chocolate and wolfing down sandwiches in blissful silence for the next few minutes. The lunch room was warm and her hands finally thawed. A beam of sunlight hit her shoulder, feeling like a hug.

Finally, Kate looked at Charlotte, who remained in the doorway, watching them with worry in her eyes.

"I'm going home to shower and change, then I'll be back to look over the interviews."

Charlotte raised an eyebrow. "I spoke to John," she said. It took Kate a moment to realize she was talking about Tourmeline. Charlotte was on a first-name basis with everyone in the station, even DC McKell. "You need sleep. The interviews are still trickling in." She raised a hand to forestall Kate's objection. "I promise to call as soon as they're all here."

Next to her, Boychuk made a noise that sounded suspiciously like a snort, but when Kate looked at him, he was busy selecting another sandwich.

A good leader knew when to beat a strategic retreat. Honestly, she didn't think she'd be able to read without her eyes crossing anyway. It was time to go home.

But first, she picked another sandwich from the container and bit into it.

CHAPTER 4

Kate paid attention to her driving and blinked her burning eyes to coax moisture into them. The police station, fire station, and city hall were within ten blocks of each other on Mendenhall Drive, a mile-long, horseshoe-shaped road bisected by Main Street. She had first arrived in Mendenhall early last summer to take the job of chief of police. Back then, the fire station's bay door would have been open to the summer day. Now the door was closed snugly against winter. She missed the friendly waves of the firefighters as they washed the fire engine.

Of course, now that Avramson had come on board as chief, there was less friendliness between cops and firefighters. She wasn't sure why, really. He was always polite and friendly to her, but a lot of her staff didn't like the man. Especially DC McKell.

To be honest, Rob McKell hadn't liked *her*, either, when she first came to Mendenhall. Not surprising, when she finally learned that he had been overlooked for the job of chief of police because he and the mayor's daughter were going through an acrimonious divorce.

It was unfair, but she and McKell had made peace, of a sort. She hoped his father would miraculously recover so McKell could get back to work. Soon.

She had come to love Mendenhall, much to her surprise. She loved that she could walk anywhere downtown and be greeted by name. She loved that the girl behind the Tim Hortons coffee shop counter knew exactly how she liked her coffee. She loved that the town sat in the middle of the Prairies like a jewel in a braided wheat crown.

It seemed to her that ninety percent of all the advertising in local newspapers, television, and radio dealt with seeding, weed control, or farming equipment. And weather conditions. Yes, indeed, she was learning that weather was God on the Prairies. Weather could make the difference between sending a kid off to university and keeping him home to help.

She could have been dropped on an oil rig and it would have felt less foreign than this world of crops, proprietary seed rights, and grain silos dotting the landscape.

She'd never lived in a small town before. All her policing work had been in major centers, the last in Toronto. But Mendenhall had a population of just under seventeen thousand people. If someone had told her a year ago that she would love being greeted by name everywhere she went, she would have called them crazy.

At the Tim Hortons, on the corner of Main Street and Mendenhall Drive, a few old-timers sat at their regular table by the steamed-up window, sipping coffee and swapping tales. Beyond the coffee shop, Main Street looked deserted. Most sane people would be staying close to their wood stoves or fireplaces on a day like today.

Kate turned left, heading for high ground and the newer developments—ten years old qualified as "newer" here—where she had bought her house.

There was no traffic. Sundays in Mendenhall were always quiet, more so in winter. The devout were busy attending one of the six churches in town. Partiers were sleeping off their hangovers. And the rest... well, the rest were enjoying a lazy day.

Kate wondered which category the dead man fit into. He was no farmer, not with those smooth hands. Probably a partier, judging by the tuxedo. Dr. Kijawa would probably find an elevated blood alcohol level. She glanced at the dashboard clock. 11:47. Still too soon to call on the medical examiner. Mid-afternoon would be better.

A yawn caught her by surprise and her jaw cracked.

The insurance companies and banks gave way to service stations and repair shops as the street climbed. She had picked her house for the view more than anything else. It sat on an escarpment overlooking the town. From her back deck, she could see halfway to Hudson Bay. At night the stars filled the sky, generating her own personal light show. Her neighbors were a little below and closer to the street so that she had the illusion of being perched alone on a mountaintop. She loved it.

The first houses in the subdivision appeared, smoke puffing out of their chimneys in straight columns. Thank God—the wind had dropped, finally. When she turned onto her street, there was no movement anywhere except for a small green Tercel parked in front of her house, its windows iced up, its engine running. She didn't recognize the car. It probably belonged to someone visiting one of her neighbors, but why park in front of Kate's house?

Six inches of snow covered the back bumper, obscuring the license plate.

She pulled into the driveway, giving the Explorer a little gas to encourage it up the slope, and stopped at the side of the house. She turned the engine off and sat for a moment, just letting the exhaustion wash over her. A warm bath and a cup of tea, then a nap. Then she'd drive over to the hospital to see what the doc had found out about the dead man. After that, she'd go back to the office to start making sense of all this.

But first she had to plug in the Explorer to keep the engine warm. The forecast was for temperatures to warm to all of minus twenty-five by mid-afternoon. Practically balmy.

She opened the door and hauled herself out, then stomped to the front of the Explorer to unwind the cord from around the license plate and plug it into the outside outlet. As she was straightening up, a voice behind her said, "Hi, Aunt Kate."

Kate whirled and almost tripped over her Sorels.

"Amanda?" She stared open-mouthed at her sister's youngest child. What was she doing here, instead of at home in Montreal? "What's wrong?"

Amanda smiled and tilted her head. "Why does anything have to be wrong?" she asked. "I came to see my favorite aunt."

"I'm your *only* aunt," Kate replied automatically. Then she glanced at the Tercel, suddenly connecting the dots. "Did you *drive* here?" Holy cow.

Amanda nodded, and for the first time, Kate realized that the girl wasn't dressed for the weather. Those high-heeled boots and cute little bomber jacket might be the "in" thing in Montreal fashion, but they spelled hypothermia here. Already Amanda was starting to shiver.

"For Pete's sake," said Kate, more angrily than she had intended. "Don't you even have a hat?"

Amanda's heavy blond braid swung as she shrugged. "It's in the car."

"And is it keeping you warm there?" grumbled Kate. Before Amanda could reply, Kate grabbed her fashionably-clad arm and pulled her up the stairs to the front door. "Come inside before something freezes and falls off."

Did Rose know Amanda was coming here? No, of course not. Rose would have called. So what was going on in her niece's life that she would drive halfway across the country in the middle of winter without calling ahead first?

A boy. It had to be a boy.

Half an hour later, with Kate shed of her parka, Sorels, snow pants, scarf, balaclava, and down mittens, they sat at the kitchen counter, nursing coffee. Kate had turned the heat up but she still couldn't seem to get warm.

Amanda sat across the counter from her, mostly ignoring her cooling coffee. She examined the kitchen with a chef's eye and Kate knew the girl would be disappointed. At 23, Amanda was a sous-chef at *L'Assiette blanche*, a prestigious Montreal restaurant, and she was used to the finest kitchen tools and equipment. Kate had bought her knives at Wal-Mart.

"Nice place," said Amanda finally.

"Thanks," said Kate, not fooled. The kitchen was pretty enough with its silver pulls, a polished granite countertop, and brushed aluminum refrigerator and stove, but she had none of the fancy gadgets her sister Rose had—no cappuccino maker or pasta maker or coffee grinder. Heck, she didn't even own an egg timer. Rose had been the homemaker among the three siblings, and she'd imbued her daughter Amanda with her love of home and cooking.

"I've wanted to see it since you moved here," added Amanda. "I've never been west of Toronto." Her gaze wandered to the dining room, an oasis of wood and upholstered chairs. The French doors led to the deck, now buried under three feet of snow. She looked reproachfully at Kate. "You don't call much, Auntie Kate. Nobody really knows how you're doing."

Kate shrugged. Her first six months in Mendenhall had been a struggle. Her constables had resisted her leadership, mostly out of loyalty to DC McKell. She and McKell had called truce when Josh Hollingsworth had gone missing, but it had still taken a major blowout, not to mention getting shot, before they finally found the boy.

Getting shot had provided her with enough excitement to last a lifetime. And it had proven to her that DC McKell was a fine deputy chief, in spite of his resentment of her. It had also shown her that her constables could work as a team and that they were well on their way to trusting her leadership. Her right shoulder twitched reflexively. She hoped she wouldn't have to get shot again to get them the rest of the way.

She hadn't told her family about getting shot. What they didn't know wouldn't worry them.

"It's been busy," she told Amanda, and didn't elaborate. She recognized the girl's ploy as one Rose used to use when they were kids. Deflect questions by going on the attack.

I learned from a master, kiddo. Kate placed a still-cold hand over her niece's. "Now, why don't you tell me why you're really here?"

Amanda tried to paste innocence on her face, but Kate just stared at her. Her niece finally looked away and swallowed hard. Were those tears in her eyes?

Definitely a boy.

The phone rang, shattering the pregnant silence and jangling Kate's already frayed nerves.

"Hang on," she said and hauled herself to her feet.

The phone was on the wall between the stove and the back door. She picked up the receiver. "Hello?"

"It's Charlotte."

At once Kate's back straightened. There was a strange note in the girl's voice.

"What is it?"

"A bad accident," said Charlotte. "A car hit black ice on the highway, just before the on ramp. It flipped over and hit a car going the other way."

Kate's fatigue fell away as she puzzled over what Charlotte had said. Or hadn't said.

"Fatalities?"

"One."

"Paramedics on scene?"

"Yes."

"Blocking traffic?"

"Both lanes."

"Who's there now?"

Charlotte knew exactly what she was asking. "John Tourmeline, Jim O'Hara and Gerry Abrams."

"Are Martins and Holmes still doing interviews?"

"They just called in. They finished and are heading to the scene. Ben and Marco are on their way, too."

"Good," said Kate. "I'm heading out now."

"Chief?" For the second time, Kate noted the queer note in Charlotte's voice.

"What is it, Charlotte?" she asked gently.

"The other driver…" She cleared her throat and went on. "It's Daisy Washburn."

Daisy. A wash of emotions swept through Kate, too quickly for her to identify.

"How badly hurt?"

"I don't know," said Charlotte.

"All right," she said and hung up.

Kate turned to look at her niece. Amanda had turned in her chair to watch her and now sat with her eyes wide and her mouth open.

"I have to go," said Kate, and headed for the hall closet to start hauling on her insulated pants. "The spare bedroom is yours. Make yourself at home. I'll call when I can."

CHAPTER 5

F RIESEN WAVED her through the barrier. His balaclava was rolled up to his forehead and his breath steamed in the cold. His grim expression was all the information she needed. Kate took a deep breath to calm herself. She hated accident scenes. It was not knowing what she'd find—survivors or dead bodies—that left her queasy. The injured she could handle. But knowing that someone was beyond her ability to rescue...

It had taken thirty minutes to get there—a trip that should have taken five. When the ice fog finally retreated back to the river, it left behind a thin layer of black ice on the highway approach. The streets in town were fine, but once she reached the outskirts she had to drive slowly or risk going off the road. She had passed three cars in the ditch and stopped to check each one out. No drivers in any of them but she still called them in.

Five cars were backed up behind Friesen's patrol car, stopped by the revolving cherry lights. Friesen finished talking to the third driver in line and moved on to the next while the driver rolled up her window.

Tattersall had already detailed Abrams and O'Hara to head off traffic at the Hayes Road and Wekusko Street approaches to the highway. Motorists could still get to and from Winnipeg, but they would have to take Highway Two or the Sixteen. The drivers behind Friesen's barricade would be stuck here until she could free up a constable to escort them back. Slowly.

Her first priority was to ensure there'd be no more accidents. She'd already told Charlotte to call the city's maintenance garage. She wanted the road sanded.

Closing the barn door after the horses were gone.

She eased down the hill, not trusting her studded tires on the icy pavement. Below was a confusion of flashing red and yellow lights and twisted metal. She separated out the lights into a tow truck and another patrol car. The twisted metal was the guard rail. The ambulance had come and gone. Tourmeline stood next to the tow truck, busy writing in a notebook. He looked up at her approach. At once his hand went up to stop her and he waved her to the side.

Kate pulled over and turned the Explorer's engine off, but kept the keys in the ignition. The moment she opened the door, a blast of cold air snatched her breath away and she pulled her scarf over her mouth and nose before stepping out. It did nothing to dispel the stink of diesel, oil, and exhaust. Frost sparkled on the tarmac and she walked gingerly along the shoulder toward Tourmeline, her breath puffing out in small, diffuse clouds.

She joined Tourmeline at the twisted guardrail and looked down the embankment. Two cars lay at the bottom. One, a black Subaru Outback, was on its roof. The driver's side was completed caved in. The other car, a red Ford Focus, looked like it had rolled a few times before landing on its side, trapping the driver's door. The front passenger side was destroyed. Both vehicles looked like a giant had squeezed them in his hand before tossing them away.

By the Subaru, something red had melted the snow before freezing.

Kate swallowed.

Tourmeline finished what he was writing and finally looked up.

"It's pretty cut and dried," he said. "Driver in the black Subaru was heading into Mendenhall and lost control on black ice." He pointed to the road and traced the tire marks in the air. Kate saw where tire tracks had left the west-bound lane to weave erratically before spinning around a couple of times.

"Then the east-bound Focus tried to avoid the Subaru." He

pointed back toward Mendenhall and she saw a thick double line in the frost where the east-bound driver had tried to brake.

"No use braking hard on this stuff," said Tourmeline matter-of-factly. He had a clipboard under his arm, and a camera swung from a cord around his neck.

"Only two?" asked Kate. Exhaustion was making her slow, unresponsive. She had to get a grip.

But Tourmeline had only been brought into the exercise when it started getting light. He was still relatively fresh. He certainly looked rested and alert. Almost cheerful. A surge of dislike spiked through her and she controlled it, knowing it was induced by sleep deprivation.

Tourmeline had automatically taken on the task of documenting the accident scene, as she had known he would. He wasn't much good at the day-to-day policing, the traffic stops, the domestic disputes, the talking to the high school kids—but nobody else on her force had his attention to detail, including her. He had the eye for what didn't fit, and the tenacity to figure out why. He had the makings of a good detective.

"Only two drivers," he confirmed. He looked away from the cars below. "The driver of the Subaru was dead at the scene, but the paramedics thought the other driver would make it."

"Daisy," said Kate, and he nodded.

Tourmeline was right, it was cut and dried. She knew from past experience that he'd taken photos to document the evidence of the accident. Still, they would have to wait for the RCMP traffic analyst to arrive from Winnipeg. The road would have to stay closed until the analyst had come and gone. Kate was pretty sure the analyst wouldn't catch anything that Tourmeline hadn't already seen.

"All right," she said finally. "When's Winnipeg getting here?"

"Might be up to a couple of hours."

Couldn't be helped. "When you're finished, escort the traffic back to Highway Two. Barriers stay up until the analyst clears the scene."

"Yes, ma'am."

* * *

The intensive care unit at Mendenhall General Hospital was on the second floor, just past the surgical unit. Kate took the stairs. Every little bit of exercise helped her keep the weight down and stay fit. Winter was a struggle for her, since she didn't run outside when it was cold, and Mendenhall didn't have an indoor track. At five-foot-three, every pound showed in her round face, although she had lost quite a bit of weight after she was shot. She was finally getting her strength and stamina back, thanks to a rigorous training session with the physiotherapist and on her own at the gym.

She reached the top of the stairs, hardly breathing fast, although she did feel the bloom of a flush on her cheeks. The curse of fair skin.

Kate had only been at the hospital once, last fall after she got shot. At the time, she had seen only the emergency department and then her room, which had been on the third floor.

As she walked down the wide corridor with its cantaloupe-colored walls and bright splashes of art work, she found herself walking faster. There was a feeling of high intensity here, as if she were walking next to a high-tension power station.

She had taken off her parka and stuffed her hat and mittens in its large pockets. A police uniform always helped in a hospital.

Up ahead the hallway split in two, and where the three hallways met was a duty desk with offices behind a glass partition. Across from the duty desk was a set of elevators. Signs on the wall told her that the maternity ward and pediatrics were on the right.

It being Sunday, the office was dark, but two nurses worked at the duty desk, heads bent over their work.

Kate paused at the junction and looked down the left-hand hallway. On one side of the hallway were three doors, and next to each door, a large window into the room. All three doors were open, and from a couple of the rooms came the sounds of equipment beeping gently and regularly. Two of the rooms were softly lit while the third remained dark. Across the hall was a door marked "Staff Only."

One of the nurses, a man, looked up from the computer screen he'd been studying. His gaze swept her up and down before he settled on her holstered gun.

"Can I help you?" he asked. His voice was low, as if he didn't want to disturb sleepers, but there was a frown on his face. Kate judged him to be in his late thirties. His hair was sandy, crinkly, and receding. Worry lines were permanently etched on his forehead, but there was a hint of a dimple in his cheek.

"I'm Chief Williams," she said.

"Yes," agreed the nurse. Kate was getting used to it. Everybody in Mendenhall knew her, or so it seemed since the shooting. His name tag read "Steinbach." She vaguely recalled that there was a town nearby with that name.

The ward was kept warm and she was glad she had taken off the parka.

The other nurse was a young woman who might have been just out of nursing college, she was so fresh. She looked up from the clipboard she was studying and her big blue eyes grew even bigger at the sight of Kate's chest badge. Her hair was up in a ponytail, reminding Kate of Amanda.

"I'm told Daisy Washburn is here," said Kate, when Steinbach just kept looking at her.

Steinbach stood up. He was a big man, at least six feet two, and the arms emerging from the short sleeves of his blue scrubs looked well-muscled. Having a big nurse around had to be handy.

"Are you next of kin?" he asked.

Was that hostility? Kate tried to think if she had ever even met the fellow, let alone offended him, but she came up blank.

"No," she said calmly. "Daisy is a friend." Well, that might not technically be true, but it would do for now. "I was here on business and thought I'd check in on her."

"I'm sorry, chief," said the nurse stiffly. "We can't release—"

At that moment, an older woman in a nurse's white scrubs walked out of the nearest room, scribbling on a clipboard. She looked up, her face a question mark, but waited until she was next to Kate before speaking, clearly not wanting to disturb whoever was in the room. Her name tag read "Kirkham".

Kate recognized authority when she saw it. This was the nurse in charge.

"Chief Williams," said the woman, her voice low and calm. "How can we help you?"

"She's asking about one of our patients, Astrid," said Steinbach. "I explained that we can only release information to next of kin."

Nurse Kirkham smiled tightly. "Seeing as no next of kin have come forward, George, I think we can share some information with the chief. After all, she can help us locate Ms. Washburn's family."

Kate's eyebrows rose. She could feel herself flushing from the heat. "Daisy has a husband in Mendenhall," she said, then racked her brains trying to remember his name. She'd never met the man, but Daisy often spoke of him. "Frank. His name is Frank Washburn, I think."

Astrid Kirkham nodded. "We've tried the home number, with no answer. And we don't leave messages of this nature, of course."

Of course. Kate took a deep breath. Just how badly was Daisy hurt?

"I'll send a car around to the house," she offered.

"Thank you, chief."

Steinbach reluctantly sat down and began punching in information on the computer keyboard as Astrid Kirkham took Kate by the elbow and led her toward the farthest room. Kate found herself reluctant to go in and was deeply grateful when Nurse Kirkham stopped in front of the window. The dimly-lit room beyond was tiny, with barely enough space for the hospital bed and the various stands and other equipment clustered around it. Kate had an impression of red and green numbers on various displays, and hoses and wires disappearing under blankets before her confused eye finally found Daisy.

Then she hissed in dismay.

Even in the dim light she could see that Daisy's face was puffy and covered in lacerations. A bandage wrapped around her head gleamed white in the gloom. Her right arm was in a cast and rested on top of the blanket.

"How bad...?"

"Broken arm, a couple of cracked ribs, some tendon damage in her shoulder. We don't think there's internal bleeding, but we want to keep an eye on it. The worst injury is to her brain."

Kate looked at Nurse Kirkham with horror. Brain damage? Her heart twisted in pain for Daisy, even though she wasn't sure she liked the woman, especially after learning that she had caused the breakup of McKell's marriage. But Daisy Washburn was smart, quick-witted, and ambitious. She would rather lose a leg than have brain damage.

"There's swelling around the brain," explained Nurse Kirkham. "We're keeping her in an artificial coma until the swelling goes down and we can assess." She patted Kate's arm. "The air bag absorbed most of the shock, but she banged her head when the car flipped. We'll know in the next few days."

Kate nodded, feeling a little bit in shock herself. Behind them, voices floated down the hallway as Steinbach spoke to someone and was answered.

Kate cleared her throat. "I'll see about finding her husband."

They turned to go back and Kate saw that the voices she'd heard belonged to Mayor Dabbs and his wife. The mayor was a tall, thin man and he loomed over the duty desk, leaning one elbow on the high shelf that obscured the work station's computers and storage crannies. He wore a suit, as always, and had a heavy overcoat folded over his other arm. His gray hair matched his wife's, although his was clipped short and hers was in a stylish bob.

Mrs. Dabbs stood next to her husband, looking worried. She came up considerably short of her husband's shoulder. The young nurse had disappeared, but George Steinbach was leaning back in his chair, a stubborn look on his face. As Kate and Nurse Kirkham approached, Steinbach said, "I'm sorry, Mr. Mayor, but the rules are there for a reason."

Mrs. Dabbs looked around at their approach. "Len."

Mayor Leonard Dabbs looked around and saw them. Immediately he straightened and headed for Nurse Kirkham.

"Are you the nurse in charge?" he asked politely. As if by

magic, Mrs. Dabbs appeared by his side. She had big brown eyes that right now were filled with determination.

"I am, Mr. Mayor," said Astrid Kirkham calmly. "Mrs. Dabbs." She nodded to the mayor's wife. "How can I help?" She kept her voice down, encouraging them to do the same by her example.

Kate almost smiled. The mayor, like the chief of police, was a public figure. In a small town like Mendenhall, everybody knew who they were.

"We've come to see Daisy," said Mrs. Dabbs without giving her husband a chance to answer. "She works for my husband and is a friend of the family. This young man," she nodded in Steinbach's direction, "says we can't."

And this is where I get off.

She nodded politely to the mayor and his wife and kept walking. As though noticing her for the first time, the mayor frowned and Kate knew she would now become another argument for them to be allowed to see Daisy.

As she headed down the stairs, she found herself thinking about Daisy Pitcairn-Washburn. Daisy didn't have any family. The mayor and his wife were probably the closest thing she had to one, except for her husband.

Kate reached the main floor landing with a troubled sigh. Now she would have to find Frank Washburn and inform him that his wife had been in a serious accident. Could have been worse, she supposed. At least Daisy wasn't dead.

* * *

Kate had never been to the Mendenhall hospital's morgue, but she knew exactly where to look for it. Sure enough, it was in the basement, past the electrical room, the secure storage, and the supply room. It was at the end of the brightly-lit, meticulously clean hallway, behind double doors. The doors had windows, but the windows were covered on the other side by blue gingham curtains.

The curtains gave her pause. She didn't think she'd even seen curtains in a morgue before.

A discreet sign by the right hand door read, "Ring for admittance." So she shifted her parka to her left arm and pressed on the button. To her surprise, a chime sounded faintly behind the doors.

Good grief.

The curtain twitched and a chocolate brown eye peered out at her. The curtain twitched back and the door suddenly opened.

Dr. Faith Kijawa stood in the doorway, one hand holding the door open. She wore a blue surgeon's gown with stains of a dubious nature, and a matching blue hat. She blinked once, then turned without a word, leaving Kate to follow her.

Nonplussed, Kate put a hand out to keep the door from closing in her face and pushed it open to follow the doctor. They had met a couple of times, often enough that they would nod at each other in recognition when passing each other on the street.

Doc Kijawa was hard to miss. She was at least five feet ten, heavy-boned, and black-skinned. She had moved to Mendenhall from South Africa about ten years earlier. Kate judged her to be in her early sixties. She stood out amid the predominantly fair-skinned, blue-eyed, Ukraine-descended population of Mendenhall like molasses on white bread.

"You are early," said Doctor Kijawa over her shoulder.

The morgue was maybe the size of two regular hospital rooms put together. At one end were the ubiquitous body drawers—four of them. In the middle of the room was a metal table with an overhead light on an articulated arm. There was a body on the table, under a heavy white sheet.

Another body lay on a gurney shoved close to the wall, also covered by a white sheet. There were red-brown stains on the sheet.

Dr. Kijawa walked past the autopsy table without glancing at it and took her seat at the desk against the far wall. She picked up a pen and scribbled something on a label.

"I do not have anything for you yet," the doctor said. Her South African accent made her sound exotic. "The body is still thawing. I have drawn blood and will send it out for analysis." She didn't look up as she kept writing.

Kate nodded. The doctor would courier the vials to the Winnipeg lab where they would be placed in the queue. No telling when the results would come in. Could be tomorrow. Could be next week.

She watched the doctor place four vials of blood in a red plastic container. She then taped the lid shut and affixed the label across the top of the container so that it overlapped the lip of the container. The container couldn't be opened without tearing the label.

The walls not occupied by drawers and desk held open shelves filled with jars and boxes, and a closed cabinet with a lock on it.

Kate had always associated the smell of morgues with death—a kind of generic, unpleasant, whirled-into-one combination of antiseptic cleanser, alcohol, and decomp.

This one smelled of cinnamon.

Dr. Kijawa finished sealing the parcel and looked around at Kate. She had a high forehead, a nose curved like a scimitar and full lips. Her hair was going gray and was cropped tightly to her skull, giving her cheekbones the prominence they so richly deserved. If not for the hair, Kate would have put her age in her early forties. Until she looked in her eyes.

"Would you like some tea?" asked the doctor.

Another first. No one had ever offered her something to drink in a morgue. Kate shook her head.

"No thanks, Doc. Did you get a chance to examine the body?"

"Of course I did," said the doctor sharply. She stood up and walked around to the head of the table. Without warning, she flipped the sheet covering the body down to its waist. The man was naked, and very white. His eyelids didn't close all the way. The underside of his arms and his back were mottled blue where the blood had pooled. Kate blinked a couple of times. He was in essentially the same position in which they had found him. The difference was he had been deliberately laid out on this table.

Had someone deliberately laid him out in the snow? Even if he was too drunk to realize he was freezing to death, wouldn't he have curled up instinctively, to conserve heat?

Kate drew in a breath then wished she hadn't. Cinnamon only masked so much.

Doc Kijawa's big hand hovered over the head, then slowly

swept down the length of the body. "He is a man in his late twenties, early thirties," she said, her voice clinically detached. "No serious scars, no broken bones." She glanced at Kate. "I was able to obtain x-rays, since they do not depend on body temperature." Then she looked down at the body again and resumed her categorizing. "His musculature is solid but lean. He visited a gym regularly. No calluses on hands or feet. Whatever he did for a living, it was not physical. He has all his teeth. What dental work is present is good quality. No contact lenses."

She sighed. "In short, Chief Williams, this man appears to be in very good physical condition. He took care of himself in life. There is no evident medical reason for him to be dead." She shrugged. "The test will tell us if there was alcohol or drugs in his blood. Very likely he died of hypothermia."

Kate nodded again. Likely he had, but she, like the doctor, would not pronounce cause of death until she had all the facts.

"When will you conduct the autopsy?" she asked.

Dr. Kijawa pulled the sheet back up. "It will be quite some time before he is thawed enough," she said. Kate could hear the tiredness in the woman's voice. She had probably been up since the exercise was called in the middle of the night. Yet her eyes were clear.

Kate wondered what kind of eye drops she used.

"All right," she said finally. "I'll check in with you later."

Dr. Kijawa shook her head. "I am going to try to sleep," she said. "Give me your number. I will call you when I am done."

Fair enough. Kate gave the doctor her cell phone number and turned toward the door.

"Chief Williams."

She glanced back at the woman.

"Have you identified him yet?" asked the doctor softly.

Kate shook her head. "Not yet," she said. "But it won't be long. We're running plates and cross-checking with DMV records." It always took more time to check with the Department of Motor Vehicles on the weekend.

The doctor nodded. She had resumed her seat at the desk and now faced Kate with her big hands folded primly in her lap. For the first time, Kate realized the doctor was wearing a woolen skirt with black tights and flat shoes. Her face lost its professional detachment and she looked suddenly much older.

"Someone is waiting to hear from him," she said sadly.

They stared at each other for a few seconds, each having had to give this same bad news to others in the past. Finally Kate sighed.

"Thank you, doctor." And she left the strange morgue behind, hearing the lock click behind her.

As she entered the stairwell to climb to the main floor, the smells of dinner reached her. She glanced at her watch. Almost five o'clock. It was dinnertime and her stomach didn't care. It seemed to her that the sandwiches she had eaten that morning at the station were still sitting like lead in her stomach.

The conversation she'd just had with Dr. Kijawa replayed in her head. The dead man might not have anyone waiting on him. No one had reported him missing. How sad that was. To die suddenly and have no one to care except the ones who found your body.

When she reached the main floor, she headed for the lobby, nodding at the admissions clerk and shrugging into her parka. She pulled her cell phone out and turned it back on as she emerged into the biting cold. The sun was setting, blessing the western sky with a rosy glow.

She stood at the hospital entrance, watching the sky and the almost empty parking lot. A big pine tree stood in the middle of a roundabout island. It still had Christmas lights on and probably would until the temperature warmed up. An ambulance drove up slowly, its roof lights off. The driver nodded at Kate then the ambulance disappeared around the back of the building.

Was the patient already dead, or were the paramedics just back from dinner break?

She shook her head and tried to decide what she needed to do now, but her brain was having trouble turning over. She had to go back to the station and check out the interviews with the witnesses at the exercise site. She had to… what? Just couldn't think straight anymore. Time for coffee.

She pulled her hood up and slipped the phone back into its

inside pocket. She was pulling her mittens on when the phone rang, startling her into dropping one of them.

She stooped to pick it up and groaned as she straightened. She'd been on her feet way too long, and now her back was going to make her pay for it.

The phone rang four more times before she finally fumbled it out of its pocket.

"Williams," she said into it.

"It's Charlotte."

Kate braced herself at the note in the girl's voice. "What is it?" she asked as calmly as she could.

"We've identified the man from the exercise," said Charlotte heavily. Kate noted that Charlotte hadn't said the word "dead."

Kate waited, listening to Charlotte breathe. When she couldn't take it anymore, she said, "And?"

Charlotte took a deep breath. There was a catch in it. "Chief, it's Frank Washburn, Daisy's husband."

CHAPTER 6

THE STREETLIGHTS were on and the temperature was already dropping by the time Kate pulled into the station's back parking lot. She dragged herself out of the Explorer and trudged to the rear door, where she paused to straighten her posture and lift her chin. She opened the door and a wave of warmth enveloped her as she walked in. She immediately began to shiver. That was tiredness more than cold, she knew.

But the cold didn't help.

The row of hard wooden chairs sat empty against the vestibule wall and the lunch room was dark. All she could hear was voices on the radio as constables on patrol checked in with each other.

She wiped her boots off and pulled off her mittens. From her angle, she could see the half-open door to the duty room, the corner of one of the common desks, and McKell's door. Wetness marked the spot on the runner in front of the duty desk where Alexandra Kowalski and Jon Avramson had stood melting earlier.

Dear lord—was that only a few hours ago? It felt like a week. Where was everyone?

She pulled her Sorels off and placed them on the horsehair mat next to the door. She probably wouldn't be here that long and the boots wouldn't be in the way. Then she pushed open the door to the empty duty room. Four desks occupied the central space, and Charlotte's made five. Her office door and McKell's were closed, as was the door to the cell area. The door to the locker room was ajar but the room beyond was in darkness. What the hell…?

Kate stood in the doorway and listened. She could hear voices coming faintly from the rear of the building. A shiver coursed up her body and she hugged her parka more tightly about her. She couldn't seem to get warm.

She sniffed. Something smelled good. Something smelled *wonderful*. She glanced around the room and saw a crockpot sitting next to the log book on the duty counter. The cord hung down over the edge of the counter. Kate stared at it, perplexed. What was a crock pot doing in her station? This one had a glass lid that was beaded with moisture on the inside.

Then she blinked. Was that *her* crock pot?

The cell room door opened, spilling light and voices into the duty room. Charlotte emerged first, looking over her shoulder.

Then Amanda walked out, followed by Tattersall, who seemed to be explaining something. All three stopped when they saw her. Charlotte was the first to recover.

"Chief. Your niece just brought over some soup." She frowned reproachfully at Kate. "You never mentioned you had company." Her eyes were bloodshot and the bags under them were even more pronounced. But her mouth had relaxed. Even Tattersall looked more relaxed. He had even combed his hair.

Clearly, Amanda's visit had given them something else to think about besides Daisy's woes, and Kate was grateful.

And yet the first words out of her mouth were, "There's nobody on the duty desk."

Tattersall's pale complexion reddened in embarrassment and Kate could have kicked herself. There were times during a shift when the duty desk was unoccupied. If there was no one at the station but the duty officer and he or she had to go the bathroom, for example.

"Sorry, ma'am," said Tattersall. He climbed up the platform and settled himself at the counter. "We were giving your niece a tour of the station."

Amanda's face was carefully devoid of expression. "I knew you were busy, so I thought I'd bring you supper."

"That was very thoughtful," said Charlotte firmly, placing a hand on Amanda's arm. "Wasn't it, chief?" The look in her eyes was stern.

At that moment, the front door opened, letting in a blast of cold air. Kate took a step back so the wall no longer blocked her view. Trepalli and Friesen walked in, stomping loose snow off their boots.

Trepalli looked up and found her staring at him.

"Hello, chief. I—" He stopped and sniffed. "What smells so good?" Next to him, Friesen pulled his hood back and took a deep breath.

"Food," he said reverently.

Like cartoon characters drawn by a trail of aroma, they floated toward the duty room. Kate barely got out of the doorway before they brushed by her and stopped to stare at the crock pot.

Which left her wondering how she hadn't smelled it when she first walked in. Was her sense of smell deteriorating along with her eyesight? And why hadn't she noticed Amanda's car in the parking lot?

And then she remembered that she had come in the back way. Amanda must be parked in front.

Trepalli was the first one to notice Amanda. As though he sensed her attention, his gaze lifted from the crock pot and tracked through the room until it found her. He looked at her and his face grew very still. Amanda stared back at him, her color high, seemingly unable to break eye contact. Next to her, Charlotte glanced from one to the other, her expression unreadable.

Charlotte and Trepalli had had a brief fling last fall, but that was over now. Wasn't it?

"Well, hello!" said Friesen, finally noticing Amanda. He stepped toward her, smiling, and stuck his hand out. "Ben Friesen."

Amanda shook his hand. "Amanda Coburn."

"The chief's niece," added Charlotte. She smiled stiffly. "She made soup for us."

Trepalli stepped forward and Friesen reluctantly let go of Amanda's hand.

"Marco Trepalli." He shook her hand once firmly and let go. "Thank you."

Amanda blushed. Kate's eyebrows rose in dismay. Time to nip this in the bud.

"Yes, thank you, Amanda," she said. "I'll be home in a little while."

At once, five pairs of eyes turned to look at her.

"What?" she said defensively.

"You should go home *now*," said Charlotte bluntly.

"I've got work to do." Honestly, that girl acted like her mother sometimes.

"With all due respect, ma'am," said Friesen, eyeing her critically, "Charlotte's right. You've been up for almost forty-eight hours."

And it's showing, his tone said.

"I—"

"There's nothing to do tonight that can't wait until tomorrow," added Trepalli.

"You're both looking rough around the edges, too," Kate pointed out. They'd both participated in the exercise and had been interviewing witnesses for the last twelve hours. Not to mention working the real crash this afternoon. They had to be tired. Of course, they were much younger...

Trepalli nodded. "And we're officially off shift. Parker and Olinchuk relieved us half an hour ago."

Kate glanced up at the big wall clock above the duty desk. It was past six. Tattersall must have ordered Colin Parker and Michael Olinchuk in early to relieve the two who'd been on duty so long. All at once, fatigue descended over her, weighing her down, as if the night had suddenly grown unbearably heavy.

"I've almost finished compiling the interviews," said Charlotte. "They'll be waiting for you tomorrow morning."

Kate opened her mouth but before she could say anything, Tattersall chimed in. "No offence, ma'am, but you're starting to look a little cross-eyed."

"All right!" she said irritably. "I get the message!" This was bordering on mutiny.

Then she was overtaken by a huge yawn and everyone in the room laughed.

She grinned sheepishly. Maybe they were right. She wouldn't be able to focus properly on the interviews and she wanted to correlate them to the rough map Charlotte had drawn. She needed to be clear-headed to figure out who was telling the truth, who was slanting it, and who was lying outright, if anyone was.

That wasn't going to happen tonight.

Amanda walked over to her. "Come on, Aunt Kate. I'll whip up some crepes for a quick dinner."

Friesen whistled softly. "What *are* you?" he asked admiringly. "Some kind of chef?"

Amanda laughed. "As a matter of fact, I am."

Kate put an arm around Amanda's shoulders and turned her away from Friesen and Trepalli. "I'll meet you there."

Amanda walked out to a chorus of good nights and Kate turned back to Charlotte, Friesen and Trepalli.

"You two," she pointed to the two constables. "You're off duty. Go home. You," she pointed to Charlotte. "Go home. Now. Don't make me tell you again."

All three nodded, chastised. The constables headed for the locker room and Charlotte for the washroom. When Kate was alone with Tattersall, she eyed him. How long had he been on? She'd lost track. Dear God, where was that damned McKell when she needed him?

"Constable, who is relieving you?"

Tattersall hesitated, then glanced at the clock. He had been on all day. Shift ended at seven o'clock. Usually the duty officer came on early to get briefed on the previous shift. Tattersall was overdue for relief.

"Dan called to say he was going to be late, ma'am," he said finally. "I don't mind waiting. It's Sunday night."

Boychuk had been on all last night with the exercise. He couldn't have gotten enough sleep and now he was due on shift again, for another twelve hours. DC McKell would have been better prepared.

But Tattersall was right. Sundays were dead, usually. Boychuk should have a quiet time of it on the duty desk. Of course, this Sunday had started with a dead body at a mock accident and ended with another one at a real accident. If she were a superstitious woman, she'd be nervous.

"All right," she said finally. "Everybody else reported in?"

"Yes, ma'am," he said promptly. "Temblay and Fallon are on patrol, and Parker and Olinchuk will be here any minute."

Her gaze fell on the crock pot and she hesitated.

"I'll put it in the lunch room for the night shift," said Tattersall, reading her mind.

Kate nodded. It was time to go home. Much as she resented it, her body was forcing her to rest. She'd have to pursue the investigation in the morning.

"One last thing," she said.

"Ma'am?" prompted Tattersall when she didn't continue.

Kate took a deep breath. "Call the hospital. Talk to Nurse Kirkham on the intensive care unit. Tell her she can stop looking for Daisy Washburn's husband."

Tattersall nodded somberly and reached for the telephone.

As she headed for her boots by the back door, Kate wondered where Daisy Washburn had been going when she had the accident. And why Frank Washburn had been dressed in a tux.

CHAPTER 7

KATE DIDN'T get a chance to talk to Amanda that night. By the time she got home, she was so exhausted that she barely made it to her bed before she crashed.

She woke up with a start to a dark room and a silent house. She lay perfectly still, her eyes wide, until she realized that the sound that had awakened her was her stomach's grumbling. With a groan, she flipped over to her side and glanced at the clock. 3:40. In the morning.

God hated her.

With a sigh, she pushed the blankets off and sat up. The room was cold and she hurriedly slipped her feet in the sheepskin slippers that had been her sister Rose's Christmas gift last year. Had she turned the furnace down before she went to bed? She couldn't remember. She felt around at the foot of the bed but couldn't find her robe. It must still be hanging up behind the door.

Finally, all the pieces fell back in place and she remembered leaving her clothes where they had dropped on the floor and pulling on her fleece pajamas before crawling into bed. Amanda must have turned the furnace down because it was the furthest thing from Kate's mind once she saw her bed.

She should have listened to the girl and eaten something before crashing.

She reached the door without tripping over her clothes and

slipped the heavy bathrobe over her pajamas. She knew from experience that there was no going back to sleep for her. She might as well get some work done.

As quietly as she could, she opened her bedroom door and glanced at the spare room across the hallway from hers. The door was closed.

Usually she kept her laptop in the spare room, on the desk. But she'd left it in the kitchen the last time she used it. She flicked on the kitchen light and headed for the kettle. This was going to be a heavy coffee day.

Ten minutes later, she had turned the heat up, turned the computer on, and scooped coffee into her Bodum. She had turned on every light in the kitchen and now, with the blind closed on the back door and the curtains drawn at the window over the sink, she had the sense of being insulated against the outer darkness. She took the kettle off the burner before it could whistle and poured the hot water over the coffee grounds, then topped the water with the plunger. In a minute or so, she would push the plunger down. The smell alone was waking her up.

She sat down at the counter, pulled the laptop toward her and punched in her password. A moment later, she had access to her work computer. On the common drive, she found the transcripts of the interviews Trepalli and Friesen had conducted, and later, Martins and Holmes.

Charlotte had wanted to compile them this morning, but Kate needed to read the raw interviews before they got filtered through Charlotte's data processing program.

She poured herself a cup of coffee and began reading.

There were almost fifty interviews in all, including the volunteers, the emergency responders, and the EMO observers. Were she a lesser woman, the number would be daunting. With a sigh, she shifted on the hard stool to a more comfortable position. This was going to take a while.

* * *

By six o'clock, Kate had read through all the interviews, jotting down notes on the back of a hydro bill, since all her pads of paper were in the spare room. On Saturday morning, in preparation for the exercise, a crane had been brought in to pull the train car onto its side and place the damaged bus in position. All that work had taken place in daylight. The workers would have seen Frank's body if it had been there.

She pulled the blind on the door up and opened the curtains. What had been cozy in the middle of the night was starting to feel claustrophobic.

Charlotte was right—the volunteers were easy. They had been bussed in, escorted to their positions in the great fake drama, and there they had stayed—except for those carried away by ambulance—until Kate called an end to the exercise. The best guess was that they had been on site for fifty-five to ninety minutes before they left. None of them were in the vicinity of the body.

Of course, someone could be lying.

She absently picked up her cup and then put it down. She'd emptied the pot an hour ago but was too involved to get up and make more coffee. She would have to move soon or pay for it with a backache the rest of the day.

As for the EMO observers, she divided them into two categories: the ones who had come on the scene with the volunteers and helped place them, and the ones who arrived on scene half an hour later to set up the observation post, just before the fake emergency call went out.

She paid particular attention to the first group, as they had wandered all over the site, setting up the exercise. They—about five of them—arrived on the bus with the twenty-six volunteer victims, and while they were all over the place, in the bus, in the train, outside the bus, even partway up the slope toward the highway, nobody could recall seeing Frank Washburn's body.

According to these interviews, none of the firefighters, emergency medical technicians, or cops had seen the body before the all clear was sounded.

Kate stared out the window of the door that led to the deck and tapped her finger on her empty cup. If she squinted past the reflection of the lit kitchen, she could make out a faint, rosy glow in the inky night. No, that was wishful thinking.

Dozens of people had swarmed all over that site, some with powerful handheld flashlights, some with headlamps. Was it possible that no one had seen the body before Avramson called it in? It was possible. That night had been very dark and there'd been ice fog.

But if so, how had Avramson's crew stumbled on Frank Washburn's body?

In her mind's eye, she retraced her own steps from the moment the two HazMat guys gave the all clear. She had been delayed by Bert's call, then Alex Kowalski had joined her on the highway. After that, she had walked down to the "accident." The part of the site facing the highway was pretty well illuminated by the floodlights EMO had set up by their tent, but when she circled the train and bus it was much darker, despite the spillover effect. And the ice fog had made everything uncertain.

How long had Frank Washburn's body lain there before someone noticed him? Was it truly possible that no one had seen him? Or had the man seen all the lights and activity and in a drunken stupor tried to reach them only to fall short?

She was going to have to go back to the damned scene and check it out again.

Who exactly had found the body? She flipped through the screens on the computer, trying to locate the information. She couldn't recall seeing any mention. Avramson hadn't known either, and he was one of the first on scene.

"Good morning."

Kate jumped and knocked the cup over on the counter, spilling the cold dregs. "Ack!" She pushed the laptop away from the small pool and righted the cup before turning to give her niece the evil eye.

"Sorry, Aunt Kate!" said Amanda remorsefully. "I thought you heard me coming." She hurried to the sink and grabbed one of the dishtowels hanging off the oven's door handle.

She deftly wiped the spill up. While she was rinsing out the towel, Kate closed down the laptop and set it aside.

Frank Washburn would have to wait while she figured out what was happening with her niece.

"How long have you been up?" asked Amanda at the sink.

"A while," said Kate.

"Tell you what. Why don't you go take a shower while I get some breakfast going?"

Kate opened her mouth to argue but her stomach rumbled in anticipation and, frankly, she couldn't think of a single good reason why she shouldn't follow her niece's suggestion.

Half an hour later, she entered a kitchen redolent with wonderful smells. Was that bacon? She didn't even *have* bacon in the house. Amanda looked up from the frying pan and grinned.

"Just in time," she said, and expertly flipped a golden brown piece of French toast onto a plate. She plucked four strips of bacon from underneath a paper towel and placed them on the plate next to the French toast. Three slices of orange completed the ensemble. Amanda's gaze travelled up and down Kate's uniform before she nodded toward the other room.

"In the dining room," she said, carrying the plate in one hand and its twin in the other.

Bemused, Kate followed the girl into the dining room and found that Amanda had set the table for two. She had found place mats and the good cutlery. The Bodum stood on a trivet between the two place mats. A small plate stacked with more French toast sat next to a gleaming silver sugar and creamer set that Kate had forgotten she owned.

"What's in there?" asked Kate, pointing to the golden liquid in the gravy boat that sat next to the Bodum.

"Warm maple syrup," said Amanda. "Sit. Eat."

Kate sat and Amanda set a plate in front of her.

"I don't have maple syrup," said Kate. "Or bacon." Those were Bad For Her.

"I went shopping yesterday afternoon," said Amanda, slipping into the chair across from her. "I should have looked through your cupboards first," she muttered. She had brushed her blond hair back into a loose pony tail and wore a pair of black leggings under a large sweatshirt that read, "Montreal Academy of Fine Foods," where she had studied. Heavy, multi-colored wool socks that Kate was willing to bet Rose had knitted for her completed the outfit. Without makeup, Amanda looked even younger than twenty-three, fresh-faced and clear-eyed and unutterably beautiful.

Yes, indeed. It was going to be hard keeping Trepalli and Friesen away from her.

The aroma was making her mouth water. She cut into the toasted bread and took a bite. A soft groan escaped her as the delicious, warm, buttery egg taste filled her mouth. Amanda had waited for her reaction and now cut into her own toast with a satisfied smile. They ate in silence for the next ten minutes and Kate polished off three slices of French toast and all the bacon on her plate.

Finally, she pushed it away and leaned back. This was going to cost her in gym time.

Only then did she notice that Amanda had barely touched her food.

"All right," said Kate firmly. "What's going on, pumpkin?" She automatically slipped into the pet name she'd had for her niece when she was little. Amanda had loved Halloween more than she loved Christmas.

Amanda stared at her for a few seconds, clearly considering her answer. Her mouth turned down slightly and her jawline hardened. She looked away.

"I'm thinking of quitting my job."

According to Kate's sister Rose, landing a job at *L'Assiette blanche* was a coup for a young chef, even if the job was as a sous-chef. Amanda loved that job.

Her niece shrugged and stepped into the pregnant silence. "I need a break. I wanted to clear my head. I knew you wouldn't mind." She still didn't look at Kate.

Kate swallowed a mouthful of coffee and considered the girl. Unlike television cops, real cops usually couldn't tell just by looking at someone if they were lying. Amanda, however, was a terrible liar. Always had been. When she lied, her face flushed and her eyes grew jittery.

The girl's cheeks were pink.

"Want to tell me about it?" Kate asked softly.

Amanda's hands tightened on the coffee mug she was clutching.

"All right." She looked up suddenly and there was determination in her eyes. "I want to quit because the chef won't leave me alone."

Kate's eyebrows rose in astonishment. "You mean...?"

Amanda nodded. "Yes. He corners me every chance he gets. The man has no shame! He's married with three children!"

"Son of a bitch," said Kate softly. She studied her niece's face, her cop's instincts telling her she wasn't getting the whole story. Amanda's cheeks were still flushed and she couldn't meet Kate's gaze for any length of time. What was going on here? "Do your folks know?" she asked slowly, watching for the girl's reaction.

"Aunt Kate—" The shrill ringing of the phone interrupted Amanda and she looked at Kate. "Who calls at seven in the morning?"

Kate shrugged. Work, probably. Everybody knew she was an early riser.

She pushed her chair back and stalked over to the kitchen wall phone.

"Williams."

"Why haven't you released the scene?"

The tight, angry voice was a little too loud and she pulled the phone away. Who...? Oh, of course. She put the phone back to her ear.

"Hello, Alexandra." It took a lot of *chutzpah* to call the chief of police at home, especially so early.

"Your people won't let me have my site back," said Kowalski. Apparently today would be a continuation of yesterday. "If you release the scene today, I can still make this work."

Kate shook her head. "You want to run the exercise today?" Holy cow. It had taken months of prep work and logistical gymnastics to settle on a date and she wanted to call a spur-of-the-moment exercise, just like that? "You'll never get all your volunteers back."

"I've called them all," retorted Kowalski. "I can get most of them back, and most of the emergency responders, too. You're the hold up."

Hold up? This was the first Kate had heard that there was a possibility of running the exercise anyway.

It didn't matter. She wasn't releasing the scene until she was ready.

"I understand, but—"

"Manitoba Rail needs their goddam track back!" Kowalski's voice rose with frustration and Kate's eyebrows rose, too. This woman did not take well to being thwarted.

"We have to clear the bus from the tracks by Wednesday morning," continued Kowalski. "That leaves tonight and tomorrow night. The sooner you release the site, the sooner we can set this rolling again!"

"Kowalski, nobody will be ready!" Who the hell had she been talking to? There was no way she could coordinate the volunteers and emergency responders for a second exercise so soon. It had taken months to figure out the first one, for Pete's sake.

"Exactly!" said Kowalski with grim satisfaction. "This will be a true test of emergency preparedness."

Kate opened her mouth only to close it again. She couldn't argue with that logic. If Alexandra Kowalski wanted to alienate every emergency responder in the area, that was her business. Kate doubted she'd be able to swing it. After all, Kowalski would have to run it by her bosses first. Just the logistics of getting the volunteer "victims" back would stop her. *Something* would stop her.

Kate shifted the phone to her other ear. "I need to take another look at the scene in daylight," she said patiently. "After that, I'll release the scene."

"About time," said Kowalski. "Don't tell anyone about the surprise exercise." Then she hung up, leaving Kate staring at the receiver. Next to Kowalski, she was Miss Manners.

"She sounded mad," said Amanda behind her.

Kate hung up the phone and turned to face her niece.

"Alexandra Kowalski is always mad." Crazy, more likely. She sighed. "I have to go to work." She studied her niece's face for a few seconds. She wanted to pursue their conversation, but the moment had passed. "Will you be all right here by yourself?"

Amanda shrugged. "Sure. I'll probably do some exploring around town."

Kate remembered the cute bomber jacket and stylish boots her niece had worn the day before. "Dress for the weather," she said. "If your car breaks down, you can get frostbite waiting for help. I have extra coats and stuff in the hall closet."

"Aunt Kate," said Amanda with a smile. "This isn't Timbuktu, you know."

Kate didn't smile. "No, it's Manitoba and it's below thirty Celsius out there. Make sure you're dressed warm enough to survive a walk to the nearest shelter."

Amanda nodded, apparently chastened, but Kate wondered if she would listen.

As she put on her winter boots—her regular ones, not the heavy white Sorels—she promised herself she'd call Rose from the office.

Her sister would want to know that Amanda was safe. Maybe together they could figure out how to deal with this chef.

* * *

She arrived at the station an hour after shift change. Tattersall was back at the duty desk, typing at the computer. He nodded a greeting when she walked in but kept working. Trepalli stood at the counter, reading through the log book. He looked up at her.

"Morning, chief."

"Good morning, constable." Marco Trepalli was a good-looking boy, with those blue, blue eyes and that thick head of black hair. When he smiled, dimples appeared in his cheeks. She definitely had to keep Amanda away from him.

She hung up her parka in her office, changed her boots for shoes and turned on her computer before heading back to the duty room. She stopped in front of Charlotte's drawing of the accident scene on the white board and stood staring at the red "X" that marked the location of Frank Washburn's body. "Trepalli."

"Ma'am?"

She looked over her shoulder at him. "Who found the body?"

"As near as I can tell, a few people stumbled on it at the same time."

"No one claimed to have seen it first?"

"No, ma'am."

Tattersall stopped typing and turned to look at them, clearly interested.

"Do you remember who they were?" he asked Trepalli.

Trepalli joined Kate at the white board. He pointed at the cluster of black numbers near Washburn's body. The boy had big hands. Clean nails, too.

"There were three firefighters and the chief, at first," he said. "Paul Arquette, Sam Higgins and Ed Pellegrino, plus Chief Avramson. Then the chief called one of the paramedics over." He hesitated a moment, then nodded. "Philip Choo."

Kate mulled over the information, replaying her arrival on the scene last night. The night before last. She didn't know the three firefighters, but she had spoken with Choo, who had confirmed Washburn was dead.

"What's the matter, chief?" asked Tattersall.

She shook her head. "Probably nothing, but I thought I saw six people around the body when I got there."

Trepalli's eyebrows rose. "I can check with Friesen. Between the two of us, we interviewed almost all the volunteers. There were only about half a dozen left when Martins and Holmes relieved us."

"Where is Friesen?" asked Kate, looking around the duty room for the first time. Charlotte was usually in by now but she had express orders to sleep in this morning. Usually a couple of constables were at the general desks, finishing up reports before they headed home, or in the lunch room briefing their replacements.

"He's driving Olinchuk home," said Tattersall. "He couldn't get his car started."

Kate nodded and glanced at the board next to the duty desk. It listed who was on duty at any given time. She saw Trepalli's name and Friesen's, showing that they were in. And Martins and Holmes were already on patrol.

"I need to go over the interviews again," she said. Clearly she had missed something.

Tattersall picked up a file folder and held it up. "I printed out all the interviews," he said. "We can split them up."

Kate nodded. "We're looking to identify who first saw the body."

Tattersall opened the folder, pulled out half the sheets and handed her the rest in the folder. Kate tucked it under her arm and headed for the lunch room. May as well be comfortable. "Coffee?" she threw over her shoulder at Tattersall.

"Please."

Behind her, Friesen's voice sounded over Trepalli's radio, "There in five."

"Ready," replied Trepalli, already moving toward the door.

CHAPTER 8

KATE WAS almost through her pile of interviews when a shadow blocked the lunch room door. She looked up, pen poised in mid-air, and found DC McKell filling the doorway. His parka was open, revealing his uniform. He held gloves in one hand and his fur hat was tucked under one arm. There were dark circles under his blue eyes and his face looked thinner. He stared at her with annoyance.

"I was only gone for a week," he said. "You couldn't have waited for me to get back?"

Kate forced herself to relax, recognizing his attempt at a joke. "How's your father?"

McKell entered the lunch room and tossed his hat and gloves onto an empty club chair. "Still dying," he said. He looked at her. "But he's not in such a rush now."

She had no idea what to say to that. He removed his parka and folded it over the top of the club chair before walking over to the coffee pot and pouring himself a cup. The lines on either side of his mouth looked deeper, as if gouged out with a knife.

"So," he said after the silence had stretched on uncomfortably. "Frank Washburn." He sat down at the table across from Kate.

She nodded. "And Daisy."

His mouth tightened. She only noticed because she was watching for it.

McKell and Daisy Washburn were not friends. He blamed her for destroying his marriage to Elizabeth Dabbs, the mayor's daughter. In a way, he was right. Daisy and Elizabeth were best friends. When testing showed that McKell would never father a child, it was Daisy who put into words the fact that it wasn't too late for Elizabeth to have children with another man.

Kate didn't understand why they hadn't adopted, and it didn't matter. Elizabeth had divorced McKell and moved to Toronto, and McKell had settled his simmering anger on Daisy. Kate couldn't blame the guy for feeling betrayed, but part of her wondered if he was just transfering his hurt and rage to Daisy, when really, Elizabeth was the one who betrayed him.

It didn't help that he didn't land the chief of police job. Kate knew he resented Daisy for costing him his marriage, and subsequently the promotion, but he never discussed it.

Which was fine by her.

"Does she know about her husband?" he asked.

Kate shook her head. "She's in a coma." An image of Daisy as she had last seen her flashed through her mind and she almost winced. Until she found out that Daisy had actively encouraged Elizabeth Dabbs to divorce her husband, Kate had considered Daisy a friend. Now she didn't know how she felt about her.

McKell took a deep breath and let it out slowly. Kate imagined she saw smoke coming out of his nostrils. He drank from his cup before replacing it firmly on the counter top. "All right," he said. "Fill me in."

It sounded suspiciously like an order, but Kate had learned to overlook McKell's overbearing attitude. It came from being a sergeant with the military police in his previous life. He was a good deputy chief, now that he was beginning to accept her leadership.

Or maybe he was just biding his time.

Despite the fact that he could be *such* a pain in the butt, she was glad to have him back. Now she would stop worrying about who was on shift and who was working overtime.

She filled him in on the exercise, the discovery of the body and the accident which had claimed another life and put Daisy

Washburn in the hospital.

During her debrief, he got up to refill his cup and hers and remained standing, one hip leaning against the counter, staring out at the pale morning.

His stillness struck her, not for the first time. It had taken her a while to notice this quality of his when she first arrived, because he had thrown up all kinds of barriers to hold her off, and she hadn't been able to see past them.

He could focus entirely on what he was being told. While his outer being was still to the point where he barely blinked, his inner self was busy listening and processing. He rarely interrupted someone who was talking, preferring to wait until they were done and then zeroing in on the heart of what was being said.

Kate finished and waited for him to speak. She expected him to comment on the discrepancy between her memory of six people around the body when only five were recorded in the interviews, but he surprised her.

"So where was Daisy going while her husband lay dead?"

The question took her aback and left a sour taste in her mouth. It was a question she had asked herself, but there was venom in his tone.

"We can ask her when she wakes up," said Kate coolly. He glanced around at her, then went back to staring out the window, at the snow-covered branches of the oak tree, beyond which was the parking lot.

"Don't you find it curious that she was heading out of town just hours after her husband was found dead?" he asked softly. "If it wasn't for the accident, who knows where she would be by now."

"Rob?"

They both turned as Charlotte came into the room, a tentative smile on her face. In her red, down-filled, long coat she looked like a blushing Michelin man.

"Hello, Charlotte," he said with a smile. As always, the transformation amazed Kate. Whenever Rob McKell smiled, she understood how he had managed to persuade three women to marry him.

Charlotte stopped in front of him. Cold clung to her and Kate shivered a little.

"Good morning, chief," said Charlotte, sparing Kate a glance. Before Kate could reply, she turned back to the DC, placing a mittened hand on his arm. "How's your dad?" Her black-and-red wool hat pushed her hair out into a glossy ring of brown curls around her face. With her cheeks red from the cold and her green eyes shining with concern, she could have been some kind of post-modern madonna.

McKell patted her hand. "My brother is with him for now," he said. "The doctors say it could be today or it could be in six months."

Kate blinked. She hadn't even known he had a brother.

Charlotte squeezed his arm and released him. "Let me know when you want me to book a flight out." He nodded his thanks and she turned back to Kate.

"Any news on Frank?"

Kate shrugged and stood up, gathering the interviews into the file folder. "The ME hasn't checked in with me yet," she said. "She probably had to wait longer than she expected to get started."

Charlotte frowned as she unzipped her coat. "Why?"

Kate hesitated and McKell forged into the breach. "Still too frozen."

Charlotte looked down at the flecked linoleum floor and swallowed hard. "Well, I'd better get to work."

Kate and McKell watched her leave. Kate glanced up when she sensed McKell's gaze on her.

"Just how frozen was he?"

Kate opened her mouth, then closed it. She was so stupid. She should have asked Dr. Kijawa that obvious question yesterday. It would have helped establish timeline.

"That's a very good question, DC McKell," she finally said grudgingly. "Let's ask the ME." She glanced out the window. It was past nine o'clock and almost full daylight. The doctor would be up. She might even be at her practice. "I'll get Charlotte to call."

She swept the file folder up and walked out, angry at herself for missing such an important detail. What else had she missed?

Tattersall looked up as she passed by the duty desk. "I just finished going over them," he said, resuming their conversation as if there hadn't been any pause. His thinning brown hair was sticking up on the top of his head from static electricity. Despite the proximity to the front door and the draft, he had taken off his uniform jacket and hung it on the back of his stool. His shirt sleeves were rolled up, revealing forearms corded with long, lean muscles. "Avramson and Arquette both say there were already people there when they arrived at the body. Choo arrived on scene after the chief sent someone to fetch him." He tapped the pile of papers with one finger. "No one seemed to know everybody who was there."

Kate nodded. "Same here." The remaining two witnesses, Sam Higgins and Ed Pellegrino, had recognized Chief Avramson but no one else.

She walked over to the diagram again and stood staring at it. Out of the corner of her eye, she saw Charlotte emerge from the washroom. McKell came into the duty room and asked Charlotte to call Dr. Kijawa's office. The phone rang and Tattersall answered.

Kate didn't stop staring at the white board with its crude black drawing and that one, blood red "X" drawing all the attention.

Avramson. Avramson would know everybody who had been at the body's location—they were all his firefighters except for Choo, the paramedic.

"What did Avramson say in the interview?" she asked Tattersall when he got off the phone.

"He identified Pellegrino, Higgins and Arquette, and described Choo. No one else."

For Pete's sake. She wasn't crazy. There'd been six people at the scene when she arrived. Not five. *Six*.

"The doctor's in with a patient," said Charlotte as she hung up the phone. "I left a message to have her call you." She was speaking to DC McKell.

Finally, Kate shook her head in frustration. "Get Trepalli and Friesen back here," she ordered Tattersall. "I want them to talk to Choo, Higgins, Pellegrino and..." She looked at Tattersall.

"Arquette," he supplied.

She nodded. "I want to know specifically who was there when they arrived at the scene, who arrived after they got there, and who left before I got there."

Tattersall nodded and turned to the radio.

McKell looked at her expectantly and she stared at him, lips pursed, until she finally made a decision.

"DC McKell, how would you like to go for a drive to the fire station?"

His eyebrows rose. "We could walk there. Save on warming up the car."

Kate shook her head. "After the fire station, we're going back to the scene."

The light in McKell's eyes was all the answer she needed. As she got dressed to face the cold, she wondered how he felt about his father dying. He never spoke of family, and while he was friendly with the staff, he never welcomed intrusions into his private life.

After his experience with Daisy, who could blame him?

Maybe she should interview Avramson alone. Avramson might think she'd brought McKell along as back up. Might make her look weak.

In the end, she decided it was the right decision. This wasn't a contest of wills. She needed information from the man, information that would be hard to get if she irritated him, which she often managed to do. McKell spoke the same language as Avramson.

It would help, not hinder, to have the DC around.

She hoped.

* * *

"Jesus H.!" said McKell. "It's colder than a witch's—"

Kate's raised eyebrow stopped him and he contented himself with, "—heart!"

The squad car had warmed for ten minutes, long enough for the oil to circulate and the engine to accustom itself to the idea of running. But the interior of the car was still frigid. The pretend-leather seats were hard as ice and her butt was never going to warm up again. Their breath plumed out to condense on the windows and McKell turned the fan on high. The engine heat indicator light didn't even budge.

McKell pulled down the fur ear flaps on his hat and let the strings dangle. He glanced at her. "Ready?"

She nodded and he put the Crown Vic in reverse. He drove slowly out of the parking lot and onto Mendenhall Drive. Seconds later, he turned in to the parking lot behind the fire station. He hesitated a moment, his hand hovering over the key, before finally sighing and removing the key from the ignition. The car hadn't even warmed up.

Kate knew exactly how he felt. A decree had come down from City Hall at the beginning of winter that no City of Mendenhall vehicle would be allowed to idle. She understood being environmentally conscious, but Mayor Dabbs wasn't the one getting in and out of cold squad cars all day long.

They emerged into the cold and hurried to the back door of the station, which opened onto a hallway painted a particularly bland green. It stank of diesel, oil, and exhaust. Double swing doors with windows opened onto a heated bay on their left. She glanced in but saw no one working on the trucks. On the other side of the corridor were three closed doors. The corridor turned left at the far end. Two bulletin boards faced each other across the hallway. One would be for union announcements, Kate knew. The other would be for everything else.

"Upstairs?" asked McKell, pointing at the metal stairs just inside the bay. There was a staff room at the top of the stairs, where the duty firefighters could doze, or eat, or whatever it was they did while waiting for a fire call.

Kate nodded, but just then the middle door opened down the hall and a man emerged. He wore sweat pants and a sweat-stained tee-shirt and had a white cotton towel rolled around his neck. While he wasn't very tall, he was powerfully built and too young to have come by that perfectly bald head naturally. He stopped, clearly not surprised to see them.

"We're here to see Chief Avramson," said Kate. Behind the man, she spied a bench press with a series of weights stacked up on the wall next to it. Then he closed the door.

"In his office," said the man. He pointed down the hallway. "Second office on your left."

She nodded her thanks and she and McKell headed down the hallway. Just before she turned left, she glanced back. He was still standing there, staring at them.

Avramson wasn't in his office, so they wandered to the front of the building and found a secretary.

"Oh, he's working out," said the Sweet Young Thing. Couldn't be more than eighteen.

"Is that so?" said McKell, smiling at the girl. But the look he gave Kate was full of annoyance.

"Just go back the way you came," said the girl. "Middle door on your left."

"Thank you," said Kate. There was no point getting mad at the girl. She wasn't the one jerking them around.

Kate led the way back down the hallway, and if there was a little more force to her footsteps, well, so be it. She didn't even pause before opening the door to the workout room. The stink of old sweat and ripe running shoes hit her like a slap in the face.

The room was about twenty by twenty and filled with workout equipment, including a brand new Bowflex in the corner.

The bald guy was nowhere in sight, but Chief Avramson straddled a wooden bench doing bicep curls. He was bare-chested, with powerful arms and pecs. His graying blond hair was clipped tight to his skull. Right now, it was dark and spiky with sweat. His torso glistened. Above his head was a big window that looked out onto the parking lot behind the fire station. She could clearly see the squad car.

McKell's irritation rolled off him in waves but the smile she gave Avramson was professional.

"Chief Avramson, I have a few more questions for you, if you've got time."

Avramson set the dumbbell down on the floor and picked up the towel from the bench. He unfolded it with a flick of his wrist before wiping his face and head with it.

"You should have called ahead, Williams," he said cheerfully. He stood up and Kate had to fight an urge to step back. The man was well over six feet tall and nearly half as wide. "I have an appointment and I need to take a shower first. Your questions will have to wait." He smiled down at her but the smile didn't reach his blue eyes.

"This will only take a minute," said Kate, raising her chin.

Avramson flicked the towel over his shoulder and bent down to pick up the dumbbell, which he replaced on the rack on the wall. Then he headed for the door.

"You're more than welcome to follow me into the shower room." He grinned, showing all his teeth. "I promise I don't bite." He clicked his teeth together. "Or you can send McKell in, if you'd rather."

Kate recognized a challenge when she heard one. How old was this guy, anyway? Seventeen?

"Stop being an ass," said McKell.

Avramson shrugged. He wasn't much taller than McKell, but he had to outweigh him by forty pounds. All of it muscle.

"Suit yourself," he said and stepped into the hallway. Kate followed him out and saw the next door down close behind him.

"Asshole," said McKell.

Kate didn't reply. Avramson wanted to play dirty? Then they'd play dirty.

"Chief?" said McKell. There was uncertainty in his voice.

Kate walked up to the shower room door, pushed it open, and found herself in a changing room with lockers and benches. The bald guy stood in front of an open locker, rubbing cologne over his neck and chest. He was completely naked.

Kate heard a snort behind her and realized McKell had followed her in. The bald guy looked around and yelped when he saw her. Kate ignored him and forged past the lockers to where she heard a shower running.

Unlike the separate showers at the station, this shower room was literally one big shower, with three shower heads and a tiled floor sloping down to a drain in the middle. Avramson stood under the hot spray of the middle one, eyes closed, letting the water run over his head and face. Steam billowed around him, but did nothing to hide the fact that he had skinny legs. The man probably never wore shorts.

"Right then," said Kate.

Avramson jumped and opened his eyes. His hands automatically reached to cover his privates.

"What the hell—?"

It was interesting how a blush started in the chest area and flooded everything north. Kate studied the effect for a moment before reaching for her notepad and pen.

She was growing uncomfortably hot in her parka, but she didn't plan to be here long.

"What the hell are you doing?" demanded Avramson, ending on a high note.

She looked at him in surprise. "I'm asking you a few questions."

"In the men's room?"

As if there was a women's room. Kate blinked at him, her best innocent look on her face.

"You invited me," she pointed out reasonably.

"I didn't think for a minute you'd follow me!"

Really, she didn't know why men covered their privates like that. Especially as she'd already seen what little there was to see.

"She's very literal," drawled McKell, behind her.

"Chief Avramson," said Kate formally, "you told Constable Friesen that you and a couple of your men found the body. Could you elaborate?"

Avramson was looking around the shower room as if hoping a door had miraculously appeared. A towel hung from a hook on the wall next to Kate. She made no move toward it.

"Elaborate how?" he asked with a note of desperation.

"Was there anyone with the body when you arrived?" asked Kate.

"Uh, no... Wait... I don't think so."

"Would that be a yes or a no?" asked Kate politely.

"No. I thought I saw someone when I got near but it was a trick of the head lamp. There was me, Arquette, Higgins and Pellegrino. We had decided to do an outer sweep of the area, to make sure no one had managed to crawl out past the perimeter."

Kate nodded as she wrote. Now that he was answering her questions, he seemed to relax.

"Who went for the paramedics?" she asked.

He opened his mouth to answer, then paused. Steam continued to billow around him. His skin was turning red under the onslaught of the hot water. Still he paused, clearly working something out.

"Chief?" she prompted.

Finally he shook his head. "I don't know who it was," he said. "I called out for someone to go get a medic and someone said he'd go, but before I saw his face, he was already gone." He peered through the steam at Kate. "He wasn't one of my guys. I don't know who he was or when he joined us."

"Did he come back?"

Avramson shrugged. "Someone came back with the medic, I think, but I was busy so I wasn't really paying much attention."

Kate didn't know what he could have been busy doing but she merely smiled and closed the notebook.

"Thank you for your time," she said. She grabbed the towel and tossed it to him. He caught it one-handed, still covering his privates with the other.

"I could report you for sexual harassment," he called as she turned away.

"Oh, don't flatter yourself," she said and left, McKell still behind her. She couldn't remember now why she thought she needed him here.

They emerged into the hallway, which was blessedly cool after the heat in the shower room. The hallway was empty and they made it back to the car without encountering anybody.

McKell started the squad car and pulled out of the station's parking lot. He whistled all the way to the exercise site.

CHAPTER 9

KATE STARED outside the windshield as the sun-dazzled prairie went by. What the hell was the matter with Avramson? What kind of game was he playing? A man was dead, for Pete's sake. Did he think it was funny?

McKell slowed down to negotiate the turn off the highway onto the Burndale road and Kate took a deep breath. And McKell. It had been a mistake to bring him. The two men clearly didn't like each other, which probably prompted Avramson to act like a jackass. And McKell's bristling attitude hadn't helped. In fact, she suspected it had egged the fire chief on.

Be honest, she told herself as the car bumped over the railroad tracks. *You got pissed off at Avramson, too.* She squeezed her eyes shut for a moment, remembering the man cupping his privates in the shower. Dear God. What had she been *thinking*?

McKell pulled over on the side of the road and they sat in silence for a moment, listening to the heater struggle against the demanding cold. Kate studied the dark hulk of the train with its flipped over car. The destroyed bus looked like a Tinker toy from this angle.

For a moment, all Kate saw in her mind's eye was Daisy's red Focus on its side, the undercarriage bent and pulled apart.

"When's the RCMP going to be finished with Daisy's accident scene?" she asked. The analyst had arrived late yesterday and hadn't finished by nightfall.

McKell shrugged. "Another couple of hours, apparently."

Kate nodded. She wanted to release the accident scene so people no longer had to detour but she had to wait for the analyst to do his job.

"Pretty impressive," said McKell, staring at the exercise site. "Where did they find the bus?"

Kate shrugged. "No idea. Kowalski found it in Winnipeg." That reminded her of the woman's phone call that morning and she sighed. "Come on," she said. "I want your eyes on this scene."

He turned the engine off and pocketed the keys. Then they both pulled down their hats, pulled up their hoods, and put on their down-filled mittens. Kate had forgotten her balaclava at home, so she pulled her wool scarf up to cover her nose and cheeks.

If she fell in this get-up, she was never getting up again.

They both got out and stood in the cold for long minutes, studying the scene. She had decided against setting up a crime scene tape perimeter. For one thing, the area was huge and she didn't want to waste manpower planting stakes and setting up the tape. For another, unless she wanted to station a constable here, a crime scene tape would only attract the curious, not keep them out.

The snow was trampled for a hundred yards around the train, a hopeless mess of boot tracks, sled tracks, and body imprints. Fake blood had frozen into splotchy red ice around the scene. A dark blob marked the spot where someone had dropped a scarf. There was even a boot lying forlornly on its side next to the track.

Kate shook her head. How did a person lose a boot and not notice?

From this angle, she couldn't see the spot where the body had been found, but she could see the blue shadow of the trails that led from the trees toward the train. Two sets of tracks paralleled it, where her constables had followed the trail back into the trees, and eventually found Frank Washburn's car.

The car had been towed to the station garage and examined. Nothing. They were still waiting on the prints.

She looked up at McKell. "Ready?"

He nodded and she stepped off the shoulder and into the ditch, following a well-tamped-down trail to the train. Ten minutes later, she hauled herself up to the flatbed car and stood looking out at the forest. The morning sun was still low in the sky, and the field leading to the forest was pockmarked with dark pools of blue shadows. McKell hauled himself up beside her and she noted with satisfaction that he was breathing hard, too.

He hadn't examined Charlotte's schematic of the scene. All he knew about the incident were the bare-bones facts she had provided him earlier that morning. Here was her chance to get a fresh perspective of what should be a straight-forward death-by-stupidity. She'd finally be able to shake the sense that she was missing something.

"Give me your analysis," she said.

He gave her a quizzical look as if to say, *Really?* "The scene's been trampled to death," he objected.

"I know." She sighed. "I just want to be sure I'm not missing anything."

He pursed his lips and shrugged, finally turning toward the forest. Kate let him look. She tilted her face up to the sky and closed her eyes briefly, enjoying the returning warmth of the sun. It had to be about minus thirty, if not colder. Not much warmer than it had been when she'd stood here on the night of the exercise. But it *felt* warmer. Amazing what sunshine could do to the psyche.

After a few minutes, McKell nodded in the direction of the wide, trampled circle about a hundred yards from the wreck.

"I've met Frank Washburn a couple of times," he said conversationally. His words sounded slurred, as if his cold lips were having trouble shaping them. "He didn't strike me as the kind of man who would wander out in the snow on a cold night."

Kate shrugged. "He was probably very drunk."

He nodded thoughtfully. "Maybe. But he's... he was the manager of the Royal Bank. You know how small towns are. There'd be rumors if the guy was a drunk."

True. Living in a small town meant that anyone in a prominent position, such as the manager of the local bank, would be constantly under a microscope. There were very few secrets.

Still. "We both know that people act out of character sometimes," she pointed out. "He could have had a reason to get drunk."

Like he and Daisy had a fight.

"True." But his tone was skeptical.

She let him study the scene in silence while she considered possibilities. There was no telling what someone might do under duress. Even the most respectable people could behave irrationally. How many times had she investigated crimes where the perpetrator was well-liked and well-respected? How many times had she heard shocked neighbors protest that the accused was a nice man who couldn't possibly have done whatever it was?

So, maybe Frank and Daisy had a blowout and he took off. As for Daisy being on the highway the morning after they found Frank, maybe she got mad when she woke up and saw that he still wasn't home. Maybe she decided to leave him. Or even go away for a few days to cool off.

Without a suitcase? And Frank was in a tux. He didn't take off. He'd been at a function somewhere. But where?

Kate made a mental note to check with Abrams or O'Hara. They were the first two constables on the scene of Daisy's accident. But a suitcase would have been noted in the log. A suitcase was a big detail to omit, and her officers were better than that.

So. No suitcase. Where was Daisy going, then? Mendenhall was home for Daisy. She had no family, but she was an ambitious woman and planned to become mayor of Mendenhall one day, maybe even go into provincial politics. She knew people all over the province, quite a few in Winnipeg, since she'd gone to college there.

So, she could have been going to see any number of friends.

"That's well out of the theater of operations," said McKell, interrupting her train of thought. His choice of words reminded her of his years as a military policeman. He traced the line of the original track with a mittened hand from the forest to the trampled circle. "That's how he got there?" he asked.

"Yes," said Kate.

He stayed silent a moment longer. "And the other two trails?"

"The constables who followed the original trail back into the woods."

He nodded without taking his eyes off the trail. She turned to follow his gaze and suddenly the evidence jumped out at her as if lined in blinking neon lights.

"Crap," she said.

McKell nodded in agreement.

"His trail is too straight for a drunk to have made." It was so obvious, she couldn't imagine how she had missed it.

"And it's wide," added McKell. "See where the two parallel trails show distinct foot prints? His isn't distinct. The prints are all muddled."

Kate stared at the shadowed trail, cursing herself for a blind fool. "I'll bet you that's the kind of trail you'd leave if you were dragging something heavy behind you."

McKell turned to look at her. There was a malicious gleam in his eye. "We should test it out."

She raised an eyebrow at him. Was the bugger suggesting he should *drag* her?

A movement out of the corner of her eye caught her attention and she turned to see a figure emerge from the trees and head straight for the center trail.

"Who the hell is that?" asked McKell. Without waiting for an answer, he shouted, "Stop!" and waved his arms.

The figure paused, staring straight at McKell, then waved back uncertainly. Kate grinned and watched Alexandra Kowalski resume her stolid march toward McKell and the train.

"Oh, for the love of..." he muttered before jumping off the flatbed. He immediately broke into an awkward run, following the path to the right of Frank Washburn's trail.

Kate's smile slowly faded and she puffed out a breath. If they were right, and someone had dragged Frank Washburn to the train site, then they were talking murder.

She replayed the scene as she had found it, trying to imagine what might have happened. The body had been left just outside the spill of light from the EMO floodlights, but close enough that someone would eventually stumble on it.

But why?

If you were going to kill someone, why ensure the body would be discovered? Remorse? Someone who cared for Daisy and didn't want her to suffer, not knowing what had happened to her husband?

Or maybe the death was accidental. Maybe the perpetrator had somehow incapacitated Frank and dragged him to the train site in hopes that he would be rescued.

She shook her head at that—too risky. Washburn had been dressed for indoors. No gloves, no coat, no hat... Unconscious on the cold ground. Anybody who had spent a winter in Manitoba would know that this was courting death.

Unless the perpetrator had expected Frank to be discovered sooner. Maybe by engineering the discovery himself. Maybe he had arranged for Avramson to find the body, but he had miscalculated and it was too late for Frank. Or maybe it had taken him longer than he expected to maneuver someone into finding Frank.

She stopped short at that. Why did she assume it was a man? A strong woman could have dragged the body into place. It would have taken a while and she would have risked discovery, but it could be done. Maybe.

She needed to find out who the sixth person had been. The person who had fetched the paramedic.

McKell had reached Kowalski and managed to get her off the track. Now she was following him back to the train. Kate couldn't read either one's body language under their heavy parkas, but she could imagine.

The body was clearly staged. No matter how drunk Frank was, if he had stumbled to the crash site on his own only to pass out, he would have ended up sprawled, at the very least. Not laid out like he was at a funeral parlor viewing.

What if the perpetrator had wanted the body discovered while he or she was on site and able to revel in the discovery?

Kate forced herself to consider that scenario, distasteful as it was. She hated the thought that someone from her small community was remorseless enough to kill a man and then stage the discovery of his body.

Of course, the perpetrator might have been anyone from Brandon or Winnipeg, too. Clearly, it was someone who knew the exercise was taking place that night. Someone who knew enough to—

"Williams."

Kate blinked and returned to the here and now. Kowalski and McKell were almost at the train, and by the look on McKell's face, he'd like to throw Kowalski under one. Preferably a moving one.

"Hello Alexandra," said Kate mildly.

Kowalski came to a stop by the flatbed and looked up at Kate. She pulled her hood back and scowled. "You said you were going to release the scene."

McKell stayed a few feet away from Kowalski, his arms crossed. He glanced up at Kate, clearly itching for a chance to respond.

"What I said," said Kate calmly, "was that I needed to take another look at the scene."

"Well? Have you had your look?" She wore a hand-knit gray wool cap that turned her face an interesting combination of pasty white and cold-induced pink.

Kate glanced at McKell, who reluctantly shrugged. There really wasn't much more they could do here.

"You're really going to try to scramble another exercise?"

Kowalski got a grim look on her face. "I'm going to do my damndest."

McKell looked like he wanted to argue, but Kate wasn't in the mood for a tug of war with the other woman. Besides, there was no way Kowalski could pull it off.

Kowalski stared up at her, waiting. Kate opened her mouth to tell her the scene was hers and then she closed it. Kowalski was a taller than the average woman, and wiry. She probably weighted one forty, one fifty. McKell, on the other hand, was a big guy, almost six feet tall, with the solidity of a mature man. He had to weigh at least one eighty.

"Tell you what, Alexandra," said Kate slowly. "I need to run a little experiment before I can release the scene." She avoided McKell's gaze. "And if you're willing to help, it should take no time at all."

* * *

Tattersall looked up when Kate walked in and she nodded a greeting. He opened his mouth to answer but it stayed open when he spotted McKell behind her. Kate didn't dare turn around.

"What happened to you?" Tattersall blurted out.

Charlotte peeked around the corner and stared. Trepalli and Friesen walked out of the coffee room, cups in hand, and stared past Kate at McKell.

"It was an experiment," he muttered and passed Kate in the hallway to enter the duty room and his office. The back of his parka was covered in pellets of snow and ice. The back of his uniform pants was soaking wet, as was his hair. His hat had been the first thing to fall off, followed shortly by his boots. He'd hung on to his mittens, however. They were soaked, too.

That Kowalski was one strong woman.

Before he disappeared into his office and closed the door, McKell gave her a look over his shoulder that told her she wasn't fooling him. She managed to keep a straight face until he closed the door, but after that, she couldn't keep the grin off her face. It had been his idea, after all.

Then she sighed. He might be pissed off, but the experiment had proved that Frank Washburn's tracks had been left by someone dragging his body to the scene, and then mingling with the emergency responders.

There was no other way it could have happened.

"What happened?" asked Friesen. He had a mug in one hand and a scone in the other.

"Is that a *scone*?" she asked. Who in town made scones?

He blushed and the hand holding the scone twitched, as if he had just controlled an impulse to hide it behind his back.

Trepalli cleared his throat. "Amanda brought them over about half an hour ago."

"They were still warm," added Friesen reverently.

Amanda had baked scones? What was she, some kind of food fairy? Through the duty desk opening she could see the doorway into the lunch room, where Trepalli still stood. His ears almost pricked up.

"Shouldn't be a problem," said Tattersall.

"Constable Trepalli."

He reached her side in five long strides. From the lunch room, she heard sounds of scrambling and a moment later, Friesen stood next to Trepalli.

Kate almost smiled at their eagerness. Patrolling was long stretches of deadly dull punctuated with spikes of adrenalin rushes. She had noticed Trepalli looking restless lately.

She'd had her doubts about him at first. But in spite of being too good looking for his own good, he was thorough and smart. And while professional in his attitude, he wasn't afraid to show sympathy. He would make a good cop.

He'd been her main support back in the fall when things were so bad between her and McKell. She had almost convinced herself that she'd made a mistake in accepting the job of chief of police, but Trepalli helped restore her faith in her abilities as a cop. And he had good instincts. He was the one who'd first suspected there actually *was* a missing kid.

"I want the two of you to canvas Washburn's neighbors," she said. "I want to know if there's been fighting between Daisy and Frank, if anyone knows where Daisy was going, where Frank was last night."

Trepalli had pulled out his notepad and was taking notes while Friesen nodded his understanding.

"After that," she said, "I want you to go to the Royal Bank and talk to his colleagues and employees. Find out if anyone had any reason to want to hurt him."

Trepalli looked up sharply. "You're thinking murder?" His gorgeous blue eyes suddenly looked bluer. He really was a very good-looking boy.

She shrugged, aware that all eyes were on her. McKell's office door suddenly opened and he stepped out into the duty room, wearing a fresh uniform. He looked around in surprise at the tableau.

"What's going on?"

Charlotte joined the little group. "The chief thinks Frank Washburn was killed." She wrapped her arms around herself as if she were suddenly cold.

Kate removed her mittens. "I'm saying we have a suspicious death," she said. She glanced at McKell, who nodded stiffly.

"We think Washburn was dragged from the trees to the train," he said. "He didn't get there on his own power."

Kate looked around at her staff. Friesen and Trepalli could barely contain their excitement. McKell looked determined, while Charlotte looked like she was going to be sick. Only Tattersall looked thoughtful.

"I guess the question is," he said, "was he dead before he was dragged there, or did he die as a *result* of being dragged there?"

Very good question, thought Kate. Hopefully she'd get an answer soon.

* * *

"You're enjoying this, aren't you?"

Kate looked up from the interviews she was reviewing yet again. She was separating them into approximate locations of where the interviewees were at the time the body was discovered. Charlotte stood in the doorway of her office, frowning.

Kate's mind went from being engrossed in keeping track of who was where and when, to being completely blank.

"This," said Charlotte, sweeping a hand at the pile of interviews. "This whole little mystery." Her eyes were suspiciously bright. Was she holding back tears?

Holy cow.

"What's the matter, Charlotte?" Kate put the papers down and gave the young woman her undivided attention.

"All of you," said Charlotte, her voice low. She crossed her arms, her fingers clutching at her sleeves, but she kept her bright, fierce gaze on Kate. "You're all excited about this. It's a game to you." She took a deep breath as if to calm herself. "You need to remember that Frank Washburn was a good man who gave a lot to this community. He coached Little League. He ran the Salvation Army Christmas campaign every year. He had a wife. Parents. I barely knew the guy, but he did *not* deserve to die like this, like the butt of a mean joke!"

She lost the battle and a few tears trickled down her flushed cheeks. She whisked them away with the palm of her hands before crossing her arms again. The look she gave Kate was reproachful.

"I..."

"As for Daisy," continued Charlotte, "She has her faults, but who doesn't? You might want to keep in mind that it's her husband lying in the morgue, and that she's lying in the hospital, not even aware that he's dead."

Kate swallowed and nodded uncertainly.

Charlotte took a deep breath and uncrossed her arms. With a last frown at her boss, she turned on her heel and marched back to her desk.

Kate stared at the empty doorway for a long time before getting up to go.

* * *

As she drove to the Mendenhall hospital, Kate went over what she knew about Frank Washburn, which wasn't a lot.

The man had just turned thirty, according to DMV records. He was the manager of the Royal Bank. Charlotte had said he coached Little League and volunteered in the community. He and Daisy had no kids.

Tattersall's cursory research told them that Washburn was born and raised in Mississauga, in Ontario, where his folks still lived. He'd gone to McGill University in Montreal and started working for the Royal Bank as soon as he graduated.

Tattersall had found a "Welcome to our new manager" message on the Royal Bank web site for Mendenhall. It told them that Washburn had started out in Montreal, then moved back to Toronto before being handed the responsibility for managing the small Mendenhall branch of the bank, where he'd been for the last three years.

Even Kate could see the man was being groomed for greater things. He wouldn't have been in Mendenhall long. She wondered how Daisy felt about that.

So much for the professional résumé. Hopefully Trepalli and Friesen would find out about the man's friends and colleagues.

Tattersall had informed Frank's family, since Daisy couldn't. Kate sighed. Normally it would have fallen to her to call them, but she'd been busy.

She was a coward. She should have told Tattersall to wait, that she'd do it when she got back to the station. But honestly, she was glad it was done. She hated informing the families.

She stopped at a red light at Main Street, keeping an eye on the pedestrians. Bundled up as they were in these temperatures, people didn't always hear cars coming up behind them. It was still technically lunch time and people were leaving their stores or offices to take advantage of the gorgeous, if cold, day. Kate glanced at the temperature display above her rearview mirror. Minus twenty five. Warming up.

The light turned green and she proceeded through the intersection, her gaze automatically scanning both sides. Her ears were getting hot. She pulled her hat off and tossed it onto the passenger seat, then glanced in the rearview mirror.

Ugh. Hat hair.

Out of the corner of her eye, she caught sight of a green car driving up Brass Street, but it wasn't Amanda's Tercel.

Kate sighed. What was she going to do about Amanda? She couldn't let the chef drive Amanda away from a job she loved. And it was against the law to kill him.

The hospital sat on a low rise across the river, so that the huge white "H" on the top floor could be seen for a long way. Kate took the bridge and turned onto the hospital road.

McKell had volunteered to interview Daisy's colleagues at City Hall. She had been impressed with his willingness until she remembered that the Mayor was out of town. Mayor Dabbs had been McKell's father-in-law for close to ten years until the divorce. McKell believed the Mayor had allowed his personal feelings to get in the way when it came time to choose a replacement for the outgoing chief of police.

Having worked with McKell for the better part of a year now, Kate was inclined to agree. He might be an ass at times, but he was a good cop, well respected by his men and by his peers across the province. It was no wonder she had faced an uphill battle for acceptance when she first arrived.

That said, the man's heart ruled him. He'd been married and divorced three times, for Pete's sake. Then she reconsidered. Maybe he did follow his heart too much, but was that such a bad thing? She allowed her head to rule her, and that wasn't much better.

The parking lot was full and Kate had to park near the incinerator. As she got out of the Explorer, her stomach rumbled loudly, informing her that Amanda's wonderful breakfast had now officially worn off.

By the time she reached the hospital's sliding glass doors, her ears were freezing. Minus twenty-five was warmer, comparatively speaking, but it wasn't *warm*.

Just as she was entering the lobby, her phone rang. She pulled it out. "Williams."

"Chief, it's Tourmeline. The prints I lifted from the car? They came back to Washburn and an unknown. My guess would be Daisy Washburn. His overlaid hers, so he was the last one to touch the steering wheel."

Kate nodded and stared down at her boots. She was dripping on the long runner that led to the Admissions desk.

"Thank you, constable," she said, and cut the connection.

A man came in behind her and she stood aside to let him pass. He stopped at the Admissions desk and was directed down the hall.

So. Only Frank's and Daisy's fingerprints in the car. Well, presumably they were Daisy's. But all that meant was that they hadn't wiped down the steering wheel since the weather got cold. Nobody drove bare-handed at minus thirty.

Someone—perhaps Frank, perhaps not—had driven his car out to the woods near the exercise site. It had been parked off road, either in an effort to hide it or to keep other cars from hitting it as they came around the bend. There was no overcoat or boots, no hat, no gloves. Nothing to indicate that Frank had planned to go outside.

The doors swished open behind her and a woman walked in holding a wailing child, galvanizing Kate into movement. She strode past the Admissions desk with a wave at the clerk and squeaked her way across the industrial linoleum to the stairwell.

Five minutes later, she found herself standing in front of the morgue doors once more, staring at the blue gingham curtains and her own blue-eyed, pale-faced reflection in the window. Her hair truly looked pitiful. She glanced at her watch. One thirty-five. She rang the bell and was rewarded with chimes again.

This time, Dr. Kijawa opened the door without checking who it was. Clearly, she had been expected.

"Chief," she said, nodding. As before, she turned and walked away, leaving Kate to follow.

The first thing Kate noticed was that there was no body on the table. The metal gleamed in the overhead light. If there were any other smells in the room, she couldn't detect them under the whiff of bleach.

Dr. Kijawa reached her desk and picked up a folder. Today she wore a white, open lab coat over a plaid, pleated skirt and a bright red turtleneck. A watch hung from a heavy gold chain around her neck.

"I conducted an autopsy on Mr. Washburn this morning," she said without preamble.

Kate unzipped her parka and pulled it open. "What did you find?"

Tiny gold hoops on the doc's ears caught the light as she looked at the contents of the file folder.

"These are preliminary findings only, you understand." She glanced up at Kate and waited for her nod before continuing. "I am still awaiting the results of the blood analysis from Winnipeg. But it seems clear to me that Mr. Washburn died of hypothermia."

Kate opened her mouth, but Dr. Kijawa raised a hand to stop her. She didn't even lift her gaze from the folder.

"We are able to conduct some blood tests here," she continued and finally looked up. "We were able to determine that Mr. Washburn had a point-oh-four blood alcohol level."

Kate's eyebrows rose. That was nowhere near incapacitation level. He could drive legally with a point-oh-four blood alcohol level.

"However," continued the doctor, "we also found evidence of a drug in his system." She closed the folder and stared at Kate. "I can't tell you the brand name, but whatever it is, it belongs to the benzodiazepine group of drugs."

Kate blinked. "Used for...?" she asked.

Dr. Kijawa looked up at the ceiling for a moment. "They are used to treat everything from schizophrenia to muscle spasms. They are also used as sleep medication."

Huh. "Could this drug be used to knock someone out?" she asked slowly.

The doctor's gaze slowly dropped until she was staring at the empty autopsy table.

"Yes, assuming it could be administered without the patient knowing." She set the folder down on her desk and abruptly sat down. She folded her hands in her lap.

Kate took a deep breath and forged ahead.

"How would Mr. Washburn have reacted to the drug?"

The doctor raised her troubled gaze to Kate's. "He would have been dizzy, uncoordinated, weak. He was a big man. It would have taken a heavy dose to knock him out."

Could he have taken the drug willingly? Whatever for? Judging by his clothes, he was at some kind of formal function. More likely, someone spiked his drink.

His drink.

"What if you combined the drug with alcohol?" Kate asked.

The doctor shrugged. It looked unnatural on her, a behavior learned since she moved to Canada. "Contra-indicated," she said. "The alcohol would magnify the effects of the drug."

So. Someone could have slipped it into his drink and within minutes, he would have been disoriented, slurring his words, acting drunk. Very drunk. An easy target.

Had Frank Washburn run afoul of someone who decided to rob him? But why not just leave Frank with the car? Why drag him all the way out to the exercise grounds?

Dr. Kijawa cleared her throat and Kate looked up.

"If that is all you needed, Chief Williams, I have a patient to see in hospital before I can resume my clinic this afternoon." Her South African accent seemed particularly pronounced.

Kate nodded. She stuck out her hand and after a moment's hesitation, Dr. Kijawa stood up to shake it. She had big hands, warm and dry.

"Thank you, doctor," said Kate. "Just one more thing. How long do you estimate his body was out there?"

The woman hesitated. "That is very difficult to estimate, Chief Williams. Once the body is frozen through and before skin damage appears..." She shrugged again. "Mr. Washburn was not completely frozen through, however. At last night's temperatures, a rough guess would be from two to three hours." Again, the awkward shrug. "A *very* rough guess."

"Thank you again," Kate said and left.

As she walked past the supply room, the secure storage, and the electrical room, she considered what she had learned from the good doctor.

Frank Washburn had been murdered. It might not have been planned, but there you had it. Whatever the original plan had been, the end result was murder. His body had been discovered at around three o'clock, give or take. By Dr. Kijawa's timeline, someone had dragged him, unconscious, to the site sometime between midnight and one o'clock.

She had to find out when EMO and Manitoba Rail had finished setting up on Saturday. The EMO observers had been on site before any emergency responders arrived, but their tent was on the other side of the highway. From there, no one could have seen Frank Washburn's body being dragged toward the wreck.

She reached the stairwell door and pushed it open. Time to check in on Daisy.

CHAPTER 10

Daisy was still unconscious, but no longer in danger, according to the duty nurse at Intensive Care. This nurse, unlike the first one Kate had met, refused to let Kate see Daisy and told her to check back in the morning, as it was unlikely the girl would be awake before then.

Put off, Kate returned to the main entrance, trying to decide what her next step should be. She pulled the zipper up on the parka and fastened the buttons. Men and women in pastel-colored uniforms walked purposefully through the hub of the main entrance. A young woman at the Admissions desk typed furiously at the computer keyboard, obviously taking advantage of a lull in the stream of injured and ill. Sensing Kate's gaze on her, she looked up and smiled. She looked vaguely familiar but Kate couldn't place her. She had that experience a lot. It came from living in such a small town. She saw the same people over and over again, but didn't really know them.

A smell of roasting chicken competed with the antiseptic smell of whatever they used to wash the floors. Not pleasant, but it did remind her that breakfast was long, long gone.

She pulled out her cell phone to check in with Tattersall and saw that he had tried calling her. She punched in his number and he answered on the first ring.

"It's me," she said, although she knew he could read her

number on the display. "What's up?"

"The RCMP traffic analyst finished with the accident scene," he said. "We can open up the highway."

She nodded. "Good. You'll take care of it?" They would have to take down the barriers and detour signs and make sure nothing had been left on the highway to cause a flat tire or other accident.

"Yes, ma'am," said Tattersall, and they signed off.

As she stepped out the doors and into the cold, she wondered guiltily what Amanda was doing. The girl had driven almost two thousand miles to see her. She should find some time to spend with her.

But this was a murder investigation. Or at least, she thought it was. And Amanda hadn't so much wanted to see her aunt as she'd wanted to run away from a hard situation at home. Kate suspected that the constant cooking and baking were yet another effort to avoid thinking about her situation.

Not that her constables minded.

As if called up by the thought, Marco Trepalli drove up in a patrol car. He pulled up to the front of the hospital and got out.

"Hi Chief," he said cheerfully. "Thought I'd find you here. How's Daisy?"

Kate finished pulling on her gloves and walked over to the boy. There was no one around the entrance, but there was no point in broadcasting their conversation. "She's out of danger," she said. "Still unconscious. Maybe tomorrow I can talk to her." She ducked down to look in the empty passenger seat. "Where's Friesen?"

"Still interviewing neighbors," replied Trepalli. "We split up. I just finished with the Royal Bank staff." He cocked an eyebrow at her. "I figured you'd want a briefing."

"All right, constable," said Kate. "Let's do it inside your vehicle." She got into the passenger side and Marco slipped in behind the wheel. He pulled away from the entrance and drove around the circle until he reached the parking lot. There were no slots open, so he parked behind a couple of cars that had been there long enough to build up frost.

"Washburn was well liked," started Trepalli. He pulled off his heavy gloves and fished through his parka pocket for his notebook. "The bank's got a dozen employees, not counting the cleaning staff." He flipped through a few pages before stopping. "Everyone I spoke to seemed genuinely upset that he was dead. Nobody could figure out what he was doing out in the middle of that field. I spoke to his assistant, a Miss..." He searched a couple pages before finding the name. "Deborah Wingfield. Older woman, in her sixties, looks like a battle ax."

Kate frowned but the boy was still reading his notes. "She said Washburn was supposed to be in Winnipeg on Saturday night. Some kind of big party. I guess he teaches a class in economics one night a week at Assiniboine Community College, also in Winnipeg. The college was hosting some mucky-mucks from China, and as one of the professors, Washburn was invited, too." He looked up from the notebook. "Funny that he wouldn't have taken Daisy with him, eh?"

Kate shrugged and nodded at him to continue. The heater was going full blast and she was getting uncomfortably hot. But experience had taught her not to mess with another cop's settings.

"That's about it for now," said Trepalli. "I think someone needs to go to Winnipeg and talk to the Dean."

Kate thought so, too, but first things first.

"Does—did Washburn stay in Winnipeg overnight on the nights he taught?" Most night classes ran from seven to ten p.m. Nobody wanted to be driving back that late, especially in winter.

Trepalli got a stricken look on his face. "I didn't ask."

Kate swallowed a sigh. Instead, she nodded. "All right. Go back and talk to Miss..."

"Wingfield," he supplied.

"Ask her about his habits. If he stayed in town, where did he stay. Who his dean is at the college. Which night he taught. If he ever spoke about the students or people he knew in Winnipeg."

Trepalli nodded. He swallowed. "Sorry, Chief."

Kate shrugged. "It's a process, Trepalli. We rarely ever get it right the first time."

"Yes, ma'am."

"What else did the folks at the bank say? Any enemies? Irate customers?"

Trepalli shrugged. "As far as these folks are concerned, Frank Washburn was first cousin to a saint. He was fair, open-minded, generous, and had a good sense of humor." He glanced sideways at her. "Makes you think he's too good to be true, maybe."

Kate didn't say anything, but yes, that was exactly what she was thinking.

* * *

McKell was already back at the station when Kate returned. She stuck her head in the lunch room and saw him pouring himself a cup of coffee. He looked up.

"Yes?"

Kate hated that look he got whenever he saw her—the one that said he could do a better job than she was doing. She forced herself to unclench her jaw.

"Let me get my coat off. I'll be right back."

She wiped her boots off on the hallway runner and nodded to Nick Martins, who was sitting at the duty desk.

"Constable," she said as she walked into the duty room. "Is Tattersall on lunch?" Whoever sat at the duty desk usually took a late lunch. It made the rest of the shift go by much faster. Except for Martins, the duty room was deserted. Charlotte's coat and boots were gone.

"Yes, ma'am," said Martins, his copper-penny eyes crinkling up in a smile. "It's his weekly lunch date with his daughter."

Kate scoured her memory and finally found the name of the girl. "Abby, right?" Martins nodded and Kate couldn't help but grin at him. It was the freckles. She was a sucker for freckles.

She'd met most of the families at the Christmas party Charlotte had organized. To her ever-lasting gratitude, Bert Langdon, the Winnipeg DC, had accompanied her and helped her keep names straight. To her surprise, the party had turned out to be a lot of fun, especially when the mystery Santa turned out to be DC McKell, fake beard, pillow, and all. She'd had just enough rum-spiked eggnog to not mind when Bert snuck a kiss under the mistletoe.

"Anything happening that I should know about?"

Martins shook his head. "Typical Monday," he said. "It'll all be in the log."

Then it could wait.

"Good," she said and headed for her office. "Charlotte on late lunch, too?" That girl rarely took lunch. When she did, she used it to run errands.

"Yep," said Martins behind her. "With your niece."

Kate stopped. She turned around. "Amanda was here?"

He nodded. "They were just leaving when I arrived to relieve Tattersall."

Well. Amanda seemed to have adopted the station. Kate didn't really know how she felt about it.

She clumped over to her office and removed her boots with relief. She had better not start resenting them now. It was only February and there was at least another month of boot weather ahead of her.

She hung the parka on the coat rack and fished the notebook out of her pocket, then grabbed a pen from her desk before heading back to the lunch room.

McKell was sitting at one end of the long table, his own notebook open on the table. Kate poured herself a coffee and joined him.

"What did you learn?" she asked.

The look he gave her was shuttered, as if he didn't want her to read anything he was feeling. Kate's pulse sped up and she raised an eyebrow expectantly.

"Turns out Daisy's been acting a little strange lately," he said without preamble. "Moody, short-tempered. The gossip around the coffee room was that she was having marriage problems."

Oh no.

Kate took a deep breath. "Go on."

McKell glanced down at his notes. "There's only about half a dozen people working in the mayor's office, and only one woman works closely with Daisy. Her name is Samantha West. Miss West does not seem to like Daisy." His voice remained carefully neutral and he kept his gaze on his notes. "She's the one who stated that she thought there was trouble with the marriage."

"Did she say why?" asked Kate. She wrapped her hands around the mug, hoping to warm them up.

"In great detail," said McKell dryly, looking up at her.

McKell was a good looking man, in an alpha male sort of way. He was about fifty, with graying brown hair cropped close to his skull. He kept himself trim and fit. She often saw him at the gym where she worked out. He had lean features and a firm jaw, but it was his way of looking straight at a person with those clear blue eyes that inspired confidence. Trust, even.

Of course, those clear blue eyes could chill like chips of ice when he wanted. While she trusted him as a cop, she couldn't get past how he had tried to undermine her when she first arrived in Mendenhall. She would never make the mistake of forgetting that aspect of him.

"She said she overheard Daisy talking on the phone to Frank," continued McKell. "Three days in a row she overheard Daisy asking Frank when he was coming home."

They stared at each other for a moment. Then Kate took a sip of coffee.

"Trepalli interviewed the Royal Bank staff," she said slowly. "Nobody said anything about Frank Washburn not living at home."

McKell shrugged. "When your marriage is breaking up, you don't necessarily want to advertise it. What else did he learn?"

Kate sorted through the information Trepalli had given her. "Washburn taught an economics class at Assiniboine Community College. One night a week. He was supposed to be attending a formal event there on Saturday night. That's why he was dressed up."

McKell thought a moment, his fingertip tapping on the side of his mug. It featured a curling rock, with the words Brandon Curling Club under it.

"Did he overnight in Winnipeg on the nights he taught?" he asked. "If so, maybe that's where he's been staying."

Kate wanted to smile, amused that they had both asked the same question. "Trepalli's going back to ask."

McKell shook his head. "Rookies," he muttered.

Now Kate did smile. "So all we've got is an overheard conversation to tell us Frank might have been staying away. Maybe Friesen will have something."

McKell nodded and leaned back. He stretched out his long legs, angling them away so they wouldn't tangle with hers under the table.

"What about you?" he asked. "Is Daisy awake?"

Kate shook her head. "No, but at least she's not in a coma any more. They've moved her out of intensive care. I might be able to talk to her tomorrow." She sipped from the lukewarm coffee. "But I did speak to Kijawa."

McKell perked up at the note in her voice.

"Turns out Frank Washburn had point oh four blood alcohol."

McKell's eyebrows rose and she saw the same grimness she was feeling reflected on his face.

"And," she continued, "There were traces of sedative in his system."

The finger tapping the coffee cup stopped and McKell stared at her. She stared back, knowing what he was thinking.

Manslaughter was one thing. A car accident causing death, sure. A misplaced punch that led to a death, yes, it happened. But drugs... they had to be deliberately administered.

"Maybe he took it himself," said McKell. "I've heard that partiers do that to increase the effects of alcohol."

Kate nodded. It was possible. Anything was possible. But how likely was it that the manager of the local bank had taken drugs with alcohol and then driven himself from Winnipeg to Mendenhall, a good hour away? Only to park the car off the road and stumble through the woods toward the exercise site? And even if he had, *someone* had dragged him to where they'd found his body. And arranged his body.

McKell shook his head, obviously reaching the same conclusion. "We need to speak to Daisy," he said.

Kate finished the coffee and stood up. "Tomorrow. In the meantime, I want to talk to Choo." At his blank look, she elaborated.

"He was the paramedic the mystery person fetched at the exercise. Maybe he knows who it was."

McKell stood up, too. For the first time, she noticed the dark circles under his eyes. The DC hadn't been sleeping well. She felt a sudden stab of sympathy for the man. His dad had lung cancer. She'd lost her own father a few years back to pancreatic cancer. At least it had been mercifully quick. She couldn't imagine how painful it was to see someone you loved wasting away over months. Years.

She wanted to tell him to go home, take the rest of the day off, but she knew better. He would hate to think she saw any weakness in him. Their relationship was too fragile still. It wouldn't withstand the burden of her sympathy.

Her stomach rumbled loudly and McKell's eyebrow rose.

"Maybe I'll grab something to eat first," she said.

McKell grabbed her cup and his and rinsed them out at the sink. "So, right now we sit with our thumbs up our wazoos and wait is what you're saying." He put the cups into the drain tray and turned around to look at her.

She shrugged off his irritability. "Unless you can think of something else. I'd like you to debrief Friesen. I want to know what he learned from the neighbors."

He nodded. "I'll call you if anything unusual turns up. In the meantime, I've got a couple of hundred emails to go through."

Martins popped his head in the door. "Chief?"

"Yes?" He had a funny look on his face. The perpetual smile was gone.

"The Washburns are here," he said, his eyes sober. "Frank Washburn's parents."

* * *

Kate indicated the chairs across from her desk and Mr. and Mrs. Washburn sat down. Only then did she take her seat. Her hands were shaking and she clasped them together on the desktop.

The Washburns were in their late fifties, maybe. Frank had clearly gotten his classical good looks from his father, who stood just shy of six feet and was silvering handsomely. Mrs. Washburn was a petite woman whose dyed red hair was cut in an asymmetrical, angled bob.

They had both removed their outerwear, to reveal dark suits. Her skirt ended just below the knee and she wore short black ankle boots. The shirt under the suit jacket was patterned black and white.

The moment she had shaken their hands, Kate had known who was in charge of that relationship. Albert Washburn's handshake was quick and over before she could really shake it back. Evelyn Washburn, however, gave a strong, firm handshake and looked Kate in the eye when she did it.

Mr. Washburn had yet to meet her eye.

"I am very sorry for your loss," said Kate. She hated these conversations. She never knew what to say, or how to say it so that she didn't sound like a public official speaking out of rote.

"Thank you," said Mrs. Washburn. Her pale blue eyes stared at Kate for a moment more, then she said, "We came to bring our son back home, Chief Williams."

Kate struggled to remember where this home might be. Somewhere in Ontario. The smell of something cheesy wafted under the closed door and she prayed her stomach wouldn't rumble.

"But the hospital won't release his body until you say so," added Mr. Washburn. His tone sounded accusing.

Kate took a deep breath. Her appetite had now vanished. She looked down at her hands. "Mr. and Mrs. Washburn," she began, "the decision about... it's not..." She stopped, regrouped, and tried again. "I believe Daisy has to decide about disposal of the body."

Red bloomed in Evelyn Washburn's cheeks, but her husband placed a hand over hers and she glanced down at the floor. Neither one spoke.

"Are you aware that Daisy's been in an accident?" asked Kate.

Mrs. Washburn nodded stiffly. "Yes."

Interesting. Did they not like Daisy? What wasn't being said here?

When the silence stretched on uncomfortably, she cleared her throat. "There are some questions surrounding your son's death."

Albert Washburn glanced at his wife, but she was now looking at Kate. She swallowed before she spoke.

"What kind of questions?" Her voice was soft, but Kate heard the steel threading through it. This was a woman who wanted to hear the truth, no matter how hard it was.

Kate's fingers tightened around each other. How the hell did you tell a parent their child might have been murdered? She wished suddenly she had let McKell handle this discussion. She was no good at this.

Mrs. Washburn waited patiently, her mouth set in a firm line. Kate finally looked directly at her. "The circumstances surrounding your son's death are unusual," she said. She took a deep breath and plunged on before the woman could do more than look expectantly at her. "He was found in the snow in shirtsleeves and pants. No coat. He'd been there a few hours. We don't know how he got there or what he was doing before he got there."

She thought of telling them what Dr. Kijawa had discovered about the drug, but decided against it. Until she learned if he had taken the drug willingly, or someone had slipped it into his drink, she didn't see the point in causing them added distress.

Mrs. Washburn's chin rose. "Are you saying Frank was drunk?"

Kate shook her head. "No, ma'am, he wasn't. He'd had maybe one or two drinks, but he wasn't over the legal limit."

Mr. Washburn suddenly looked at her directly. He, too, had blue eyes. Unlike his wife's pale blue, his were almost navy, they were so dark.

"Are you going to autopsy him?" He tried to keep his voice steady, but it rose on the last word. Mrs. Washburn's hand immediately covered his.

"I think they have to, Albert," she told him softly. Then she turned her gaze back to Kate. "Do you suspect he was murdered?" Unlike her husband's, her voice was steady, but there was a glitter of unshed tears in her eyes.

"We have to investigate all possibilities, ma'am," said Kate. Then, helplessly, "I'm so sorry but I have to ask. Do you know of anyone who would want to hurt your son?"

The Washburns stared at her, the same bemused expression on their faces. It was Evelyn Washburn who replied finally.

"I know it's a cliché, Chief Williams, but our son was a good man. People loved him."

In the ensuing silence, Albert Washburn sighed brokenly. "How could anyone have done this?"

* * *

After the Washburns left, Kate sat in her office for a long time, the door closed, staring out the window.

* * *

The phone rang, startling her and she picked it up. "Chief Williams," she said, only then glancing down at the display. "Hi, Bert," she added, suddenly cheered.

"Hi yourself," he said at the other end. "How's your investigation going?"

Kate shrugged, even though he couldn't see her. "It's going."

"Anything I can do to help?"

Kate smiled. "Don't think so," she said. "But thanks."

"Don't thank me," he said in a low voice. "I'm looking for an excuse to see you."

The intimacy of his voice sent shivers up her scalp. He'd made his intentions clear at the Christmas party, and she'd been holding him at bay ever since, although right now, she couldn't remember why.

"We'll always have Whiteshell," she whispered and laughed when he groaned.

Late last fall, before the leaves were all gone, Bert had taken her canoeing in Whiteshell Provincial Park. It had been a perfect day—warm and sunny, with no wind—and they had even brought along a picnic, which they had eaten on the beach. Bert had coddled her, refusing to let her paddle or do any of the work because of her healing shoulder. Their conversation had lasted all day, interspersed with long periods of comfortable silence. By the time they returned to Winnipeg, it was late and Bert offered her his guest room, but she'd taken one look in his copper-penny eyes and seen that he had no intention of letting her sleep alone.

She'd gone home, much to his disgust.

"You are a hard, hard woman, Katie Williams," said Bert.

"Yes, I am," said Kate firmly. "And that's why you should go find yourself a softer one."

"I should," agreed Bert and she was surprised at the pang of disappointment she felt. Then he added, "unfortunately, I happen to like hard women."

She grinned. "And on that note, I have to go interview a paramedic. Talk to you later."

He promised he'd call her in a few days, then hung up.

She got up to put her parka on, the smile lingering on her face.

* * *

Philip Choo was at least six feet two, with hard hands the width of a shovel blade. He engulfed Kate's hand in his and gave it a firm shake before releasing it.

"Sorry I missed you earlier," he said, indicating she should take a seat.

The paramedics' lounge was brand new, with three square tables instead of the one long one they had at the police station. The paramedics had a stainless steel fridge and even had a stove, with a matching microwave above it. One corner of the lounge boasted a floor lamp and two easy chairs. Kate looked closer at the brown leather chairs. Were those La-Z-Boys?

Must be nice.

She dragged her attention back to the paramedic. Choo's black hair fell in a shock over his forehead and he was forever pushing it back. While his skin was darker than hers and his brown eyes had a slight tilt to them, there was nothing obvious—aside from his name—to identify his Asian heritage.

She slid into a chair and he sat across from her. His shirt sleeves were rolled up, revealing corded muscles. He was a lanky guy, but strong.

"I hear you had a Winnipeg run," she said, not bothering to correct his misunderstanding. She hadn't come by earlier. Trepalli or Friesen had.

Choo leaned his arms on the table and laced his fingers together. "Just a patient transfer," he said. "The patient will likely come back in a couple of days after they've finished running tests on him in Winnipeg."

Kate nodded. Mendenhall had an x-ray machine and that was about it. The lab at the hospital could handle some testing, as evidenced by Dr. Kijawa's discovery of the drug in Frank Washburn's system, but most complex tests had to be done in Winnipeg. The town couldn't afford the capital costs of an MRI, or the costs of a tech to operate one.

"So, the body was Frank Washburn, eh?" said Choo.

"Did you know him?"

He shook his head. "No. I know his wife, of course."

Of course. Daisy was well known in Mendenhall. Kate had come to think of her as the driving force behind City Hall, while Mayor Dabbs was simply its figurehead. Dabbs gave pretty speeches, but Daisy got things done. Kate would have been lost without her help last fall when it came to organizing the Cop Games.

"Mr. Choo," said Kate, removing the notebook from her parka pocket. On second thought, she removed the parka, too. "It's my understanding you didn't find the body."

Choo nodded. "That's right. I was working on the highway side of the train."

A man came into the lounge and nodded a greeting at them. By tacit agreement, Kate and Choo waited until he had poured himself a coffee and left before resuming their conversation.

"How did you learn that there was a real victim?"

He took a deep breath and sat back. He stared up at the ceiling for a minute.

Kate glanced around the room while he thought. This lounge might be snazzy with its new furniture and bright yellow paint job, but her station's lunch room had nice big windows. She decided she wouldn't switch.

"Someone came to get me," he said finally, dropping his gaze down to her. He had a wedding ring, she noticed with surprise. He didn't look a day over nineteen. "I was just coming out of the bus and the guy grabbed my arm. Must have seen the armband." All the paramedics wore the reflective armbands with the bright red cross on their parkas.

"Who was it?" she asked, and held her breath waiting for his answer.

Which came immediately. "I couldn't tell," he said. "He was wearing a balaclava."

Damn. Of course he was. Everyone else was, too, except for Avramson, who was much too manly for one.

"Did you recognize his voice?"

Choo shrugged. "No. But there were lots of people there from Brandon. And there were EMO observers, too, so there were lots of people there I didn't know."

"You're sure it wasn't one of the victims?"

He shook his head. "No."

"What?"

He looked at her. "What?"

"Are you saying you're sure he was a victim, or that he wasn't?"

"He wasn't," he said firmly.

"How do you know?"

He hesitated.

"Was he wearing a parka? Was there a cross on it?"

He shook his head. "I honestly don't remember, Chief," he said regretfully. "All I know is, I was sure he wasn't one of the victims."

"Can you recall anything else about him?" she asked. But she'd run out of hope. If Choo didn't remember, she had no idea how they were going to track down the person who had alerted the firefighters and gone to fetch him.

Damn, damn, damn. She would dearly love to find the man and ask him a few questions.

Choo looked at her with sympathy. "I'm sorry, Chief. I was focused on getting to the victim. He was taller than me, if that helps. Oh, and I think he had an accent."

Kate's eyebrows rose and she began to smile.

CHAPTER 11

"What kind of accent?" asked McKell. He was seated at his desk and had his colored index cards out. He used them when he was setting up schedules for the next month. Kate hoped he wouldn't die suddenly and leave it up to her. She could never figure out his system.

She shrugged out of her parka and let it fall on the back of the chair. She leaned back, wondering why she didn't have comfortable guest chairs, too.

"Australian," she said. "Or maybe New Zealand."

McKell pursed his lips and twiddled the pencil between two fingers. The light from the window over his desk gilded the side of his face, revealing a hint of a four o'clock shadow. "A few British dialects sound like Aussies."

"I know," she said. "It's not much to go on, but honest to God, an Aussie in the middle of the Prairies will stick out. We'll find him."

McKell's office had that lived-in feel to it. He had set up a bulletin board across from his desk where he posted faxes and printouts of wanted felons and runaways. On the wall closest to his desk was one of those individualized calendars that people sent at Christmastime with pictures of the family or of special trips taken in years past.

Kate hoped no one ever made one for her.

Behind him, where he would see it whenever he worked on his computer, was a framed photo collection featuring a man who looked a lot like McKell, only older, and a variety of younger men and women and children. Presumably his family.

He even had plants. Real ones.

He pushed away from the desk but kept his hands on the edge. "That EMO woman came by while you were gone."

Kate barely hid her wince. "Alexandra Kowalski? What did she want?"

"Don't know." He shrugged. "She wouldn't talk to anyone but you."

Kate's eyebrows rose. What could Alexandra Kowalski possibly want now?

"I heard she was some pissed at you for canceling the exercise." A small smile quirked the corner of his mouth. She had come to suspect that for all of his love of rules and order, Rob McKell secretly liked it when people shook things up a little. Especially if she was the one being shaken.

She shrugged. "She's over it. I just hope she doesn't spring a surprise exercise on us."

The smile slipped a little. "Can she do that?"

"I don't know," admitted Kate. "I know she planned to do that this morning. I'm hoping someone talked some sense into her."

"I hate zealots," mumbled McKell, looking down at his hands. "It's going to be another cold night."

Kate refused to worry about it. She had other things to concern her.

"Did Trepalli and Friesen report in?"

McKell crossed one leg over the other. "Just Friesen. He didn't get to talk to all the neighbors because some of them were at work. He's back out there now, trying them."

That would make him popular. "Did he learn anything interesting?"

McKell fished under a file folder and slid his notebook out. While he flipped through the pages, he said, "Not really. The Washburns are..." He started again. "The Washburns were a quiet couple, took part in neighborhood barbecues, entertained regularly. There weren't any arguments or loud parties." He finally found the page he was looking for and read silently for a moment. Then he looked up.

"The retired accountant across the street said both of them worked long hours. They each have a car, but we knew that already. And she said that Frank Washburn didn't come home on Thursday nights."

"That would be the night he teaches, then," said Kate.

McKell nodded. "But the woman told Friesen that she hasn't seen Frank's car in the driveway since last Thursday."

Huh. Well, that could mean anything, of course. The car could have been in the shop. He could have lent it to someone.

Or he could have moved out of the house.

"We have to talk to Daisy," said McKell.

Kate nodded. "We do."

* * *

Charlotte looked up from zipping her coat as Kate left McKell's office. Working late again. Maybe it was time Kate lobbied for more admin support.

It was dark out and the windows reflected back the image of the duty room. Kate sighed. She was *so* ready for spring.

At the duty desk, Tattersall was talking on the phone and typing at the same time. The radio crackled on low in the background. Kate couldn't tell who was talking. Holmes sat at one of the desks clustered in the center of the room, filling in a form and scowling.

"What's the matter, constable?" she asked.

He was one of the shortest members on the force, maybe five feet eight, and she doubted he weighed more than a hundred and thirty pounds, but he had huge hands. She'd seen him wade into a brawl and break it up without getting a bruise on him. He had short blond hair that always seemed to spike out—or maybe he styled it that way, she wasn't sure—and startlingly dark, bushy eyebrows over piercing blue eyes. He was thirty-eight, divorced with one little girl, but unlike McKell, he and his ex-wife seemed to get along fine.

He looked up at her in surprise. "Nothing, ma'am. Why?"

Charlotte piped up behind Kate. "Kyle always looks like that when he's filling out requisition forms."

He grinned sheepishly and returned to his form.

"All right, I'm off," said Charlotte.

"Goodnight," said Kate, looking up at the clock. It was almost six-thirty. What the heck was taking Trepalli so long?

"Do you need anything before I go?" asked Charlotte hesitantly.

"No, I'm good. Have a good evening."

That young woman was too young and too pretty to spend so much time at the station. She needed to get out and have some fun. And suddenly, Kate remembered that Charlotte had had lunch with Amanda, which reminded her that she really had to go back home and spend some time with her niece.

Charlotte left with a wave and Kate turned to Tattersall. "I have to go, too," she said. "When Trepalli reports back, tell him to call me at home to fill me in."

"Yes, ma'am."

"DC McKell?" she called. McKell came out of his office. He would be working for a while longer, until after shift change.

"The guy with the accent?" he asked.

She nodded. "Can you start calling around tonight? Shouldn't take that long—we have the list of everyone who was involved in the exercise, after all."

"We'll take care it," said McKell. "You going to Winnipeg tomorrow?"

"If we can find out who Washburn's dean was, and if he's around, then yes, I'd like to talk to him." She pulled on her coat and zipped it. "I'm home if anything comes up."

* * *

The smell that greeted her when she opened her front door almost swept her off her feet. She closed the door on the cold and took a deep breath. Was that roast pork?

Amanda came out of the kitchen wiping her hands on a dishcloth. She had another one tucked inside the waistband of her jeans like an apron. She wore a red, long-sleeved, vee-necked tee-shirt with the sleeves pushed up to her elbows. Her feet were in hand-knitted socks that looked a lot like the ones Rose had sent Kate at Christmas. With her hair up in a swingy pony tail, she looked completely adorable.

"Hi!" she said. Her cheeks were flushed with the warmth in the kitchen.

"Hi yourself," said Kate. She started taking off her outerwear. "What smells so good?"

"Pork loin," said Amanda. "And risotto with a Waldorf salad."

Kate's stomach growled so loudly that Amanda heard it and laughed. Kate hung up her parka and stored her boots on the plastic runner lining the floor of the closet. Only then did she notice that the house was warm. She usually kept it in the low sixties while she was at work and only turned up the heat when she got home, which meant an uncomfortable half hour of walking around chilled. She had tried setting the timer on the thermometer, but her hours were so irregular that half the time she ended up heating the house for hours before she showed up to enjoy it.

It was nice coming home to warmth, and to supper ready.

"I could get used to this," she said, following Amanda into the kitchen. She watched her niece pick up the wooden spoon from the spoon rest and resume stirring the rice concoction. "I haven't had risotto in years."

Amanda grinned over her shoulder at her. "It's easy to make, you know. I could show you how."

"Sure. Right after I learn how to hang glide," said Kate.

Amanda laughed again and kept stirring.

"I'm going to change," Kate said and headed down the hallway toward her room.

The back bedrooms were cold. She didn't heat the spare bedroom unless she had to use the desk, and she kept her bedroom cool because she preferred sleeping in a cool room. Still, there was cool and then there was minus thirty. She turned up the heat on the electric baseboards to chase the chill and sat down on the side of her bed.

The phone sat on her night table. It was time to call Rose and figure out what exactly was going on with Amanda. Kate couldn't shake the feeling that her niece's story wasn't true, or at least not the whole truth. If her boss was putting the moves on her, well then, Kate favored the direct approach. She would go over there and slap the man silly.

But if that was true, there was no way Amanda could have kept the truth from her mother. And Rose would have told John, Amanda's overprotective father, who would have marched right over to the lecherous chef and put the fear of God into him.

So why was Amanda *really* here?

Whatever it was, Amanda clearly hadn't told her parents about it or Rose would have called. Realization curled her toes. Rose and John didn't know their daughter had left Montreal for Mendenhall, or they would have called.

What was Amanda into?

Kate pictured her sister sitting at her desk in the tiled-and-granited, brushed stainless steel kitchen of their lovely St. Lambert home on Montreal's south shore of the St. Lawrence River. With the kids grown and gone, the house was too big for John and Rose, but they loved entertaining and lived in hope that the kids would eventually give them grandchildren.

Kate tried to picture Amanda with a baby and shook her head. Amanda's brother Sean was even less ready. Having recently graduated from McGill, he was spending a year traveling through Europe and having a blast, judging by his travel blogs and emails.

With a sigh, she plucked the handset out of its cradle and punched in Rose's number from memory. It wasn't ten o'clock yet in Montreal. Rose and John would still be up. Unlike her, they were night owls.

The phone at the other end rang three times before being picked up.

"Hello?"

"Rose, it's me," said Kate in a low voice.

"What's the matter?" asked Rose, suddenly alert.

"Nothing," said Kate. "Relax." She should have realized that calling at this time would raise all of her sister's alarms.

"Why are you calling so late?" There was a hint of anxiety in her sister's voice.

Kate glanced at the bedroom door, hoping Amanda couldn't hear her. "This is the first chance I've had," she explained. "How's everyone?"

There was a pause. "Fine," said Rose finally. She waited.

And waited.

The woman should have been an interrogator. When they were kids, Rose was the one who could wait for *hours*, poised over the fishing hole Dad had cut into the ice, waiting for the fish to bite, while Kate whined about going home.

"All right," she said testily. "I'm calling about Amanda."

"What about Amanda?" asked Rose. There was a funny note in her voice. In the background, Kate could hear John asking what was going on. "Shhh," said Rose, presumably to her husband. "What about Amanda?" she repeated.

"Do you know where she is?" asked Kate.

"At work, I would guess," said Rose cautiously. "Or at home if it's her night off. I've lost track of her schedule." And Amanda had her own apartment in Old Montreal, so Rose wouldn't necessarily know if Amanda was home or not.

Kate closed her eyes. Damnitall.

"She's here," she said bluntly. She opened her eyes and stared at the pine highboy in the corner. Rose remained silent. John's questioning voice came through faintly from the background.

"Is she all right?" Rose finally asked, breaking the silence.

"Seems to be," replied Kate, surprised that Rose was taking it so well.

There was an even longer pause this time. "What is she doing there?"

Now it was Kate's turn to pause. Rose wasn't reacting at all the way she had expected. She had expected a flurry of questions, exclamations, something to indicate shock and surprise. Not this cautious calm.

"She got here yesterday around lunch time," said Kate finally. "Did you know she's thinking of quitting her job because her boss is coming on to her?"

"Really?" Rose sounded as if she'd just learned that Kate preferred tea over coffee.

And that's when Kate realized the truth. "You knew she was coming, didn't you?" she blurted out. "What's going on, Rose? Why is Amanda here?"

Rose sighed. "I was going to go myself," she said. "But I couldn't get away for another few weeks. *L'Assiette blanche* is closing down for three weeks for renovations so Amanda said she'd go. I wanted her to fly but she wanted a road trip."

Kate pulled the phone away from her ear and stared at it, baffled. Her sister *seemed* to be speaking English, but she wasn't making any sense, kind of like when she used to sleepwalk. Except that she was awake and still not making sense.

"What are you talking about?" she asked as calmly as she could. "*Why* was it so important to come here?"

"To see if you were all right, of course," said Rose. There was an edge to her voice. "For months we've been calling and leaving messages. When we do speak to you, you're vague and don't tell us anything."

"But Rose," said Kate in complete bewilderment, "I'm always like that. Why the sudden worry?"

"Because you were *shot*!"

Oh.

Kate closed her eyes, and this time they stayed closed as she listened to her sister breathe at the other end of the line. Rose was five years younger and they hadn't been particularly close while they were growing up. As adults, however, they became friends and spent as much time together as they could. Rose hated the fact that Kate was a police officer. She always worried that Kate would get hurt, and had been thrilled when Kate accepted the position of police chief in Mendenhall.

Oh God.

"Rosie, I'm so sorry," said Kate as abjectly as she could. Rose was right. Of course she was right.

What had she been thinking?

Rose remained silent on the other end, except for a few snuffles.

"Rosie?"

"I'm still here," said her sister. "I'll always be here, Katie."

Now Kate felt tears pricking her own eyes. "I know," she whispered.

This was getting maudlin. Kate cleared her throat. "You know, you could have called instead of making poor Amanda drive for two days."

"Ha!" said Rose. "We all know how honest you are over the phone, don't we? No, we wanted to see for ourselves what was going on. And according to Amanda, your shoulder may have healed but you're not eating enough."

Amanda had been calling in reports? Dear God.

"It's ready!" called Amanda from the kitchen.

Amanda's determination to feed her suddenly took on new meaning. "I've got to go," said Kate. "Amanda's got supper ready."

Having determined that Kate was too thin, Rose wasn't about to keep her from dinner. They said their goodbyes and Kate hung up the phone, then buried her face in her hands. The road to hell...

"Aunt Kate?"

"Coming!" she called and stood up. She was going to have to call Mom, too, but not tonight. Tomorrow.

As she hurriedly stripped off her uniform, her thoughts whirled uselessly around the fact that Amanda had lied and spied on her and yet Kate was the one feeling guilty. She was down to her underwear when the doorbell rang, startling her. Nobody ever came to the house.

Not that she was home much to hear if someone *did* ring her doorbell.

"I'll get it!" cried Amanda before Kate could step into her jeans. She pulled them up over her hips and zipped them, noting that yes, they were looser than she remembered. She grabbed a clean sweatshirt from the middle drawer of the highboy and pulled it over her head.

Damn, it was *cold*!

She heard the murmur of voices coming from the front of the house as she looked around for her sheepskin slippers, finally finding them by the door. She took the time to hang up her uniform before finally padding down the hallway toward the living room. Before she got there, she heard laughter coming from the kitchen and detoured to follow the sound.

Trepalli stood next to Amanda at the stove. He still had his coat on, but his feet were clad only in heavy gray wool socks. Amanda was feeding him a spoonful of risotto. He closed his eyes in bliss as he savored it.

"That's delicious," he said reverently. He opened his eyes and looked down at her, smiling.

Amanda smiled back at him, her head tilted up. They were so close, all he had to do was lean in a few inches to kiss her. For a moment they stood frozen, poised halfway to a kiss, then Kate cleared her throat and they sprang apart guiltily.

My, my, my.

"Chief!" said Trepalli, for all the world as if he'd forgotten whose house he was in.

"Constable," said Kate equably. She raised her eyebrows at him. She'd had constables drop her off or pick her up at home before, but this was the first time anyone from the station had been inside her home. She didn't know how she felt about it.

Uncomfortable, she decided.

Amanda stepped into the breach with a brilliant smile. "Marco came by to see you," she said. "I think he should stay for dinner."

Kate's eyebrows rose so high she felt they might climb off her face. Trepalli's face bloomed red and he stammered, "I couldn't... That's very nice... I can't..." He looked at Kate, desperation writ large all over his face.

"Oh nonsense," said Amanda grandly, oblivious to the finer subtleties of chief/constable relationships. "There's a ton of food." She suddenly seemed to sense something and hesitated. She looked at Kate. "Right, Aunt Kate?"

Kate looked at Trepalli. The poor boy looked like he wanted to crawl underneath the tiles. What the hell. It wasn't as if *she* was inviting him to dinner. And it would postpone the inevitable discussion with Amanda.

"Of course," she said. It came out a little stiffly. "Stay for dinner, constable."

"I'm still on duty, ma'am," he said. The color was receding from his face and now he was beginning to look a little hopeful.

Kate sighed. "You're almost off shift," she said. "Let Tattersall know where you are and take your coat off."

She caught his wince and turned away to hide her smile. The boy clearly wanted to spend time with Amanda, but he hadn't taken into account the ribbing he would get back at the station when they found out he'd had dinner at the chief's house.

Ten minutes later, they were seated at the dining room table with a steaming platter of sliced pork loin and a bowl of risotto in the middle of the table. Amanda brought in the salad and seated herself across from Trepalli.

"Help yourselves," she said regally and in the next few minutes, the only sound to be heard was the clinking of cutlery as they applied themselves to the meal.

It was, bar none, the finest meal ever served in Kate's dining room. The pork loin was so tender she didn't need a knife to cut it. The risotto was creamy and cheesy and hot. And the Waldorf salad had just the right crunch factor with the walnuts and sweet factor with the apples and grapes.

Trepalli polished off his plate with the single-minded determination of a bachelor who had never learned to cook. Kate watched him eat with admiration. She remembered that he came from a big family. It must have been pretty cutthroat at dinner time to train him to that level of efficiency.

When he finally looked up, his gaze went unerringly to Amanda.

"I may have to marry you," he said solemnly.

Amanda blushed and pushed the tray of pork toward him. "Have more."

Kate almost rolled her eyes. "Yes, constable," she said. "Have some more. And while you're at it, maybe you can tell me why you dropped by."

He started and looked mortified. Good grief. The boy had

forgotten that he had come here for a reason. Aside from seeing Amanda, of course.

"Yes, ma'am." He cleared his throat and glanced at Amanda.

Seeing her cue, Amanda stood up. "I'll go refill the risotto," she said, and left the dining room.

Kate almost smiled. Rose had raised the girl well.

"I finally tracked down Mrs. Wingfield," he said, his voice low. At the look on her face, he clarified. "Washburn's assistant at the bank." Kate nodded for him to keep going. "She's been looking after Washburn's parents, getting them settled in a hotel, that kind of thing."

"What about Daisy's parents?" Kate asked. Then she remembered that Daisy was an orphan. And apparently, the Washburns weren't going to take her under their wing. "Never mind," she said. "I remember now. So what did Mrs. Wingfield have to say?"

"She said Washburn went to Winnipeg every Thursday night and left straight from the bank. He always had an overnight bag with him and was always at work the next day."

Well, that confirmed that.

"Did she tell you where he stayed?"

He shook his head. In the soft light of the dining room chandelier, he looked very dashing with his dark hair and deep blue eyes. The uniform he wore seemed to have been tailored especially for him, displaying his wide shoulders, narrow hips, and long legs to advantage. No wonder Amanda was attracted to him.

But in the short time she'd known Trepalli, he'd dated at least six women that she knew of, including Charlotte at the station. At least, she was pretty sure they had dated. And that was just the women she knew of. There were others in Winnipeg and Brandon, she was sure.

Hmm. Now *there* was an idea...

"I asked her," replied Trepalli, oblivious to her burgeoning plans for him. "But she said she didn't think he stayed at a hotel." Before Kate could ask why, he continued. "She submits his monthly expenses to the college—you know, mileage, photocopying, that kind of thing. She says she's never seen a bill for a hotel."

"So," said Kate, drawing out the word. She stared at the dining room wall above Trepalli's head. It needed a painting or something, she noted absently. If Washburn didn't stay at a hotel, and he didn't drive back home on the nights he taught, then he stayed with someone he knew.

Her gaze drifted down to Trepalli. He was looking at her steadily, the same speculation in his eyes.

"We need to find out where he was staying," she said softly.

"And who he was staying with," added Trepalli.

"You mean who he was having an affair with," said Amanda bluntly, entering the dining room carrying a pot of coffee, creamer and sugar bowl on Grandma's silver tray. Amanda's great-grandmother's silver tray.

Trepalli raised one eyebrow in silent acknowledgment and got up to take the tray from her.

"No seconds?" he said mournfully.

Amanda smiled and patted his arm. "Something better," she said and disappeared back into the kitchen. Before Kate and Trepalli could do more than look at each other questioningly, she returned carrying a cheesecake. In the other hand, the girl carried a small glass bowl that Kate didn't even know she owned. In it was some kind of berry compote.

"Dear God, child!" A bubble of panic rose to the surface of Kate's mind. "Are you trying to kill me?" It was one thing to eat well but she couldn't even *calculate* all the crunches she'd have to do to work off this meal.

Amanda smiled serenely. "Aunt Kate, you don't have to have a piece, if you don't want it."

Sure, Kate grumbled silently as she watched Amanda cut into the cheesecake. Might as well tell her she didn't have to breathe, if she didn't want to.

"Did you find out who she submitted Washburn's invoices to?" she asked.

Trepalli jumped up and left the room, returning a moment later with his notebook. He flipped through until he found the right spot. "Dean Marilyn Deverell," he said.

Good boy, she thought, but didn't say. *You're learning.*

Half an hour later, Trepalli left, a happier man. Amanda stood in the open doorway and waved him off until Kate bit her tongue against the desire to yell, "Shut the door!"

Despite the impromptu company of her young constable, it had been a pleasant meal. It had certainly put a sparkle in Amanda's eyes. They quickly cleared off the table and cleaned the kitchen, stacking all the dirty dishes in the dishwasher, which rarely got used. All the cooking and cleaning had steamed up the window over the sink so that all Kate could see was a ghostly reflection moving between the curtains. She closed them.

"I've made more decaf," said Amanda, wiping down the counter top. "Feel like a cup?"

Kate took a deep breath. "Pumpkin, you don't have to do this, you know."

Amanda looked over her shoulder at Kate. "Do what?" She seemed genuinely puzzled.

Kate waved at the kitchen, then at the dining room. "This. I spoke to your mother and she told me why you're really here."

Amanda took a deep breath but didn't say a word. A chip off the old block.

"You're sweet to be concerned, and I love having you here, but you don't have to feed me, or bring food to the station. You don't have to work while you're here." Which was going to be for how long, exactly? The full three weeks of the restaurant's renovations?

But Amanda just looked at her uncomprehendingly. "Aunt Kate," she said, "this is what I *do*." She hung up the cloth over the tap and made shooing motions at Kate. "Now, go sit down and I'll bring out the coffee."

"One more thing," said Kate. "Is there really a married chef who's a lech?"

Amanda blushed and grinned sheepishly. "The chef *is* married," she said, "but he's married to another man."

Kate shook her head and abandoned the kitchen to her niece. The living room felt cold after the warmth of the kitchen, but she resisted the urge to turn up the heat. There was a fireplace in the middle of the wall, but she'd never used it. It made her nervous. She watched her reflection in the big picture window and tried to see beyond to the darkness. Her house was between streetlights, but she could faintly make out the house across the street, mainly because the lights were on on its front porch. She pulled on the cord to draw the curtains, slowly eclipsing the dark reflection of the room.

A sudden image of Daisy Washburn as she had last seen her popped into her mind. Had Daisy suspected that her husband was having an affair? Was that why she was on the road to Winnipeg yesterday? Was she going to confront her husband and his lover?

The phone rang, startling her, and she headed for the kitchen just as Amanda headed into the living room with the coffee pot and fresh mugs. Kate stepped aside to let her pass.

She picked up the receiver on the third ring. "Williams."

"So now you're showing preferential treatment to one of your constables?" drawled McKell.

Kate almost groaned. He wasn't about to lecture her, was he? She leaned against the wall, phone tucked between her shoulder and her ear.

"Did he get ribbed?"

"He certainly did," said McKell and she could hear the grin in his voice. "Although there was more than a little jealousy in the kidding. I hear that niece of yours is a good cook."

A swell of pride filled Kate. "She's a *chef*, I'll have you know. She works at one of the finest restaurants in Montreal."

"Well, excu-u-use me..." said McKell and she relaxed. Apparently McKell thought it was funny.

"So what do you have for me?" she asked, bringing them back to business.

"Two possibilities," he said at once. "One Brandon paramedic, by the name of Steve Osbrig. He's originally from Australia. And Henry Beverington is a Winnipeg firefighter, originally from England."

"Did you cross-reference..."

"I did," he confirmed. "Neither mentioned finding the body in their interviews."

She knew they hadn't. She had read those damned interviews three times and correlated them with Charlotte's board. No one had claimed finding the body.

"All right," she said. "We'll do it the hard way."

"I'll take Osbrig, since you're already going to Winnipeg," said McKell.

Kate nodded, even though he couldn't see her. She straightened up and plucked the black marker from on top of the white dry erase board she had mounted on the wall next to the phone. "Who's on days tomorrow?" she asked.

"Same as today," he said at once. "Trepalli and Friesen, Martins and Holmes, with Tattersall on the duty desk."

Kate wrote down the names as he said them, and added Osbrig and Beverington. It always helped her think. She'd already decided she was taking Trepalli with her but wasn't sure about which of the others should accompany McKell to Brandon.

"I want Trepalli with me tomorrow," she said. "How much experience does Friesen have in interviews?"

McKell remained silent for a few seconds. She could hear his slow breathing. "Not much," he admitted. "All right, I'll bring him with me, but that'll leave us short."

"We can stagger," said Kate. "You go first thing, I'll go when you get back."

"Hang on," said McKell. She heard pages rustling. "Osbrig is on nights. He'll be off at six tomorrow morning. We can catch him at home in the afternoon, after he wakes up."

"What about... Beverington?" she asked, glancing at the white board to find his name.

"Days off," said McKell. "No telling where he'll be."

"All right," she said. "I'll head out first thing with Trepalli. We can check Beverington's home, then the fire station if I don't find him. Do you have a home address for him?"

The doorbell rang and Kate heard Amanda get up to go answer it while she jotted down the address. If that was Trepalli, she would tear a strip off the boy.

"Are we good for now?" she asked.

"Yes, ma'am," said the deputy chief. "We can touch base when you get back from Winnipeg."

Kate hung up and padded toward the living room. She wouldn't have been surprised to see Friesen at the door, either, but she emerged from the kitchen in time to see Amanda let Alexandra Kowalski in.

What the hell was that woman doing at her house?

"Sorry for—" began Kowalski, looking down at Amanda, then she caught sight of Kate. "Hello, Kate," she said. "Sorry to disturb you at home." She stayed on the mat in front of the door and clutched her gloves in her red, chapped hands.

Kate opened her mouth to say something polite, if untrue. Then she got a good look at Kowalski's face.

"What's the matter?" she asked, forgetting her irritation.

Kowalski's thin face was mottled red. She was still wearing the heavy red parka with its reflective EMO armband, but she had taken her hat off to reveal mousy hair in a braid down her back. Her eyes were bloodshot and narrow. Had the woman even slept since the exercise?

Amanda pushed the door closed and hovered uncertainly next to Kowalski.

Deal with this quickly, Kate told herself, *before Amanda invites Kowalski in for tea.*

"I just wanted to tell you that there won't be another exercise," said Kowalski.

Kate sighed. "I'm sorry, Alex," she said. "I know you put a lot of work into it."

Kowalski smiled without showing her teeth. There was no humor in it. Kate couldn't figure out why the woman was here. She could have called with the news. She just kept staring with those bloodshot eyes. It was creepy.

"Is it true?" Kowalski asked softly. "Was it Frank Washburn?"

Kate nodded. Kowalski had seen him at the scene but hadn't recognized him. Because she'd never met him or because he was unrecognizable? "Did you know him?"

Now Kowalski dropped her gaze and swallowed hard. After a moment, she nodded. "Yes. I hadn't seen him in a few years." She shook her head, still looking down at the floor. "I didn't even recognize him," she said in a voice so low it might have been a whisper.

Kate almost reached out to place a hand on Kowalski's arm, but there was something so contained about the woman that her hand fell away. She had never seen anyone look as lonely as Alex Kowalski did in that moment.

Then Kowalski looked up and skewered Kate with her brilliant, bloodshot gaze. Kate caught her breath at the fierceness in the woman's eyes.

"Is it true he was murdered?"

Kate considered her words carefully. "We're still investigating," she said finally. "But it's beginning to look that way."

Kowalski's face twisted in a flash of pain, quickly erased. "In that case," she said softly, "you might want to ask yourself what Daisy Pitcairn had to gain from her husband's death."

Without another word, she opened the door and stepped out into the night, leaving Kate and Amanda open mouthed behind her.

CHAPTER 12

THE NEXT morning as she was getting ready to leave, Kate told Amanda not to open the door to strangers.

"Honestly, Aunt Kate," said Amanda reprovingly.

"Don't "honestly" me," said Kate. "You opened the door last night without checking."

Amanda shrugged. "I knew you had a gun."

Kate clamped her mouth closed on a retort. She wrote down her cell phone number on a scrap of paper and handed it to her niece. "I'll be back in town in the afternoon." She closed the door on Amanda's amused expression. "Honestly" indeed.

The temperature had plummeted to minus forty again overnight, but the Explorer started up without much of a protest.

Her neighbors were friendly but minded their own business. They seemed happy that she had moved in and she saw why when she realized how many teenagers lived on her little cul de sac. Nothing like having the chief of police as a neighbor to keep the wild parties down.

As she drove slowly away from the house her thoughts circled back to Kowalski. She didn't know much about the woman except that she lived in Winnipeg and worked for the Emergency Measures Organization. She seemed to know most of the people at the tabletop exercises, including McKell and Charlotte.

It had been Kowalski's idea to run the exercise in rural Manitoba. Her idea to do it in February. And her idea to simulate a train accident. The woman might be a pain in the butt, but she knew her job. She had all the details of the exercise at the tip of her fingers and grew irritated when others at the tabletop didn't.

Aside from the two tabletop exercises in preparation for the on-the-ground scenario, Kate had had no dealings with Kowalski. They hadn't even shared coffee, principally because Alexandra Kowalski didn't seem capable of doing two things at the same time. If she was working, that's all she did. If she was socializing... actually, Kate couldn't imagine the woman socializing. There was something off-putting about her intensity.

There weren't many vehicles on the streets yet, but there would be. Mendenhall's public transit system was a joke. If you didn't have a car, you walked. The town was surrounded by farms and low, rolling hills. Before moving here, she had thought she would find the place flat and boring, and had been willing to put up with it for a few years until she retired.

But to her surprise, she had come to love it. The prairies weren't flat at all—at least, not here. The land rolled like a wrinkled blanket. Last summer she had seen thousands of sunflowers turning their heads as one to follow the sun. She had seen thunderstorms sweeping in from miles away. In her explorations, she had found hidden lakes and even a desert.

Even now, when snow squeaked like styrofoam underfoot and the least little breeze risked frostbite on exposed skin, she admired the pale pink of the eastern sky as the sun began its ascent.

This really was beautiful. Deadly, but beautiful.

She arrived at the station just after shift change. Friesen and Trepalli were already on patrol, but Martins was in the lunch room, filling a thermos cup.

"Morning, chief," he said when she walked in.

"Morning," she replied and took a mug from the cupboard. "Where's Holmes?"

"With Tattersall," said Martins. His freckled face broke into an infectious grin. "Seems Tattersall can't approve Holmes' requisition until he can *read* Holmes' requisition." He filled her cup while he had the pot in hand, then added sugar and cream to his coffee and screwed the lid on his thermos cup.

Kate was smiling when she walked into the duty room. Holmes and Tattersall were standing by Charlotte's empty desk, bent over a sheet of paper, thinning brown head next to blond head.

"This doesn't even look like an eight," grumbled Tattersall.

"Well, what else could it be?" replied Holmes. He glanced up at Kate. "Morning, chief."

"Gentlemen," she nodded in passing, and got an absent-minded nod back from Tattersall.

"Kyle, if you don't know what you wrote, how the hell am I supposed to guess?"

She hid her grin until she got to her office and set the mug down. The door had been closed all night and the heat turned down so that it was frigid in there. She kicked her Sorels off and slipped her feet into her black work boots. They were frigid, too. With a sigh, she turned the thermostat up, grabbed her mug, and left the office, closing the door behind her.

Tattersall and Holmes were still working on the requisition form. She grabbed the log book with her free hand and called over her shoulder, "In the lunch room if you need me."

Only a few minor incidents had been recorded: a drunk brought in to spend the night in the drunk tank; two teenagers involved in a fender-bender; a woman reported a prowler outside her house, but the responding officer saw no tracks anywhere around the house and found himself invited in by the homeowner. Kate checked the name and nodded to herself. Mrs. Simmons. At least once a month, the old lady called to report a prowler. McKell had informed Kate that she had started doing it shortly after her husband died. He always sent a constable out to her place to check it out, and it was understood that the constable would spend half an hour chatting with the elderly woman. They always left with a bagful of homemade cookies for the station.

Kate tried to imagine that happening in Toronto.

At eight-thirty, after her second cup of coffee, she closed the log book and returned to the duty room. Tattersall was on the phone, so Kate returned the log book to its place at the end of the counter and waited.

At that moment, Charlotte arrived in a gust of cold air. She wore a long, green, wool coat and a multicolored scarf that wound around her neck three or four times. A matching hat was pulled down over her ears but couldn't contain the mass of dark curls. She had cut her hair a month ago, much to the chagrin of the male constables, but Kate found the hairdo very becoming. It showcased Charlotte's green eyes and heart-shaped face.

"Good morning!" said Charlotte. "Another glorious day in paradise!"

Still on the phone, Tattersall rolled his eyes at her and she grinned. "Good morning, chief," she said.

"Charlotte, I'm sure there's a rule somewhere about being so cheerful in the morning," said Kate.

Charlotte laughed and began unwinding the scarf. She normally came in at morning shift change, but was owed so much overtime that she had decided to come in later every day.

Tattersall hung up and Kate turned to him but at that moment, a young man came in looking for a security check for a job he was applying for. Kate sighed and returned to her office, which was thankfully warm. She worked on her monthly report to City Council until Tattersall came to her office, twenty minutes later.

"Were you looking to talk to me, chief?"

The phone began to ring again and he made a move to go answer it.

"I want you to call Trepalli back in," said Kate quickly. "He's coming to Winnipeg with me."

Tattersall nodded and hurried back to the duty desk, but Charlotte had already answered the phone.

Fifteen minutes later, Trepalli returned to the station and stood in her doorway.

"You wanted to see me?" he said uncertainly.

"Yes," she answered, standing up. "We're going on a road trip."

The uncertainty cleared from his face and his eyes lit up. "Winnipeg?"

She nodded. "We're going to talk to Dean Deverell and try to find a paramedic who has an accent."

He stared at her, a half-smile on his face. "An accent, ma'am?"

"It's a long story," she said, bending over to change her boots. "I'll fill you in on the way."

"Yes, ma'am," he said happily. "Squad car?"

Kate straightened up and considered. After a moment, she shook her head. "We'll take my car," she said. She never liked announcing her presence in another jurisdiction. She'd stop by the Winnipeg Police Department headquarters and chat with Bert. That would be her notice that she intended to interview a witness in their jurisdiction.

She fished through her parka pockets until she found her car keys and tossed them to Trepalli, who plucked them out of the air.

"You can drive," she said. Once McKell arrived, they would leave.

"Yes, ma'am," he said and left to go start her car.

* * *

Once in the car, Kate kept her hat and mittens on but Trepalli removed his fur cap the moment he sat down and tossed it into the back seat out of habit. The last time they had driven to Winnipeg together had been last fall, when they'd both had witnesses to interview, for different cases.

She had needed to interview that dentist—what was his name, again? He'd helped an old flame out by giving her a place to stay in Mendenhall and a job with a colleague in Winnipeg. Kate wondered if the dentist's marriage had survived.

She sighed. She'd ended up with a bullet in her shoulder on that case. She still had nightmares about it, sometimes.

Trepalli glanced at her. "Thinking about the last time we did this?" he asked gently.

She smiled to herself. Trepalli's intuition had led directly to her shooting, but it had also led to the unraveling of the case, so she couldn't complain too much. And she'd learned that Marco Trepalli was smart as well as sensitive. A good combination.

"Yes, I was," she admitted. "I was thinking that it all worked out in the end."

"Right," he said. He glanced at her and she caught his look.

"So who's the guy with the accent?" He changed the subject.

Kate reached for the travel mug in the holder and sipped her coffee. "His name is Henry Beverington. He's a firefighter at Station Six on North Main." She briefed him on the reason the accent was so important, and they spent the rest of the trip discussing the case.

Winnipeg was almost an hour east of Mendenhall on the Trans-Canada Highway. Once in town, they had to thread their way to the Winnipeg Police Department headquarters, which was on Albert. An uglier building she had rarely seen.

The five-floor monstrosity was made of concrete and had long, narrow windows made to look like bars on a jail cell. Kate hated it and suspected most Winnipeggers hated it, too. It squatted on the block like a fortress: uninviting and fear-inspiring. She much preferred her post-World War II era station house. It was small and drafty, but it didn't put the fear of God into visitors.

"Courtesy call?" asked Trepalli when they finally pulled up to a parking meter on the other side of the street. "Chief Stendel?"

Kate's teeth automatically clenched. She willed herself to relax her jaw. Stendel was narcissistic and arrogant and was more of a politician than a real cop. Still, he had come through for her last year in the missing kid case. But the man dated women young enough to be his daughters, for Pete's sake.

As far as she was concerned, Bert Langdon was the real driving force behind the WPD.

"Or are we going to see DC Langdon?" continued Trepalli innocently.

She refused to meet his gaze, instead opening the door and stepping out into the cold. Trepalli hurriedly shut off the engine and followed suit.

"I'll just be a few minutes," she said, pulling her fur hat down around her ears. Already the cold was chipping away at her cheeks. "I'm sure you can find a female constable to give you a cup of coffee."

Trepalli fell in behind her and wisely chose to remain silent.

Five minutes later, Bert greeted her as the elevator doors opened onto the third floor.

"Hi," he said, grinning at her.

"Hi yourself," she smiled back. "Thanks for agreeing to see me on such short notice."

The duty officer downstairs had called and Bert had told him to allow her up. Now that she was here, she wondered just how presumptuous she was being. Bert was the deputy chief of a major Canadian police department. He was a busy man.

And yet, he had dropped everything to meet her at the elevator.

"Anything for you, Katie," he said, waggling his eyebrows meaningfully.

She laughed and only then became aware that there were people in the hallway and that they were being observed through the glass walls of the offices.

Apparently oblivious, Bert Langdon put a hand on her back and guided her down the hallway to the employee entrance. He punched in a quick code and the door unlocked. The smell of burnt coffee immediately put her at ease. This building might look like something out of a bad science fiction movie, but it *smelled* like a cop shop.

This was part of the reason Kate was reluctant to take their relationship to the next step. She liked Bert. A lot. But they were both cops. Not only cops, but chief and deputy chief. There was no way their relationship could proceed like a normal relationship. They would always be under the microscope of their respective police forces.

And cops dating cops... that was never a good idea. She'd seen too many cop marriages fail. Besides, she didn't know *how* to be in a relationship. The few times she'd tried, she'd failed miserably. She was getting too old for that nonsense, anyway.

No. It was better to stay friends. She just needed to convince him of that.

He led her past a lunch room where a woman sat at a round plastic table drinking coffee and flipping through a magazine. The fingers of her left hand drummed against the cup and Kate could almost feel the woman's need for a cigarette.

The hallway opened up into a common office with a couple of dozen cubicles hiding men and women. The investigative arm of the WPD lived on this level of the building—the detectives and crime scene techs. Stendel's office was on the top floor, with the administrative wing of the force.

At last they reached the far end of the room and Bert motioned her ahead of him into his office. She'd been here once before, in summer, and had admired the view from the bank of windows giving onto Albert and Laster. Right now, the view consisted of hundreds of rooftops with smoke rising straight up from chimneys and vents, punctuated by the odd five- or six-story building. The sky was clear and blue and the snow on the rooftops looked impossibly white.

Bert took her parka and hung it up on the coat rack by the door before closing the door. Then he turned and gathered her in a hug, followed by a quick peck on the cheek. Before she could do more than start in surprise, he released her. "Sit," he said, indicating one of the comfortable black leather chairs he kept for guests. She sat and he dropped into the chair's twin, facing her. He leaned forward and rested his elbows on his knees.

"How's it going, Katie?" he asked gently. Like Martins, Bert had red hair and copper-penny eyes, but his hair was fading to gray, and his copper-penny eyes could see right into her.

Her stomach fluttered and she told it to settle down. She wasn't a girl anymore and Bert wasn't a boy.

"I'm fine, Bert. Your mother?"

His mother was ailing. She was in a nursing home in Winnipeg. Bert had invited her to move in with him a few years ago when her second husband died, but last year they had both decided it was time for her to move into an assisted-care facility. Bert just couldn't give her the level of support she was beginning to need. And then, a few weeks ago, she had come down with pneumonia. His mother had just turned eighty-one and he was her only child. All her siblings were dead and his father had been an only child, too. When she was gone, he would be completely alone.

He broke into a smile and she caught her breath at the young man she saw just beneath the surface, full of charm and happiness.

"She's recovering, would you believe."

Kate smiled, happy for him. He had been a late surprise for his parents, while hers were young when she was born. Dad had died a while back, but if she was lucky, she would have Mom around for a long time.

"I'm glad to hear it," she said, and meant it, even though part of her felt sad anticipating his inevitable grief.

Her inevitable grief.

His office suited him. One wall was covered with bookshelves. She could see the Criminal Code of Canada and a leather-bound set of the Statutes of Manitoba—familiar books in any law enforcement office. The fact that he kept books when they were all available online warmed her. That's what she did, too. She always found it much easier to find what she was looking for in a book than on a screen.

In the corner was a round table with four chairs, perfect for small meetings or for spreading papers out, like now. Bert had travelled extensively and the photographs of African sunsets, Thai temples, and South American jungle flowers added splashes of color to the drab gray walls of his office.

"I'm sure you didn't drive all the way here to ask about Mum," he said, sitting back. Something in his eyes told her he regretted that she had so obviously come on business, but it couldn't be helped. She *had* come on business.

She shrugged and smiled. "It's more of a courtesy call," she said. "I need to interview a witness who lives here."

Bert smiled and she blushed. A phone call would have sufficed. He knew and she knew that she had stopped by because she wanted to see him.

"About Washburn?"

Kate nodded and studied his features. "Did you know him?"

Bert nodded. "Met him once or twice, with Daisy. How is she doing?"

"Recovering," said Kate. "Haven't had a chance to talk to her yet."

Bert's gaze found the window and the snowy landscape beyond. "Hell of a way to go."

They were back to Frank Washburn. "Oh, I don't know." Kate shrugged at his look of surprise. "After a while, I'm told, you just fall asleep." And never wake up.

Bert shook his head again, his expression serious. "I've seen a couple of cases of death by hypothermia. They lose their senses and start taking their clothes off. In the final stages, they try to dig themselves into the snow. It's called burrowing."

Kate stared at him unseeingly while she recalled how Frank Washburn had been stretched out as if he had laid himself down, his hands by his sides.

"Not Washburn," she said slowly. "He was definitely underdressed for the weather, but I didn't get the sense that he'd been stripping. He still has his shirt on and his pants. He had a bow tie and a cummerbund. We didn't find a jacket or coat or shoes." She shrugged. "And he definitely didn't burrow."

Bert looked at her, waiting.

"He had point oh four alcohol and a sedative in his system," she said.

"Ah." He didn't need to add anything else. They both knew what it meant. "Any leads?"

Kate hesitated. She had already told him more than she normally would have, but he was a colleague, after all.

"Nothing solid," she admitted. "I'm down to looking for a guy with an accent." When he looked at her skeptically, she elaborated. "We're trying to find the person who first discovered the body, but so far, no luck." She went on to explain about Choo identifying the person who'd fetched him as having an accent. "And the only two people it can be live in Brandon and Winnipeg."

"Do you need any help?" he offered but she shook her head.

"No. Thanks, but I think I can still handle an interview. If I can find the fellow."

"You think he's in the wind?"

She shook her head again. "Days off. He's a firefighter. We're going to try his house first."

"Let me know if you need to track him down," said Bert. "Do you have time for lunch?"

She smiled gently, surprised at the regret she was feeling. "Can't. Trepalli's with me and I can't leave him alone too long or he won't have any room left in his little black book." She stood up and reached for her coat.

Bert laughed and stood up, too. He took the parka from her to hold it while she put it on. "I hear you have company."

Kate finished sliding her arms into the sleeves and turned to look up at him. She didn't have far to look. He was only a few inches taller than she, something she found most attractive in a man. She hated having to crane her neck to look up at a six-footer. Waste of a man, as far as she was concerned.

"Now how would you know that?"

He quirked an eyebrow at her. He was so close she could smell the coffee on his breath. "Police grapevine."

Kate rolled her eyes, but she knew it was true.

"My niece is visiting," she confirmed.

"I'd like to meet her one day," he said casually.

She glanced at him then glanced away, suddenly flustered. He wanted to meet her family?

"Maybe when I wrap up this investigation, and if she's still here, you could come for dinner." Even as she spoke the words, she couldn't believe she was saying them. "She's a chef, you know," she added hurriedly.

"So I hear," said Bert placidly. Was that satisfaction she saw in his eyes? Feeling like she had just been outmaneuvered, Kate opened the door, then impulsively closed it and turned to face him.

"How well do you know Alexandra Kowalski?" she asked.

He hadn't been expecting that. He thought for a moment, lips slightly pursed, before answering.

"Not that well, really. She's been with Emergency Measures for a few years, but this is the first time she's been involved in organizing an exercise. She was admin until now. I think." Curiosity just about shone from him. "Why do you ask?"

She shrugged. "Just wondering. She seems very... intense."

Bert laughed. "Oh, she's that, all right. Heaven help you if you try to cross her. She once called Stendel and yelled at him for not providing paperwork he had promised. And that's when she was in admin!" He sobered. "You could talk to Daisy about her," he said. "I think they went to high school together in Mendenhall."

Kate smiled and nodded, and turned away before he could see the surprise on her face.

* * *

She found Trepalli deep in discussion with a man, a uniformed cop, in the coffee room. They both looked around when she walked in.

"Ready, constable?" she asked, nodding politely to the other cop.

"Chief." The cop's gaze fixed on her so steadily that she immediately wondered what they had been discussing. He was maybe ten years older than Trepalli, his uniform pants and shirt crisply ironed, his hair freshly cut.

Trepalli gathered his parka from the chair and headed out behind her.

They took the stairs down to the lobby and exited onto Albert. The cold air snatched the breath from her and had she been alone, she might have cursed.

"Did you want to drive?" asked Trepalli as they crossed the street. He unlocked the doors and started the engine from her remote control.

"Nope," she said. "You're doing a fine job."

Trepalli grinned. "That would mean so much more if I didn't know how much you hate driving in town."

Cheeky thing.

The Explorer's leather seats had warmers, but she was still glad she had invested in sheepskin covers for the driver and the passenger seats. The bloody car was like an icebox, and they'd only been gone maybe thirty minutes.

"Where are we going next?" asked Trepalli, oblivious to the

eyeball-freezing cold in the car. He took off his gloves and dropped them between the seats before pulling her map of Winnipeg out of the side door pocket.

Damn. She was going to have to fish her notebook out of her pocket. She pulled the heavy lined glove off her right hand and dug through the outer pocket of her parka. She located the notebook and pulled it out. Her fingers fumbled the pages but she finally found the next to last one.

"113 Stephen Street," she said. "It's off North Main, I think." She returned the notebook to her pocket and quickly donned the glove again. She flexed her fingers, trying to convince them that they were warm.

As Trepalli looked for Stephen Street on the map, she buried her chin in her collar and frowned. Thoughts swirled in her head and every time she thought she grasped one, it eluded her only to be replaced by another.

Was Washburn murdered, or was it a weird accident? Did someone spike his drink, hoping to rob him? Realizing something was wrong, did Frank Washburn try to drive home? There were no other fingerprints on the steering wheel except his and Daisy's, which meant nothing. It was winter. Anyone driving the car would wear gloves.

Speaking of which, where *were* his gloves? His coat, his boots? Would they find them in the spring, after the snow melted?

It was highly unlikely that a doped Frank Washburn would have driven out of Winnipeg, down the highway for almost an hour to the scene of the exercise, parked off the road, and walked through the forest only to end up just beyond the reach of the lights.

No. He had been dragged. And left to die. Bert was no medical expert, but he was a long-time cop. She would check with the medical examiner, but she trusted that he knew what he was talking about. Frank Washburn had been completely unconscious by the time he was laid out. There'd been no stumbling, no burrowing.

"Got it," said Trepalli. He folded the map and tucked it back into the door pocket. The defroster had mostly cleared the windshield. "Got your seatbelt on?" he asked, his breath puffing out. He pulled on his gloves.

Kate wordlessly buckled herself in and he pulled out. Within seconds, she stopped paying attention to the road, falling back into speculation over Washburn's death.

She'd been feeling around the edges of this case for two days and it was time to get serious. Someone had deliberately murdered Frank Washburn, or at the very least, drugged him, which led directly to his death. She had to follow this where it led. Wherever it led.

With a sigh, she took her glove off again and unzipped the parka so she could reach the inside breast pocket. She pulled her Blackberry and turned it on, then carefully punched in the number for McKell's phone. Out of the corner of her eye, she caught Trepalli's curious glance.

McKell answered on the first ring. "McKell," he snapped.

"It's me," she said, knowing that he would recognize her voice.

"Everything all right?"

"Yes," she said. "We're in Winnipeg, on our way to find Beverington." She took a deep breath and expelled it silently. "I want you to get a warrant for Washburn's cell phone records and his land line, if he has one. The phone at his office, too."

She could hear him writing at the other end of the line. "What about Daisy's phone?" he asked quietly.

She hesitated, but this was no time for sentiment. "Daisy's, too," she said crisply. "You've got enough to justify the warrants."

"Got it," said McKell. "Anything else?"

"That's it. See you in a few hours."

"Yes." And he hung up.

She tucked the phone back into her inside pocket and zipped up her parka.

Trepalli's silence was so tense she could almost feel him biting his tongue to keep from speaking. Well, let him bite it. She didn't feel like talking any more.

* * *

North Main was a rough section of town, but the families living on the residential streets on either side of it had been there a long time and didn't scare easily. Where many of the businesses on North Main sported papered-over windows or for sale signs on the doors, the homes in the area didn't change hands often.

113 Stephen Street was an older, detached home on a short residential street that dead-ended at a chain link fence, beyond which the ground fell away to a ravine. All the homes were of the same generation, at least fifty years old, but well kept. They sported pastel-colored siding with contrasting trim and front doors, as if the owners had all watched the same decorating show. All the driveways were well-shoveled, the walkways precisely shoveled up to the grass.

It was spooky.

Trepalli laughed. "Looks like an enterprising teenager cornered the market on snow clearing."

At once, Kate's perspective changed and she realized he was right. "Is that what you used to do?"

He shrugged. "My parents couldn't afford allowances," he said cheerfully. "We had to show a little initiative or we'd never have dated."

A little initiative? With his interest in women, he probably had run his own business, with employees.

Beverington's house was halfway down the street. It was white, with blue trim around the windows and a darker blue door. Trepalli parked in front of it and turned the engine off.

"Looks like no one's home," he said, nodding toward the empty driveway.

"Maybe he doesn't drive," said Kate.

"He's got kids," added Trepalli and Kate followed his line of sight. A kid's sleigh stood upright against the cast iron railing on the porch.

Kids. She didn't do well with kids.

"Well, come on," she said, already grumpy.

Trepalli shot her a surprised glance but got out of the Explorer. Kate closed the passenger door behind her and looked at the house. A picture window on the left of the front door and a smaller window that opened, on the right. Living room, bedroom. Without turning to see if Trepalli followed, she made her way up the walkway and up the short flight of stairs and rang the doorbell.

A dog immediately started barking and Trepalli muttered, "Oh great," behind her. Then the door swung open and the barking stopped. An older woman stood before them, dressed in black slacks and a white turtleneck, clutching a pink woolen sweater around her thin frame. There was no sign of a dog. Her mouth was a slash of pink lipstick.

"Can I help you, officer?" She had a strong English accent. Her face was as thin as her body, but it seemed to Kate the kind of thinness you lived with all your life, not the kind that came with illness. The woman's wispy white hair was pulled back in a bun at the back of her head. Clearly, she was freezing, but she didn't invite them in. The house had an arctic entry and the inside door was closed, preventing her from seeing inside.

Kate had her identification already in hand. She showed her badge to the woman and said, "I'm Chief Kate Williams of the Mendenhall Police Department, and this is Constable Marco Trepalli. Is this the home of Henry Beverington?"

The woman's chin rose. "Henry is my son," she said proudly. "What do you want with him?"

"We were hoping to talk to him about Saturday night's exercise," said Kate, opting for discretion. She didn't want to spook the woman with talk of bodies.

"Oh, you mean the dead man," said the woman, nodding her understanding. "Do come in." She stepped back to allow them access to the small space. "Henry is running errands. He should return shortly." Once Trepalli had managed to turn himself around and close the outside door, she opened the inner door and gave them room to remove their boots.

"Would you like tea?"

Kate glanced up from pulling up her sock, but the woman was looking at Trepalli. He glanced at Kate for approval before saying, "Thank you, Mrs. Beverington, that would be great."

"Have a seat in the living room," said the woman. "I won't be a moment."

Kate and Trepalli closed the door to the arctic entry behind them and looked around. The living room was small but comfortable. A red, plush couch below the picture window seated three people and faced two club chairs in brown leather across from a long, low coffee table. At the far end of the couch, a small dog—a mutt, really, with shaggy hair falling into its beady black eyes—lay on a blanket. It blinked up at them.

"Do sit," said Mrs. Beverington, entering the room carrying a tray with a brown betty, china cups, a creamer and sugar set, and a plate full of lemon squares.

"That was fast," said Trepalli, hurrying to take the tray from her.

She smiled her thanks. "I always keep the water hot."

Trepalli placed the tray down on the coffee table. Kate sat down in one of the club chairs so she could keep an eye on the picture window, and he sat in the other one. On the far wall was a fireplace, with no fire. Maybe it didn't work.

"The insurance company made us stop it up," said Mrs. Beverington regretfully, following Kate's gaze. "Such a shame. I do like a fire in winter, don't you?" She sat down next to the dog on the couch and absently stroked its head. Her fingers were twisted with arthritis.

Kate nodded, even though the woman had addressed the question to Trepalli. "You live here with your son?" she asked.

"Actually, this is my house," said Mrs. Beverington. She reached for the brown betty, but Trepalli leaned forward.

"Allow me," he said.

Mrs. Beverington leaned back and smiled approvingly at Trepalli's bent head. "Such lovely manners," she murmured. The dog stared balefully at Trepalli.

"So your son lives with you," prompted Kate, hoping to keep this from deteriorating into a Trepalli love fest.

"Since the divorce, yes."

Trepalli placed a cup and saucer on the table in front of Mrs. Beverington and indicated the cream and sugar. She shook her head and clasped her hands in her lap. "He should never have married that woman," she said softly. Then her face brightened. "But if he hadn't, we wouldn't have little Anna, would we?"

"Anna is his only child?" asked Kate politely and accepted a cup from Trepalli.

"My only grandchild," said Mrs. Beverington. "She's in grade one. Would you like to see a photo?"

Kate hesitated but Trepalli said, "Sure."

Half an hour later, Kate knew more about Henry Beverington's early life in Bristol, his move to Canada with his mum, his shenanigans as a teenager, his decision to become a firefighter, his getting "that woman" pregnant, his failed marriage, his wonderful daughter and his move back to mama's house, than she could ever have wanted to know.

Mrs. Beverington nattered on about little Anna's accomplishments, but a movement outside the picture window caught Kate's attention.

A gray four-door Focus drove up the driveway and a big man got out. He glanced at her red Explorer as he walked around to the hatchback and pulled plastic bags out. Then he slammed the hatch closed and made his way up the driveway toward the back of the house. Mrs. Beverington, her back to the window, saw none of this.

A moment later, a door somewhere in the back of the house opened and cold air swirled around Kate's feet. A clunk of cans and a thump as bags were placed on a table or a counter.

"Henry!" called Mrs. Beverington, looking toward the kitchen. "We have company."

Kate heard a zipper being pulled down and a softer thud as a coat dropped to a chair. Then the padding of stockinged feet. She got to her feet and Trepalli did the same, setting the photograph album on the coffee table.

The man who entered the living room was at least six feet three, very blond, with a friendly open expression. He rubbed big hands together to warm them and smiled at his mother.

"Mum, what have you gotten up to now?" He had an accent, too, but not as strong as his mother's.

Mrs. Beverington laughed. "Henry, this is Chief Williams from Mendenhall and Marco Trepalli, one of her officers."

Beverington nodded acknowledgement of the introduction. "You were at the exercise," he said, looking at Kate. He was all legs and shoulders, and was dressed in jeans and a heavy red sweater that looked handmade. It hadn't been made by Mrs. Beverington, not with those hands.

"That's what I was hoping to talk to you about, Mr. Beverington," said Kate.

He indicated the chairs behind them and they sat down while he maneuvered his way around the coffee table to sit down next to his mother. He put an arm around her and squeezed gently.

Kate glanced at Trepalli and saw the same doubt in his eyes.

"What did you want to know?" he asked, helping himself to a lemon square. His cheeks were still ruddy from the cold. He might be thirty-five, thirty-six, a man clearly in the prime of his life.

Now that he was sitting in front of her, Kate realized she hadn't given any thought to how she would approach him. She hesitated, and felt more than saw Trepalli turn to look at her.

"Is it about the man they found?" prompted Beverington soberly.

The cautious friendliness in his blue eyes decided her.

"Yes," she said, nodding. "We've been trying to establish a timeline for the discovery of his body." She glanced at Trepalli meaningfully and he stared back uncomprehendingly.

"Constable, could you take notes?" she finally asked.

The poor boy blushed in embarrassment but jumped up and went to the arctic entry. Like her, he kept his notebook in his parka. While he was trying to pull it out, Kate turned back to Beverington.

"Can you tell me when you first saw the body?" she asked. Trepalli closed the door to the entry and came back to his chair.

Beverington pursed his lips and shook his head. "I didn't," he said. "I never actually saw the body."

Frustration rose like a slow tide in Kate. For Pete's sake, was she *ever* going to find Witness Zero?

"You were described to us as the person who went to find a

paramedic," she said cautiously. Pointless to let him see her frustration. Mrs. Beverington glanced from Kate to her son, frowning.

Beverington frowned, too. "I was," he confirmed. "I was heading back inside the wreck to pull out more 'victims',"—he curled his fingers in the air to indicate quotation marks—"and someone told me they needed a paramedic for someone who was hurt for real on the other side of the train." He shrugged. "I collared the first free medic I saw and told him he was needed."

"You didn't go with him," said Kate.

"Never got the chance," he said. "I got called over to help with a couple of litters." He raised his eyebrows. "And the next thing I knew, the all clear sounded and the exercise was over. It's only when I got back to the station that I found out someone had died."

Trepalli kept scribbling but Kate sat back in the chair and stared at Beverington. He was telling the truth, damn it. What a wild goose chase.

"Who told you a paramedic was needed?" she finally asked, knowing it was useless.

He shrugged helplessly. "No idea," he said. "Never saw her face."

"*Her* face?" exclaimed Trepalli. "It was a woman?" His pencil remained poised in mid-air. Kate understood his reaction.

Beverington nodded hesitantly, looking from one to the other.

"What can you tell us about her," said Kate. "Tall? Short? Anything distinguishing about her?"

Beverington absently popped another lemon square in his mouth and stared up at the ceiling as he chewed. His expression grew doubtful. "It was pretty dark," he warned. Kate nodded encouragingly. "She was tall," he glanced at her, "came up to my nose."

That would make her roughly five nine.

"She wore the same parka we all did," he continued, "but I didn't notice any markings or name tags. She had a scarf pulled up over her nose and mouth, even over her balaclava." He shrugged again. "Wish I could be of more use," he said.

Kate smiled. "You were a great help, Mr. Beverington." She stood up and he scrambled to his feet, then helped his mother up. Well-raised. Kate pulled her business card from her uniform pocket and handed it to him. "If you remember anything else, anything at all, please give me a call."

He looked down at the card for a long second before looking back up at her. "She had a deep voice."

"Deep how?" asked Kate. "Kathleen Turner deep?"

He looked at her strangely and she realized it was a reference he was probably too young to get.

His mother patted his arm. "As if she had drunk a lot of whiskey in her life," she explained.

"I don't know how to describe it," he said. "It was deep, but I knew it was a woman."

"All right," said Kate. She couldn't remember any women in the exercise except for Alex Kowalski and Samantha Paterson, the only woman on the Mendenhall Police force. Besides herself, of course. And Paterson wasn't particularly tall, nor did she have a particularly deep voice. Kowalski was pretty tall, but she didn't have a deep voice, either.

"It wasn't an accident, was it?" asked Beverington softly.

Kate felt Trepalli moving up behind her but she held Beverington's gaze. "No, sir. It wasn't." She smiled at Mrs. Beverington. "Thank you for your hospitality, ma'am."

"My pleasure, Chief Williams," said the woman gravely.

For the first time, Kate noted that her son had inherited her deep blue eyes and frank, direct gaze. He escorted them to the door and stood in silence while they got their coats and boots on. Then, just as Trepalli was reaching for the door, Beverington asked, "Can you tell me who it was?"

Trepalli glanced at her and she nodded. It wasn't a secret.

"Frank Washburn," said Trepalli.

Beverington's expression went from solemn to shocked.

"Did you know him?" asked Kate, suddenly alert.

He nodded. "My hockey team has played against his for years.

He's a good guy." His ruddy cheeks stood out starkly against the sudden pallor of his face.

Kate finished putting her gloves on while she examined him. "Can you think of anyone who might have wanted to hurt him?"

Beverington stared at her but she could tell he wasn't really seeing her. Finally he shook his head. "Honestly? No. He was a good player, but he was there for the love of the game. Never any dirty tricks. He always made sure anyone who got hit wasn't hurt. Took his turn buying the beer." He shrugged. "A good guy."

A good guy didn't get himself killed, thought Kate sourly.

"Where did you play?" asked Trepalli suddenly.

Mrs. Beverington wrapped her sweater around herself more snugly and Kate realized they were cooling down the house by standing in the arctic entry to chat, but she didn't want to lose this train of enquiry.

"Here and in Mendenhall," said Beverington. "We like playing in Mendenhall because we can usually get early ice and be home at a reasonable time."

"You play later here?" asked Kate.

"Often the only ice time we can get is around ten or eleven at night. Makes for a late night when you've been playing for a few hours and then have to drive home, especially to Mendenhall."

"If that was me," said Trepalli, "I'd probably spend the night in town and drive home in the morning."

Beverington nodded. "A lot of the Mendenhall players do that," he agreed. "Cram themselves into cheap motel rooms or spend the night at a friend's."

"What about Washburn?" asked Kate. "What did he do?"

Beverington shook his head. "Sorry. I didn't know the guy well enough to know."

All right, then. Kate took her glove off and shook hands with the guy. He'd been helpful. "Thanks again, Mr. Beverington," she said. She nodded at his mother. "And thank you, ma'am."

Ten minutes later, she and Trepalli were driving away from the Beverington home, heading for Portage Avenue.

"Well, hell," muttered Trepalli finally. "We're no further ahead than we were when we started out."

"Nonsense," said Kate. She felt unaccountably cheerful, awake and alive. "We're getting closer and closer all the time." They had learned something important. She could feel it in the singing of her blood.

Now if she could only figure out what it was.

CHAPTER 13

DEAN DEVERELL was out for lunch when Kate called to ask if she could see her. Not only that, but the dean would be in a meeting for the rest of the afternoon. The dean's secretary was polite, but firm. No, it was not possible to obtain a few minutes of the dean's time. Kate would have to make an appointment. The first available one was a week Wednesday.

Kate refused politely, thanked her for her time and broke the connection. Trepalli glanced sideways at her then returned his attention to the traffic on Portage Avenue. "No luck?"

"The good dean is apparently unavailable," said Kate. She was irritated at herself. She had hoped to save time by making sure the dean was around. Instead, she had put the dragon at the gate on alert. It was always better to show up in person and brazen it out.

"So we go back home?" asked Trepalli.

She looked at him in surprise. "No. We go to the college." Did he really think she'd give up this easily?

* * *

Assiniboine Community College had been built twenty years ago. At the time, it was on the outskirts of the city, in farm country. Since then, the city had expanded out to it and beyond. Now the college was surrounded by car parks, malls, and businesses.

Like the Winnipeg Police Department Headquarters building, Assiniboine Community College was built mostly of concrete and glass. Unlike the WPD Headquarters, the look was airy and inviting, with large windows and outside artwork.

Trepalli found the visitor parking and parked. They walked up to the entrance, keeping their chins tucked inside their collars. To the right of the wide walkway was a deep indent in the pristine snow. That would be the student smoking pit, reasoned Kate. Trees huddled around it, and now that she was paying attention, she thought she saw staggered steps all around.

Then Trepalli opened the door and they were out of the wind.

The reception desk was to the left. A young woman sat behind the glass, looking at them inquisitively. Kate smiled at her but didn't move toward her. Just ahead, under an open stairway, was another pit surrounded by benches. Another gathering place for students, clearly. To the right of the pit was the bookstore and to her immediate right, a big sign announced the registrar's office.

There was nobody in the lobby, although she could see a few people working in the bookstore.

Kate removed her gloves and her hat and stomped her feet clear of snow.

"Want me to ask where the dean's office is?" asked Trepalli. He had removed his hat and gloves and tucked them under his arm.

"No," said Kate, giving him a look as she set out. Good grief. Why not just put it on the PA system that she was coming to the dean's office?

"How will we find her...?" he asked, stretching his long legs to keep up with her.

She climbed the stairs quickly and waited for him at the top. When he stood next to her again, she pointed at the signs on the walls.

They were in a sunny atrium, the hub of the college. It had a glass ceiling and glass walls all around. Three wings led away from the atrium, each with a sign above the corridor. The one behind her read Liberal Arts while the one to her right read Management Tourism and Hospitality and the third sign read Business and Management.

"My guess is we'll find Dean Deverell somewhere down this

hallway," said Kate, pointing to the Business and Management sign.

The sound of footsteps on the stairs caused them both to turn around. A young man clutching a small backpack that looked heavy was running up the steps. He paused when he saw them waiting for him at the top. His face paled and Kate wondered what he was carrying in his pack.

She put on her best smile and his step faltered on the top step. He clutched the handrail.

Oh, for Pete's sake. She stopped smiling.

"Excuse me," she said, "could you direct us to Dean Deverell's office?"

Relief flooded the student's features and Kate fought an impulse to roll her eyes. At his age, she had thought the world revolved around her, too.

"The administrative offices are at the far end of that hallway," he pointed toward the Business and Management hallway. "There's a reception desk there. They can show you to the Dean's office."

"Thank you," said Kate but she was already talking to his back as he retreated down the Liberal Arts hallway.

They both stared after him. Finally Trepalli said, "Kinda makes you wonder what he has in that backpack, doesn't it?"

Kate smiled and turned away.

The hallway connected to a wing with classrooms on either side. Sure enough, at the far end was a counter that spanned the width of the hallway, behind which were desks, only one of which was occupied. The Sweet Young Thing at that desk looked up when she heard them approach and her gaze immediately fastened onto Trepalli. She was cute, in a tiny, blonde, and very young way. She watched, her mouth slightly parted, as he approached and finally came to a stop at the counter.

Kate opened her mouth to speak, but Trepalli beat her to it.

"Good afternoon," he said, giving her a smile.

The girl blushed.

This time Kate did roll her eyes but it didn't matter. The girl only had eyes for Trepalli.

The girl got up and walked over to the counter. "Hello," she said, a quaver in her voice. "Can I help you?"

Trepalli smiled again and damned if the girl didn't blush again. "Are you Dean Deverell's executive assistant?" he asked.

For the first time, the girl seemed to notice that Trepalli wasn't alone. She glanced at Kate, who knew better than to smile, and then back to Trepalli.

"Oh no," she said. She was regaining her composure, although her hand did stray to her hair, as if to make sure it was still there. "That's Mrs. Barker." She glanced to the right, where a bank of offices could be seen through a glass wall. "She just left for a late lunch."

Trepalli laid his hat and gloves on the counter and rested his hands next to them. He leaned forward a little. "Actually," he said conspiratorially, "we're here to speak with Dean Deverell herself. Can you tell us where to find her?"

The girl blinked rapidly and Kate could have sworn she saw a flutter at her throat. "The dean is in a meeting with the other heads of divisions," she said. "It's the monthly division meeting. They'll be in there all afternoon."

Come on, Trepalli, thought Kate. *Don't fail me now.*

"This won't take long," he said. "Do you think you could call her out?"

"Oh no!" The girl shook her head vigorously. "They don't like to be disturbed during their meeting."

Trepalli nodded soberly. "I can understand that..." He looked at her and smiled this time sticking his hand out. "Sorry, I'm being rude. My name is Marco Trepalli and this is... Kate Williams."

Kate nodded at the girl's brief flicker of acknowledgement but she didn't offer her hand. The girl was too busy having her hand engulfed by Trepalli's. Kate noted Trepalli's avoidance of her rank and decided she didn't mind. The mention of the word "chief" might have set off the girl's alarms.

"I'm Nicole Beringer," she said, and Trepalli finally released her hand.

"Nice to meet you, Nicole," he said warmly. "How about this as a compromise. You tell my colleague where the meeting is being held and she can hover outside the door until they take a break."

"What about you?" asked the girl, staring up at him.

"Oh, I don't think we both need to go," he said. "If it's okay with you, I'll just wait here."

"Well, I guess that would be all right," she said, not taking her eyes off Trepalli.

Two minutes later, Kate found herself standing outside a boardroom that was tucked in a recess of the Liberal Arts wing. Without the girl's detailed directions, she would never have found it. The door had one of those sliding signs that indicated whether or not the room was occupied. Right now it read "occupied," and Kate could hear voices murmuring through the heavy wood.

Taking a deep breath to calm her sudden nerves, she knocked at the door. A moment later, a young man opened the door, a forbidding expression on his face. He looked like he was wearing his dad's suit and tie.

Then he noticed her uniform and his eyes widened.

"Yes?"

"Is Marilyn Deverell inside?" She spoke loudly enough for anyone in the room to hear.

The young man flinched and moved just enough for Kate to catch a glimpse of the room beyond. It was smaller than she had expected, with a table big enough for ten, but seating only five at the moment. There was only one woman at the table, a blonde with a short, tailored hairdo that looked razor-cut. Her gaze was fixed on Kate.

"What is it, David?" asked the man to the woman's right.

The young man at the door turned to look at the table. "This police officer would like to speak to Dean Deverell."

One empty spot at the table held a laptop. David was the meeting recorder.

Dean Deverell stood up and smiled at her colleagues. "Let me see what this is about," she said and walked toward the door.

Dean Deverell wore a beautifully cut, knee-length business suit in gray wool, with a lavender silk blouse underneath, that told the world she was all business; while the four-inch spike heels she wore told the men in the room that there was more to her than just business.

"Thank you, David," said the dean as she reached the door. She waited until he cleared the doorway then closed the door behind her.

The face she turned to Kate was not friendly.

"I'm Chief Williams from the Mendenhall Police Department," said Kate.

"I believe my secretary told you I was unavailable."

And yet, here you are, thought Kate.

"This should only take a few minutes of your time, Dean Deverell," said Kate. "Would you like to do it here or in a more private location?"

The woman's brown eyes—probably not a natural blonde, then—narrowed at the implication that she would rather have privacy for what Kate had to say. Her lips thinned and she nodded sharply.

"Very well." She turned on one of those very high heels and left Kate to follow her.

The dean led Kate out of the small nook and back into the main hallway, and finally stopped at a closed door. There was a narrow window in it revealing a darkened classroom. She opened the door and flicked on the lights, then stepped back to let Kate in before closing the door.

"Pick a seat," said the dean.

A faint scent of baby powder reached Kate, throwing her for a moment. She was having trouble reconciling the powerful, sexy woman with the baby powder. She sat at the nearest student desk.

To her credit, Deverell didn't choose the teacher's table at the head of the class but sat in the student desk nearest Kate. Her estimation of the woman went up. Not enough to make her apologize, but enough to temper her remarks.

"Thank you, Dean Deverell," she began.

"Don't thank me," snapped the woman, and for the first time, Kate realized how angry she was. She hid it well. "Just tell me why you pulled me out of my meeting."

Fair enough.

"Do you know Frank Washburn?"

Surprise swept the anger away from the dean's face. "Frank? Yes, of course. He's one of my contract professors."

"What does that mean?" asked Kate. It was clear the woman didn't know Washburn was dead, but Kate didn't want to tell her quite yet. She wanted information before she had to deal with the emotional reaction.

"We pull in professionals from the community to teach in their area of expertise," said the dean. She shrugged. "He teaches economics to my Business and Management students."

Kate nodded. "How often?"

"One night a week, on Thursdays." The dean stopped and looked at Kate, a sudden dire knowledge in her eyes. "Something's happened to him, hasn't it?"

Kate studied the woman's stricken face. "Why do you say that?" she asked softly.

The dean's clasped hands flew apart, birds suddenly released.

"Why else would you be here, asking about him? He's gone missing, hasn't he?" She blinked rapidly, obviously trying to control tears.

Was this the woman Washburn was having an affair with? If he was having an affair?

"No, ma'am," said Kate gently. "Mr. Washburn is dead."

Both hands flew to the woman's mouth as if to keep a scream from coming out. Her eyes widened in horror as she stared at Kate. Finally her hands dropped away and lay curled on the desk top, forgotten.

"How?" she whispered. "When?"

"We're still investigating," said Kate, moved in spite of herself by the woman's distress. "We found him at the site of an Emergency Measures Organization mock accident, early Sunday morning. It appears he froze to death."

"But..." the dean stopped, then started again. "Sunday morning? How early?"

"Around three in the morning," said Kate.

Dean Deverell frowned. She was a lovely woman, really, in spite of the harsh haircut. She was in her mid to late forties, with a trim figure and nice legs—although that was probably from the shoes. There was a gold band on her left hand.

"I saw him that night," said the dean. She clasped her hands in her lap. "He came to a cocktail party the college hosted. He seemed perfectly fine."

"Was he drinking?"

The dean shook her head and her hair fell back perfectly into position. "Frank never drank, that I could tell. In any case, he wouldn't drink because he was planning to drive back to Mendenhall that night."

Well, he'd had a drink at some point before he died.

"Was he with anyone?" she asked.

Dean Deverell shook her head again. "No. I got the impression he really didn't want to be there, however."

"How do you mean?"

The woman shrugged. "I overheard him talking to his wife on the phone, in the coat room." She blinked, and blushed. "I had left my cell phone in my coat pocket. I wasn't trying to eavesdrop."

I do it all the time, thought Kate, waving a hand for the woman to continue.

"He was obviously trying to calm her down. He said he'd be there soon."

"What time was that?"

Dean Deverell looked up at the ceiling. "I wanted to check up on the kids..." she murmured. She looked at Kate. "New babysitter." She remained silent a moment longer, clearly figuring out her times. "It would have been around ten-thirty, eleven o'clock. He left soon after."

And less than four hours later, Frank Washburn lay dead in the snow.

"Where was the cocktail party?"

"At the Burma Tree, on Ellice." The dean took a deep breath and shifted slightly in her seat. "It was an accident?" The look she gave Kate was direct.

"We don't believe it was."

Dean Deverell closed her eyes and shook her head. "Frank is—was—a good man. He didn't deserve to die like that."

Kate blinked. That was almost word-for-word what Charlotte had said.

"Can you think of anyone who might have wanted to hurt him?" she asked.

A face peered in through the window but the dean ignored it. She shook her head. "Honestly, no. I'm not exaggerating when I say he was a good man. He had honor, you know? He always did the right thing for the right reason. And he was also a lot of fun. His students loved him. Oh God. His students."

The personal shock was passing. Now she had to think like a dean. By Thursday night, she had to find someone to replace Frank Washburn.

"Is there anything else, Chief?" She glanced at the clock at the front of the room. "I'm afraid there's a class in here in the next few minutes."

"Just one more question," said Kate as the dean made to get up. "Did he have any friends in town? Do you know where he stayed on Thursday nights?"

She looked at Kate blankly. "I'm sorry, I have no idea." She stood up and watched Kate get up. "I could check with Mrs. Barker, my secretary. She handled all the payments. If he stayed in a hotel, she would know which one."

"Thank you very much for your time, Dean Deverell." Kate stuck her hand out and the dean shook it firmly.

"I wish I could say it was a pleasure," said the dean.

Kate fished through her uniform pocket and came up with a business card, which she handed to the dean. "For when your secretary finds the information we need."

Dean Deverell nodded and tucked it in the pocket of her suit.

"Oh, one last thing," said Kate before the dean could open the door. "I need a list of the people invited to the reception."

The dean hesitated, then nodded. "I'm not sure who would

have it," she said, "but I'll get it to you."

"Thank you."

They opened the door to find a cluster of students milling around the door, waiting to go inside.

Kate watched the dean walk away then made her way back to the Business and Management wing. Students now thronged the hallways, their voices filling the space with chatter and laughter. They made way when they saw her coming, and by the time she turned down the Business and Management wing, she felt like an old time gunslinger come to town. Trepalli saw her and gave the girl at the counter a little wave before joining Kate. There were now three more women, apparently returned from lunch, at the desks behind the counter. All four watched Trepalli walk away.

"How did she take it?" he asked when he finally reached her.

"Hard, I think," said Kate. The dean was a woman used to keeping her emotions to herself.

This wing, too, was filled with students hurrying to classrooms or sitting on the center benches and chatting. None of them paid Kate or Trepalli any mind. Apparently business and management students were harder to impress.

"I saw a picture of her on the wall behind the counter," said Trepalli. "Good-looking woman. Do you think Washburn was having an affair with her?"

Kate shook her head. "No." She could be wrong of course, but no, she didn't think so. They reached the staircase and started down, passing a dozen late students running up the stairs.

"I had no luck finding out who he stayed with when he was in town," Kate added when there were no young ears nearby. They paused in the entrance lobby to zip up their coats. "The dean's going to get her secretary to dig up the information." She sighed, thinking of Mrs. Barker's unwillingness to help. "The dean doesn't know anything about Washburn's private life."

"Well," said Trepalli, "Nicole—the receptionist—does." He gave her a wicked grin before pushing his way outside.

* * *

"Ash Mann," said Trepalli, as they sat shivering in the Explorer, waiting for it to warm up. The window fogged over faintly from their breathing. From their spot in the visitor parking lot, they could see students popping out of side doors and propping them open while they had a quick smoke. Most of them didn't have a coat on.

"Who is he?" she asked, tucking her chin into her scarf. The temperature gauge read minus twenty-four Celsius, and this was the warmest time of the day.

"The receptionist didn't know," Trepalli admitted. "But she said he came to the college once when Washburn was in class to drop off a laptop he had left at Mann's place." Trepalli looked up from his notes. "Apparently Mr. Mann is 'hot'."

Kate frowned. Who was Mann? According to Dean Deverell, Washburn hadn't planned to spend Saturday night in town, but Mann might know something important.

"Is that all you've got?" she asked. She meant it literally, but realized how it sounded when she saw the disappointment on his face. "I mean," she corrected, "are you finished reporting?"

He nodded stiffly and she smothered a sigh. Fragile ego. "Drive me around to the front."

Without a word, he put the car in gear and drove out of the parking lot and around the loop to stop at the edge of the walk that led to the front doors.

"I'll be right back," she said and left the car. When she got inside the college, she walked up to the reception desk and asked the woman if she could borrow her phone book. Without a word, the woman handed over the three-inch thick Winnipeg phone book. Kate kept a Southern Manitoba directory in her car, but the Winnipeg one was too big to fit in her door pocket. She flipped to the *M*s, then narrowed down her search to the right page and column. There were three Manns, but no Ash or A. Mann.

Of course not.

She thanked the receptionist and headed back outside. Fine. She'd ask Daisy.

* * *

It was well past two by the time they got back to Mendenhall. When they pulled up at the station house, Kate's stomach growled loudly.

"Me, too," said Trepalli, getting out. He handed her the keys to the Explorer before opening the door to the station house for her. The glass outer door was still iced over. Kate was beginning to despair of ever seeing spring again. Maybe this was the Icelandic hell. Lord knew, there were enough Icelanders who had emigrated here.

The warmth inside chased all thoughts of hell—Icelandic or otherwise—away, and Kate sighed with pleasure at being out of the cold wind.

Behind her, Trepalli stomped his feet to remove the excess snow and she heard him take a deep breath.

"Amanda's been here," he said.

Kate glanced over her shoulder at him and then the smell hit her—something rich and spicy and *meaty*. Her stomach growled in instant response.

"Hi, Chief," said Charlotte, leaning over the duty counter to stick her head through the opening. "Hello, Marco."

Was that her imagination, or did the temperature in the station just drop a degree or two?

"Charlotte," Kate acknowledged as she walked past the counter and into the duty room. She pulled her gloves and hat off and began to unzip her parka. She paused when she saw Kyle Holmes sitting at one of the desks, talking to an older woman who occupied the witness chair. The woman talked in a low voice and clutched her black down coat around her body as if she was freezing. Holmes looked up when Kate walked in. He nodded a greeting but turned back to the woman immediately.

"Where's Tattersall?" she asked Charlotte.

"Late lunch," said Charlotte. "Kyle was on the desk when Mrs. Berryman came in." The headphone kept Charlotte's glossy curls out of her face and made her look all of fifteen.

Kate glanced at the woman again, noting the knitted hat pulled down to her eyebrows, the downturned mouth, the fluttering hands. So that was the famous Mrs. Berryman. The woman called the station at least once a week to complain about something. Usually it was kids loitering around her house, but she'd also reported suspicious strangers, strange noises, strange lights, strange cars... The list went on.

McKell had left standing orders that the constables were to respond to her complaints promptly and with respect. She had been a nurse in the Korean war, and as far as McKell was concerned, that gave her a free pass. According to him, the old and the lonely were as much in need of police services as anyone else. Maybe more.

A bit sentimental for Kate's taste, but it wasn't as if her officers were run off their feet with calls. They could afford to humor the old woman.

She wondered what it meant that Mrs. Berryman was now coming into the station to lay her complaints.

"Dear God," murmured Trepalli reverently. He took a deep breath. "What did she bring?"

Charlotte seemed to forget to be mad. She dimpled in a smile. "Stew and bannock," she said. "It's in the lunch room. And she made the most amazing cookies for dessert."

"DC McKell is gone?" asked Kate as Trepalli made a beeline for the lunchroom.

"Yes, ma'am," nodded Charlotte. She settled herself in the duty chair. "He and Ben left for Brandon about half an hour ago."

Kate had called McKell when they were on their way back to Mendenhall and told him what she'd learned. She still wanted the DC to check out Steve Osbrig, the Brandon paramedic, and told him to go as soon as he was ready, and not wait for her return.

All right, then. McKell would be back in an hour or so. In the meantime, she was going to check on Daisy. But first, food.

"What's bannock?" she asked.

"It's a kind of flat bread—Good afternoon, Mendenhall Police," she said suddenly. She nodded at no one and said, "Yes, Mr. Mayor, she's here. Just a moment, please, and I'll see if she can take your call."

Kate pointed to her office in the back and Charlotte nodded.

Mrs. Berryman looked up at her suspiciously as she passed

the desk. Kate nodded and kept going. She removed her parka and dropped it on the guest chair just as the phone began to ring on her desk. She pushed her door closed, rounded the desk, and caught it on the third ring.

"Hello, Mr. Mayor," she said, sitting down.

"Chief, how are you?" asked Mayor Dabbs. He always had time for the niceties and Kate had learned not to rush the process.

"I'm fine, sir. How can I help you?"

"Have you determined how he came to be out there?"

"Not yet," said Kate. "Did you know Mr. Washburn?" It seemed she was always asking that question.

"Yes, of course," replied the Mayor. "He came to all our functions with Daisy. Nice chap."

Nice chap? What an odd thing to say.

"So, how long have you known him?" she probed.

The mayor paused. "I didn't call for idle chit chat," he said sternly.

"All right," said Kate, her bullshit radar suddenly going off. "Why *did* you call?"

"To see how you were coming with the investigation, of course!" The mayor sounded aggravated, and Kate drummed her fingers on the cold, smooth surface of her maple desk, wondering why he was so flustered. A chair scraped on the tile floor of the duty room.

"We're working a few leads," said Kate noncommittally. "I'll let you know as soon as we learn anything definite."

"Good," said the mayor and rang off.

Kate stared at the receiver for a few seconds before putting it back in its cradle.

What was that all about?

* * *

It was beef stew, and it was heavenly. The beef cubes were tender and juicy, the gravy thick and spicy, the chunks of carrots, onion, and potato just firm enough. And bannock was indeed a flat bread that had been fried.

Kate tore off another chunk and used it to sop up the last of the gravy in her bowl. Across the table from her, Trepalli had just scarfed down his second bowl and now sat back in his chair looking blissfully sated.

"I could get used to this," he said.

Kate frowned. That was exactly what she was worried about.

CHAPTER 14

"What do you mean, she's gone?" asked Kate. The nurse stared stolidly up at her from his seat at the Intensive Care nursing station. He shrugged then nodded at the screen in front of him. "According to this, she discharged herself this morning," he said, "before I came on shift."

Kate stared at the man, trying to understand what he was saying. He was the same nurse she had encountered the first time she had come to see Daisy. Steinbach, that was his name. He was no friendlier now than he had been then. She wished Nurse Kirkham, the older nurse, were there, but the ward was eerily empty. The only activity was behind the nursing station, where half a dozen women and men worked at desks in the administration area.

"Two days ago, she was in a coma," said Kate clearly.

Steinbach nodded.

"Yesterday she was still unconscious."

The worry lines deepened on his forehead and he ran a hand through his receding hair, leaving barely a dent in the crinkly curls.

"It *is* unusual," he admitted, scanning the screen. "She was awake and responsive last night," he read. "She was well enough to be transferred to the general ward. I see here that the doctor wanted her referred to a neurologist in Winnipeg." He looked up at Kate. "Your best bet is to talk to Dr. Avery. He's her doctor." There was a hopeful note in his voice. She suspected he was worried about Daisy.

Well, so was she.

"All right," she said. "Thanks for your help."

She walked down the hallway toward the stairwell, then stopped and turned back. "Is Dr. Avery still in the hospital?" she asked Steinbach.

He shook his head. "I doubt it. He would have done his rounds and then gone back to his clinic."

"Which is?"

"Mendenhall Medical Clinic."

She knew the place. It was a newer brick building, on the corner of Nelson and Tenth. It had a pharmacy attached to it. She'd had to go there to see Dr. Christiansen when she was recovering from her bullet wound.

"Can you page Dr. Avery, just in case?"

He hesitated, then nodded. He picked up the phone and punched in a couple of numbers. A moment later, Kate heard his voice over the loud speakers, "Dr. Avery, call eight two one two. Dr. Avery, eighty-two twelve."

She waited around for ten minutes. A nurse emerged from one of the rooms and visitors from the elevator. They spoke to Steinbach, who directed them to a room down the hall. The phone at the nursing station rang, and he picked it up on the first ring, but shook his head at her. Finally she handed Steinbach her card.

"If the doctor shows up, please call me and I'll come back."

Steinbach nodded and she left. She took the stairs down to the main floor, noting again the smells of supper wafting up the shaft. This time, she was inured, thanks to Amanda's stew. She made a mental note to reimburse the girl for all the money she'd been spending.

She fastened her coat and pulled on her hat before braving the cold, but to her surprise, the temperature had moderated. Or maybe she was just getting used to it. She used the remote control to start the Explorer and watched it come to life in the parking lot, its headlights winking on welcomingly.

Still, she hesitated outside the door of the hospital, staring into the growing gloom. The streetlights had come on, although there was still well over an hour before full dark. From its perch on the rise, the hospital had a great view of the bridge and the downtown area. As she watched, lights came on in office buildings. Mendenhall had a bylaw that limited building height to four stories. Kate liked the idea.

She breathed deeply of the cold air, letting it wash the hospital smells—good and bad—out of her lungs.

Why on earth would Daisy have checked herself out of the hospital? She was in no shape to look after herself. She didn't have any family, and the Washburns clearly weren't going to be there for her. Maybe her friends would rally to her aid, or the Dabbs, but why put herself through that when she could be well looked after at the hospital, for free?

She pulled off her glove to reach for her phone just as it rang, startling her. She fumbled it out and pressed the talk button on the third ring.

"Williams."

"We interviewed Osbrig," McKell said, without preamble. "He was inside the wreck, pulling victims out when the body was discovered."

"Did you—"

"Yes, confirmed with other witnesses who were with him when the siren went off. It wasn't him."

Kate nodded and started walking toward the parking lot. "We had to check it out," she said. "Beverington never actually saw the body." She unlocked the door of the Explorer and slipped in behind the wheel.

"And he doesn't know who asked him to get the paramedic?"

"He said it was a woman," said Kate. "No one he knew."

McKell already knew this. She had briefed him on her way back from Winnipeg. He was just thinking out loud.

"A woman," mused McKell.

"A woman with a deep voice," she amended. "Beverington said he was sure it was a woman, but that her voice was low."

"Well, hell," muttered McKell.

Kate knew exactly how he felt. For two days she had been running around, chasing one lead after another, and she was no nearer to finding out what happened the night Frank Washburn died.

"What's happening with the warrants?" she asked.

She heard a drawer close at the other end and the creaking of McKell's ancient wooden roller chair. Through the air vents, she caught a whiff of wood smoke from someone's fireplace or wood stove.

"We got 'em," he confirmed. "Tattersall's working with MTS to get the records."

"Good." Kate nodded to herself. Once they had those records, they would have a much better sense of who Frank Washburn had been talking to in the days leading up to his death.

"Daisy checked herself out of the hospital this morning," said Kate.

"Holy crap," said McKell, the shock clear in his voice. "Is she nuts?"

"That's a good question," said Kate grimly. "Send a patrol car out to her place to see if she's there. If she is, have a constable call me. I want to talk to her."

"Where will you be?"

Kate glanced at the dashboard clock. Four sixteen. "I'm going to see her doctor at the Mendenhall Medical Clinic," she said. "I want to know exactly what's going on with Daisy Pitcairn-Washburn."

* * *

The door to the clinic was locked, but the lights were on and Kate could see a woman sitting at the reception desk, her gray head bent over paperwork. Kate knocked on the glass door but the woman didn't raise her head. She knocked more loudly and the woman looked up, frowning. She peered in Kate's direction, but obviously couldn't see who it was in the gloom. She stood up and disappeared from view, only to reappear a moment later when she came around the desk. While she didn't wear a uniform, Kate guessed from the short, no-nonsense haircut and practical, crepe-soled shoes that she was probably a nurse.

The woman unlocked the door and cracked it open. "The clinic is closed for the day," she said. "Is this an emergency?"

Kate had her identification out. She flipped the leather wallet open and held it up at the woman's eye level.

"Kate Williams, chief of police," she said. "I'd like to come in."

The door cracked open wider, but not so wide that Kate felt welcomed in. The woman examined the identification then pushed the door open. Once Kate was inside, the woman locked the door behind her.

"What can I do for you, Chief Williams?"

Her voice was low, but not particularly deep for a woman. Kate shook herself mentally and focused on the task at hand. "Is Dr. Avery here?"

The woman nodded. "He's catching up on some paperwork in his office. I'll tell him you want to see him."

The woman left Kate standing in the middle of the waiting room while she disappeared into a hallway at the back.

Kate looked around. Toys were heaped in a basket in the corner, under a series of empty coat hooks. Hard wooden chairs lined up against the wall. In the opposite corner, pamphlets offered information on everything from quitting smoking to the importance of wearing a condom. All the magazines were neatly stacked.

All the offices she could see were dark, their paper-covered examination tables gleaming ghost-like in what little light reached them from the main office.

"Chief Williams?"

Kate jumped, spooked by the deep voice. She turned to find herself facing a man dressed in a doctor's coat over a shirt and tie.

He was barely her height and completely bald. His face was lined with fine wrinkles and speckled with age spots, but the brown eyes that peered at her through thick glasses were penetrating and intelligent.

"Dr. Avery, thank you for seeing me," said Kate, regaining her composure.

He raised an eyebrow. "It's not every day the chief of police comes to see me," he said. "How can I help you?"

The nurse had resumed her place behind the desk and Kate glanced at her before looking back at the doctor.

"This involves one of your patients."

He was a sharp one. "Mrs. Sullivan knows everything about my practice," he said. "Whatever you tell me, I'll probably end up telling her." Mrs. Sullivan didn't look up but she smiled. "However," continued the doctor, "you might be more comfortable in one of the examination rooms?"

Kate shook her head, reluctant to enter one of the ghostly rooms. Better to stay here in the brightly-lit waiting room, with Mrs. Sullivan pretending she wasn't listening.

"I understand that Daisy Washburn is your patient," she said.

The doctor's expression grew somber. "I don't think I'd be divulging anything private if I said yes, she is," he said. "Her husband was, too, God rest his soul."

That surprised her, although she couldn't say why. Maybe it was because this man seemed a natural fit for female patients.

"Can you tell me why you discharged Daisy today?"

He frowned, and a dozen thin lines formed between his brows. "I did not discharge her."

"Well, she's gone," said Kate.

"I know she is gone," said the doctor testily. "The hospital called me to let me know she had discharged herself. Against my orders, I might add."

Kate half raised a hand as if she was still in school. "Why would she do that?" she asked. "Wasn't she seriously injured?"

Here the doctor hesitated and she realized she had ventured into uncomfortable territory. He glanced at Mrs. Sullivan, who was watching him.

"Why do you need to know?"

Fair enough. She was asking him for information he felt uncomfortable sharing. Maybe she needed to give a little first.

"She's a person of interest in the investigation into her husband's death."

The words dropped into the room like stones in a deep pool. The doctor and his nurse stared at her as if waiting for her to qualify the statement. She set aside the twisty feeling in her gut. She wasn't being disloyal to Daisy. She was doing her job.

"I doubt Daisy would have done anything to harm him," said the doctor finally. His expression didn't change, but she got the sense that he had withdrawn from her.

"Do you know her well?" She didn't mean it to sound challenging but the nurse's back stiffened and the doctor's lips pressed tightly together. She raised a hand to forestall any objection, although these two were pros in their own right, and used to playing off each other. They wouldn't give anything away. "Seriously. How long has she been your patient?"

"Five years, Anna?" He glanced at Mrs. Sullivan, who shook her head.

"Six, Doctor."

"I became her doctor when her doctor retired."

Daisy would have been twenty. A grown woman. He probably knew very little about her personal life.

"Did she ever talk to you about her husband?" she asked. "Were they having trouble?"

"I really cannot discuss this with you," he said firmly. "That would be breaching patient confidentiality."

Yes, it would. And it didn't matter. Kate was forming her own opinion about Daisy Washburn's marriage based on the woman's coworkers and neighbors.

"Was she depressed?" she asked. "Having trouble sleeping?" The doctor remained stubbornly mute and Kate sighed. "All right," she said. "At least tell me how badly injured she is."

Dr. Avery crossed his arms, having clearly decided he didn't like her. "She has a broken arm and two cracked ribs. Her shoulder was injured. Some bruising. Fortunately, the swelling to her brain went down and she is recovering well. She needs to be checked out by a neurologist, however. The concussion was the worst of it. She was lucky. The airbags protected her from worse injuries."

"*Should* she be on her own?"

"Well, no," said Dr. Avery. "But then she's not, is she?"

Kate frowned. "What do you mean?"

"She's not alone," he clarified. "Her sister was with her when she discharged herself from the hospital."

Kate blinked at him. "How do you know?" she asked slowly.

He looked at her in silence for a long moment before finally speaking. "I spoke to the nurse in charge," he said. "She told me Daisy's sister had arrived to help her out."

Something cold and heavy settled in Kate's gut.

"She doesn't have a sister," she said slowly.

The doctor's face paled. "Then who—?"

"Who was the nurse you spoke to?" Kate interrupted.

He glanced at Mrs. Sullivan.

"It was Astrid Kirkham," said the woman.

That was the same nurse Kate had spoken to yesterday. With a curt nod to both of them, she thanked them and left.

* * *

Steinbach wasn't at the nurses' station when Kate returned to the intensive care ward. A thin young woman in pale blue scrubs was typing away at the computer. Through the glass wall behind her, Kate could see two women and a man turning off computers and putting their coats on. She glanced at her watch. Past five.

Crap. Had there been a shift change?

The nurse looked up from her typing. "Can I help you?" She had pretty green eyes and a round face that put Kate in mind of the Icelandic heritage of the province.

"Is Nurse Kirkham still here?" she asked, mentally crossing her fingers.

"She's helping with dinner," said the young woman. "We're a little short-staffed."

Only then did Kate become aware of the quiet activity in the hallway. An industrial-size metal tray trolley waited outside the room farthest down the hallway. While it had room for at least thirty trays, she counted only five.

At that moment, Steinbach emerged from the room and grabbed the trolley to push it to the next room. Kate stared at him, trying to figure out the way they ran their shifts. If Nurse Kirkham had been on duty when Daisy "discharged" herself but Steinbach hadn't, that must mean they had staggered shifts.

He looked up and caught her eye.

"Chief Williams," he said. "Forget something?"

"I need to talk to Nurse Kirkham," said Kate.

"How can I help you, chief?" said Nurse Kirkham behind her.

Kate jumped and turned. Nurse Kirkham smiled apologetically and stepped around her to get to the trolley. She slid one of the trays out and checked the name on the card. Steinbach did the same with another tray and headed for the next room down the hall.

"Can you spare a minute?" asked Kate.

"Yes, of course," said Kirkham. "Just let me deliver this tray. George can handle the others." The tray held a covered plate, a glass with milk and a crimped paper lid, and a small bowl of green jello under a plastic film. She disappeared into the room and returned a moment later, closing the door partway.

"Now," she said. "Let's go into the waiting room."

Kate followed her past the nursing station to the juncture of another wing, which, judging by the pastel colors of the walls and the wide window halfway down, was the maternity ward. A man in a flapping white coat rushed by them, one hand holding the end of the stethoscope against his chest to keep it from bumping against him. He pushed open one of the rooms and a woman's loud moans escaped, only to be cut short when the door closed behind him.

"In here," said Nurse Kirkham, ushering Kate into a room painted a cheerful yellow, with a television high on the wall in one corner and half a dozen padded chairs surrounding a low coffee table strewn with magazines. Next to the door was a vending machine with pop and juice on display.

Kate didn't even give the woman a chance to close the door.

"Daisy Washburn," she said.

Nurse Kirkham waited, her expression patient. Kate realized she was taking up the woman's valuable time and took a moment to marshal her thoughts.

"What time did you discharge her?"

Nurse Kirkham shook her head. "I did not discharge her," she corrected. "In fact, I counseled against it."

"But she still left."

"That's right," said the woman. "Her sister assured me she would look after her." She shrugged. "We can't keep a patient against her will."

"What did her sister look like?" asked Kate. She held her breath while the nurse stared at her, perplexed. When the woman realized Kate was serious, she shrugged again.

"Nothing like Mrs. Washburn," she began. "Tall, about five feet nine or ten, with straight, dark-blonde hair, maybe thirty years old. Attractive."

"And how was Daisy?"

Nurse Kirkham's eyebrows rose in surprise. "How do you mean?"

"Did she seem comfortable with the woman?"

The eyebrows rose even higher. "She didn't speak much," she said slowly. "And she allowed her sister to do most of the talking, but she did answer a few questions directly." Two spots of color appeared high on her cheeks. "Is something wrong, Chief Williams?"

The two women stared at each other. Finally Kate sighed. "I don't know. All I know is that Daisy Washburn doesn't have any brothers or sisters."

The other woman swallowed hard and clasped her hands tightly in front of her waist. "Then who...?"

Kate smiled mirthlessly. "That's what I would like to know."

She turned to leave, then remembered something else. "Did Daisy have any visitors?"

Nurse Kirkham shook her head. "Flowers and phone calls, but we discouraged visitors. You, the mayor, and his wife were the only ones until this morning when her... sister... showed up."

"I'm going to need a record of her incoming and outgoing phone calls."

The nurse shook her head. "That's above my pay level," she said. "You'll have to take it up with the Chief Admin Officer."

Kate swallowed her frustration and bit her tongue to keep from swearing. This woman had done nothing wrong.

"What about her voice?" she asked.

Nurse Kirkham frowned. "Whose voice?"

"The sister's voice," said Kate. "Was there anything special about it?"

She thought for a moment, then shook her head. "Nothing. A little deep, maybe, but that's all."

* * *

"There's no one here, chief," said Kyle Holmes.

Kate had pulled over to take the call. Now she sat in the car and watched as cars turned off River Road onto residential side streets. People going home for dinner. Grabbing a bite before taking the kids to hockey, ballet, or 4-H. People unaware that a good man had been murdered in their midst. And that his wife was now missing.

"Have you asked the neighbors..."

"Martins is knocking on doors, but there's fresh snow on the driveway and the walk. No one's been here."

Where the hell was she?

"I want to find her, constable. She may be in trouble."

"Yes, ma'am," said Holmes before hanging up. Kate slipped the phone back inside her pocket and stared at the street and its oblivious residents. She had questioned the admissions clerk and the security guard, and the paramedics in the ambulance station next to the parking lot. No one could recall seeing two women matching Daisy's description and that of her "sister" leaving the hospital.

Daisy wasn't under arrest. According to Nurse Kirkham, she hadn't appeared to be under duress.

Kate didn't care. Something about the whole situation didn't sit right. Much as she hated relying on "feelings," she had learned to listen to the little voice warning her something was off.

She pulled the phone out again and called McKell.

"McKell."

"No one knows where Daisy is."

There was a long silence. When he spoke again, there was a hint of satisfaction in his voice. "She's running."

"We don't know that," said Kate sharply. It irritated her that he was always willing to believe the worst of Daisy. She filled him in on what she had learned about the "sister."

"She could be Daisy's accomplice."

"Or she could have taken Daisy under duress," Kate pointed out.

"Unlikely," drawled McKell. "You said yourself Daisy appeared to go willingly with her."

Kate shrugged. "Appeared."

"Come on," said McKell. "First she hightails it out of town the day her husband's body is found and now she disappears the moment she can get out of bed?" He took a deep breath. "Let me put a BOLO out on her."

Kate shook her head. "We don't have any evidence connecting her to her husband's death," she pointed out. "And she can check herself out of hospital if she wants."

She could almost feel his frustration, but she was right and he knew it. He was too biased to see clearly when it came to Daisy Washburn.

"We need to get a record of Daisy's calls while she was at the hospital," she said into the silence.

McKell didn't say anything for a while. "I know the Ethics Officer there," he finally said. "If we get his okay, we shouldn't have to get a warrant."

"Good," she nodded. "Maybe then we can figure out who the hell took her out of the hospital. How's Tattersall doing with those warrants?"

"He got the MTS manager to call his boss in Winnipeg, who called the MTS lawyers, who said they had to honor the warrant. MTS is pulling the information now, but we probably won't have it until morning."

Kate stared at nothing while she thought. She had exhausted every avenue of investigation she could think of for the moment.

"Hello?"

"Still here," she said, and sighed. "I guess there's nothing else to do until we get those phone records."

"I guess," agreed McKell glumly.

"All right," she said. "Tell the patrols that we're looking for Daisy. Have them swing by her place a couple of times tonight, just in case. If they find her, they are to report in to me."

"Got it," said McKell. "That it?"

She hesitated but decided against telling him what she had in mind.

"That's it, DC. Call me if anything comes up. I'll be at home."

"Will do."

* * *

The mayor's house was a new construction in The Meadows, a subdivision that had gone up in the last year to accommodate the growing population of Mendenhall. The Dabbs house was red brick and gray stone and had to be close to three thousand square feet. The man's children were grown and out of the house. Why buy something that big?

Elaine Dabbs answered the door. She was a petite woman who refused to dye her gray hair. She kept it in a face-framing bob. Unlike her husband, she dressed for comfort, rather than for style. Tonight, she wore a pair of navy stretch pants and a hand-knit sweater with tiny red and white hearts all over it.

"Chief Williams," she exclaimed when she saw Kate at the door. "Come in!"

Kate smiled at her and stepped inside onto the mat. A smell of fried onions, garlic, and meat greeted her as Mrs. Dabbs closed the door. She smiled up at Kate. Maybe that was why Kate liked the woman. There weren't too many adults who had to look up at her.

"Do you have time to come in?" asked Mrs. Dabbs. "I'm just making spaghetti sauce to send to George at college."

George was the youngest, if Kate remembered correctly. The other boy had graduated a few years ago. Elizabeth, McKell's ex-wife, was the eldest.

The entrance was laid with flagstones that cut off diagonally and became an oak floor at the hallway. A darkened room opened to her left and a wide staircase with a sturdy white wooden handrail led upstairs. The hallway beyond Mrs. Dabbs led to a brightly lit kitchen. No doubt there was a "family" room somewhere, too.

"I hear your niece is in town," said Mrs. Dabbs. "And that she's a wonderful cook."

Kate's eyebrows rose. She knew she lived in a small town, but still!

"Amanda is visiting for a few days," she said. "She's a chef in Montreal."

"Very impressive," said the woman. "And apparently she's a beauty, too. You'll be lucky if the lads in this town let her leave."

Kate smiled. "I won't keep you, Mrs. Dabbs. I was hoping to speak with the mayor."

"It's Elaine," she said. "Mrs. Dabbs is my mother-in-law." She shuddered delicately and Kate laughed.

"Leonard isn't here right now. He had a Board of Variance meeting."

Kate had no idea what that was. "Do you know when he'll be home?"

Elaine shook her head. "Afraid not. Is it urgent? Do you want me to pull him out of the meeting?"

Kate hesitated. She wanted to ask the mayor if he knew of anybody in Daisy's circle who matched the description of the woman who had taken her out of the hospital. She wanted to ask him if he knew of anywhere Daisy might have gone. But was it urgent?

"No," she said finally, regretfully.

Elaine Dabbs studied Kate's face. "Are you certain, Kate?" she asked softly. "Is it something I could help you with?"

Kate laughed a little sheepishly. It was warm in the house, but she didn't want to open her coat. She wouldn't be here long.

"I'm looking for Daisy Washburn," she explained.

Mrs. Dabbs blinked. "Isn't she in the hospital?"

"She checked herself out this morning," said Kate.

"Really?" said Mrs. Dabbs with dismay. "She didn't call us to come pick her up."

"To take her home?" asked Kate.

"Of course not," said Elaine Dabbs. "To bring her here. I wouldn't want to come back here right away if Leonard died."

Could it be that simple?

"Do you have any idea where she could be staying?" asked Kate.

Elaine ran a hand through her gray hair as she thought. She was probably five or six years older than Kate, but Kate doubted the woman had ever worked outside the home. They were from different generations, no matter their age difference.

"I don't know that she has that many friends," she said slowly. She looked up at Kate quickly. "Isn't that a sad thing to say about someone?"

Kate didn't answer. She didn't have a lot of friends, either. Those she had were mostly cops. Maybe Daisy liked it that way.

"I can't think of a single person she could turn to at a time like this, except for us," said Elaine. "Maybe Leonard would know."

Kate didn't want to worry the woman but now that she was embarked on this line of questions, there was no turning back.

"Daisy left with a woman," she said. Really, there was no need to mention that Daisy had passed the woman off as her sister. "Maybe you know her. Tall, good-looking, with straight, dark-blonde hair. She had a deep voice."

Elaine thought for a few moments, then shook her head. "Not that I can recall," she said. "Maybe she's someone Leonard knows."

Kate stifled a sigh. Another line of pursuit that would have to wait.

"In that case, Elaine, could you ask him to call me when he gets home?"

"Of course."

Kate handed her a business card with her cell phone number on it and let herself out, leaving the woman to her spaghetti sauce. She stood on the stoop for a moment, looking up and down the street. The landscaping was hidden under a deep blanket of snow, but a few saplings dotted the lawns around her, wrapped in burlap and supported by anchors to keep the trees straight under the weight of snow. Another ten years and those saplings would be sturdy and tall.

Lights were on all along the street and suddenly, Kate was exhausted. She wanted to crawl under a blanket and sit in front of a warm fire. Unfortunately, she didn't have a fireplace. Well, she did, but she didn't have any wood to burn. With a sigh, she walked down the steps and crunched through the snow and ice to the street where she had parked the Explorer.

Time to go home.

* * *

The house's windows shone with light, and a wave of delicious, warm air hit her when she walked in.

"Hello?" she called. Something jazzy was playing on the stereo. A dozen or so CDs were strewn on the coffee table. She couldn't remember the last time she'd pulled one out.

"In here," called Amanda. She stuck her head through the kitchen doorway and grinned at Kate. Her cheeks were flushed. "I'm trying out a new recipe," she said, and disappeared into the kitchen again.

Kate smiled and took her coat off. Of course she was trying out a new recipe. For as long as she'd known the child, she'd been trying out new recipes.

"What is it?" she asked as she set her boots on the plastic liner in the closet.

"Wiener tort," said Amanda.

"A hot dog pie?" wondered Kate. "Surely not." She entered the kitchen and stopped, mouth open. Someone had set off a bomb in her kitchen.

"Vinarterta," corrected Amanda, spelling it out. "A Vienna cake. It's essentially a prune cake, with lots of layers. I had it once in a café in Austria." She was oblivious to Kate's dismay.

Cake pans and cookie sheets littered the counters. A wooden cutting board was covered in flour, as was the cupboard door below it. A food processor stood abandoned on the table, along with a dishcloth that looked beyond rescue. There were dirty glass mixing bowls in the sink, as well as a wooden rolling pin.

She didn't own ANY of these items.

"Good lord, Amanda, did you buy out the store?"

Amanda turned from where she was trimming what looked like a stack of thin pancakes and followed Kate's gaze. She frowned reprovingly.

"Aunt Kate, your kitchen is pathetic."

Kate's eyebrows rose. "I *have* a coffee pot."

Amanda laughed. "That and the crock pot are your only saving grace. I'm almost finished with this last torte, then we can have dinner."

Kate glanced around the disaster that was her kitchen, looking for what might end up being dinner. Finally, she caught a whiff of something cheesy and tomato-y and decided it was in the oven.

Well, first things first. She went into her room and changed into her jeans and sweatshirt, then went back to the kitchen to start cleaning up.

Dinner turned out to be the best lasagna Kate had even tasted. Amanda had whipped up a green salad with nuts and seeds and chopped up grapes, and a light, zingy dressing that was the perfect counterpoint to the pasta. Kate absolutely refused dessert, however. She settled for decaf coffee while Amanda had a slice of last night's cheesecake.

"Now," began Kate as they relaxed at the dining room table. "Tell me about *L'Assiette blanche*." She'd never been there but according to Rose and John, it was on all the best dining lists in Montreal.

Amanda grinned around a mouthful of cheesecake. "I was so lucky to be hired there! Chef Brabant is a bit of a tyrant, but a genius with meats and sauces. He's part owner of the restaurant, you know. And he treats us all like his children, even the baker, who's much older than him. Did I tell you that we've been ranked at five stars for over six years now?"

Kate sipped her coffee and wished she could feel some of Amanda's enthusiasm. It was beyond her that someone could be so excited about cooking.

"Now," said her niece firmly. "Why don't you tell me why you're all broody?" She got up to draw the drapes on French doors.

Kate sighed. "It's just this case," she said. "It's like a big tangled ball of wool. I know I could unravel it, if I could just find the loose end."

Amanda sat back down and poured herself a cup of the decaf before topping up Kate's. She was wearing a plaid flannel shirt that Kate was pretty sure had come out of her closet, but she had to admit it looked a lot better on Amanda.

"Tell me about it," suggested Amanda. She took a sip of coffee and grimaced, then added more sugar. "It might help to sort out everything in your mind."

Kate hesitated. She was always reluctant to discuss an active case with a civilian, but really, what could it hurt? There was no way Amanda could be involved, so she didn't risk becoming a witness. And maybe it would help Kate to lay the facts out in front of just about the only person in town who had never had anything to do with Frank or Daisy Washburn.

She sipped her coffee and put the facts in order in her mind.

"You know about Frank Washburn," she started.

Amanda nodded. "The man who died."

"The man who was killed," corrected Kate. "Someone spiked his drink with a sedative and dragged him to the site of the emergency exercise." She stopped, thinking it through. "At least, that's what we suspect happened. He may have taken the sedative himself, but that's unlikely."

Amanda stayed quiet, allowing Kate to tell the story in her own time.

"That was Saturday night," continued Kate. "Well, Sunday morning, technically." Feeling chilled, she wrapped her hands around the mug to warm her fingers. "Whoever it was may not have intended for him to die." In fact, whoever it was probably hadn't intended that at all. If they had, why leave him somewhere where he was likely to be found and rescued? Really, it was just bad luck that no one had stumbled on Frank earlier.

Like when EMO was placing the volunteer "victims"—surely there would have been a lot of lights around. Someone would have seen Frank's dark trousers against the white snow. But no one had. Was it because of the ice fog or because he wasn't put in place until after all the volunteers were in position?

If so, the killer had taken a hell of a chance. He could have been discovered dragging Frank into position. A person wouldn't take a chance like that unless they really wanted Frank to be found.

"We haven't been able to pinpoint who exactly found his body," she finally continued, glancing at her niece. Amanda leaned forward on her elbows, her expression attentive. "Whoever it was seemed to be with a group of firefighters, although none of them know who it was. This mystery person volunteered to fetch a paramedic, but actually got someone else to get the paramedic." She sighed in frustration. "No one can give me a description. The best I've got is that it was probably a woman around five foot nine with a deep voice." She shrugged. "No other description. It could have been a man."

She suddenly remembered Henry Beverington telling her and Trepalli about Washburn being a "good guy"—she had forgotten to follow up on the hockey team angle. She glanced at her watch. Almost nine o'clock. Too late to start interviewing people tonight. She made a mental note to talk to McKell tomorrow about interviewing Washburn's teammates.

"I suppose you've talked to friends and family?" prompted Amanda when Kate fell silent.

Kate nodded. "And neighbors and co-workers. Nothing, except maybe a little tension in Frank and Daisy's marriage." That had come from the work colleague, she remembered, and was corroborated by the dean who had overheard Frank talking to Daisy on the cell phone the night he died.

She told Amanda about it, just so all the facts would be laid out. She didn't think a jealous colleague and an overheard one-sided conversation in a coat room were valid clues.

"Later that day, the same day we found the body," she continued, "Daisy was in an accident on the Trans Canada. She ended up in the hospital." She didn't elaborate because that was the day Amanda arrived—was that really on two days ago?—and she already knew about the accident and Daisy.

"Did you talk to Daisy?" asked Amanda. She had pushed her dessert plate off to one side and her arms were crossed on the table, her hands rubbing her arms as if she was chilled, too.

Kate shook her head. "Never got the chance." She described how Daisy had been in an induced coma for Sunday and Monday. "When I went to the hospital this afternoon to see her, she had checked herself out, with a mystery woman who said she was Daisy's sister."

"Could it have been...?"

"No. Daisy doesn't have any family."

Amanda's eyebrows rose. "Do you think it's the same woman who was at the exercise?"

Kate's hands tightened around the mug. "I don't know," she said clearly. "But it could well be."

They stared at each other across the dining room table. Kate saw the same concern and doubt on Amanda's face as she was feeling.

"You think she's in danger?" asked Amanda.

Yes, thought Kate. But she didn't know why she felt that way. By Nurse Kirkham's account, Daisy had not been under duress and the other woman's behavior had not been threatening. And according to McKell, the woman was probably Daisy's accomplice.

But there was a lump of ice in the pit of Kate's stomach that disagreed with their logic.

"So, if she's in danger, too," said Amanda, "that would mean that someone wanted to hurt both of them. Unless..."

Kate looked up from her white knuckles to find her niece staring off into space.

"Unless what?"

Amanda looked back down and found Kate's gaze. She shrugged. "Well, if you want to hurt a woman, what better way than to attack someone she loves?"

A tingling began in the base of Kate's spine and worked its way up to her scalp. She stared at Amanda but was seeing instead all the facts of the case rearranging themselves in a different pattern.

A ringing began at the other end of the house and it took Kate a moment to recognize her cell phone's ring tone.

"Excuse me," she said and hurried to her room, where she'd left her cell phone on the bed when she changed. She scooped it up.

"Williams."

"Hello, chief," said Leonard Dabbs. "Elaine tells me you wanted to talk to me." His voice sounded cautious, but it could have been the tinny effect of the cell phone reception.

"Thanks for calling," she said, glancing at her watch. Nine thirty. The mayor kept late hours. "You heard that Daisy checked herself out of the hospital?"

"Yes," he said. Kate waited but he didn't add anything. She frowned.

"You don't seem surprised," she said, heading back toward the kitchen.

The mayor gave a forced laugh. "I'm not, really. I knew she'd want to get out as soon as possible. She has a thing about hospitals."

Amanda walked quietly by, carrying the dessert plate and their cups.

"Why?" asked Kate.

"I think she remembers the car accident that killed her parents," he said. "She was very young, but I think she spent time in hospital, recovering. Many people associate hospitals with death, you know."

Kate blinked at the yellow kitchen wall, trying to figure out what the mayor was talking about. "She checked herself out in the company of a woman who claimed to be her sister," she said abruptly.

There was a long silence at the other end and Kate cursed herself for having done this over the phone. Right now, she desperately wanted to see the mayor's expression.

"She doesn't have any family."

"I know," said Kate. "Do you have any idea who it might be? Dark blonde, shoulder-length straight hair, five-feet-ninish, deep voice."

Amanda returned to the kitchen with the cutlery, creamer and place mats.

"No," he said finally. "It doesn't sound like anyone I know."

Kate remained silent. There was something he wasn't telling her.

"Mayor Dabbs," she said gently, "I am very worried about Daisy. She's in no shape to be on her own right now and I have no confidence that the person's she's with has her best interests at heart."

The mayor sighed. "Daisy is a grown woman and can make her own decisions, Chief Williams."

Well, that was an odd answer. "Do you have any idea where I could find this woman?" she asked bluntly. "Or who Daisy's friends are who might know this woman?"

"No," said the mayor, and there was no disguising the sadness in his voice. "I'm not sure Daisy has many friends, certainly nobody she would turn to in a difficult time. I would have hoped she would turn to us."

Kate's heart squeezed at the regret in the man's voice. The mayor was genuinely fond of his assistant.

"All right, Mr. Mayor," she said gently. "If you hear from her or learn anything about her whereabouts…"

"I'll call you," he promised. And without another word, he hung up.

CHAPTER 15

To Kate's surprise, John Tourmeline was on the duty desk when she got to the station the next morning. That must mean today was transition day and she had lost track of the shifts again. Tattersall's crew would start on their four nights tonight.

"Good morning, Tourmeline," she said as she stamped the snow off her boots. It was relatively mild at minus twenty-two Celsius.

"Hi, chief," said Tourmeline cheerfully. He swiveled on his stool to face her as she entered the duty room. She could see scalp gleaming through his combed brown hair. He probably didn't even know he was starting to go bald.

His uniform jacket hung neatly on the back of the stool. His shirt was pressed and buttoned at the wrists. The top button was open, as per regulations, and she could see a white undershirt peeking out. In any other man, Kate would have suspected that his wife had ironed his uniform, but not Tourmeline. The man would never trust his uniform to someone else.

He made her tired just looking at him.

She glanced around. "Where is everyone?"

"Johnson is taking the GMC to the shop and Fallon is on his way to Winnipeg to testify in traffic court. Paterson and O'Hara are at the exercise site. Manitoba Rail is moving the wreck today."

Oh yes. She had forgotten about that.

She hadn't gotten enough sleep. The facts of the case kept rearranging themselves in her head until she could make no sense of anything. When she finally had fallen asleep, sometime after three o'clock, she'd had nightmare after nightmare of Daisy Washburn being dragged through the snow in her hospital gown.

She nodded her thanks and headed into her office to remove her boots and her coat. Her door was already open and it was actually warm in the office. More of Tourmeline's doing, no doubt. She had just laced up her black boots and turned on her computer when Tourmeline walked in, holding a thick sheaf of papers in his hands.

"Phone records," he explained when she looked at him blankly.

"Thank you," she said with feeling. "When did they come in?"

"An hour ago," he said. "To the general email inbox. It's copied to your email, too."

Good. "I want to see DC McKell as soon as he gets here."

"Yes, ma'am," he said. She wondered if he'd had time to catch up on everything that had been happening. Probably.

She followed him out the door. The emails and reports could wait. She would go through the records in the lunch room, close to the coffee pot.

A thought occurred to her. "Tourmeline, call Paterson and O'Hara," she said. "Tell them to keep an eye out for a cell phone at the exercise site. We never recovered Washburn's phone or wallet."

"Yes, ma'am," said Tourmeline.

The chances of finding the cell phone were close to nil. With all the feet tramping through that field over the past week, it was probably buried under two feet of snow. She knew from the dean that he'd had a cell phone on the night he died because she overheard him talking on it in the coatroom.

She paused before leaving the duty room and flipped through the pages in her hand until she found what she was looking for. "This is his cell number," she said, and gave it to him. They could try calling it. If the phone was on and the battery still charged, they might hear it ringing.

Two minutes later, she went back to her office, scrounging for highlighters. There wouldn't be any local numbers on the land line print-out, since MTS didn't bill for those, but long distance numbers were listed.

Not that there were that many. In the last month, Daisy and Frank had made only five long distance phone calls, and received three, all from the same number in Toronto. With a sigh, she went back to the lunch room, gathered up her papers and coffee, and returned to her office. She was going to need the computer and her calendar for this.

Half an hour later, she had identified the Toronto number as Albert and Evelyn Washburn's phone number. Frank's parents.

She heard the outer door open and close, and the stamping of boots on the bristle mat. A moment later, Tourmeline said something unintelligible and Kate heard Johnson reply. He was back from dropping off the GMC. A clank of keys and then the door opened and shut again. He was going out on patrol.

Five minutes later, a woman's voice sounded in the duty room, then Charlotte stuck her head in the doorway. "Good morning, chief."

"Mornin', Charlotte," muttered Kate, still poring over the phone records. The land line records told her nothing, but cell phone records were ridiculously complete.

She riffled through the papers until she found the list detailing Daisy's incoming and outgoing calls. Most of them were to and from city hall. A couple were to local take-out joints. She had made half a dozen calls to Frank's cell phone, and received as many back.

Kate studied the list, frowning. If she went by the cell phone record alone, she would suspect that Daisy Washburn didn't have many friends. But for all she knew, the Washburns' land line was constantly ringing with invitations for them.

Daisy didn't strike her as a loner, no matter what these cell phone records said. She was outgoing and friendly, and very professional. McKell would argue that she was also ruthless, but his judgment was suspect when it came to Daisy.

Amanda had said that if someone wanted to hurt a woman,

they would hurt someone she loved. Kate didn't need any special sensitivity to know that Daisy Washburn had loved her husband. Kate had seen the look on her face whenever she talked about him.

The question was, did someone hate Daisy enough to kill Frank?

It was possible, of course, but it didn't feel right. Premeditated murder, especially the kind of cold, calculating decision to murder someone in order to hurt someone else, was rare. Usually, murder was a thoughtless, impulsive act. Not the act of someone who would then risk dragging the body to the scene of a mock accident. No. Whoever had dragged Frank out to the train wreck had done so hoping he would be found quickly.

Poor Frank.

She glanced at her watch. Past nine. Where was McKell? She wanted him to contact his source at the hospital to find out who Daisy had called—and who had called her.

She flipped through the pages until she found Frank Washburn's cell phone records. Her eyebrows rose. Dear God. The man had lived on his cell phone.

With a sigh, she sat back and started studying the numbers.

After a moment, she thought of something and began flipping through the pages. When she didn't find what she was looking for, she stepped into the duty room.

"Tourmeline."

"Chief?" He swiveled on his chair to face her.

"Did you forward all the emails from MTS?"

"Yes, ma'am."

"Get in touch with them, please. They didn't include the text messages."

He nodded. "Will do." He reached for the phone and Kate returned to her review of Frank's cell phone records.

Half a dozen phone calls to the Royal Bank, usually over weekday lunch times. Most of the other calls were also local, with a few Winnipeg numbers. She looked up the Mendenhall numbers, most of which were land lines, in the reverse directory and made a note of the names and addresses. All the names were male. She would get Tourmeline to check them out. She recognized a couple of the names. One was a farmer, the other owned one of the two hardware stores in Mendenhall.

McKell arrived five minutes later. She heard his deep voice rumbling in the duty room and Tourmeline replying. A moment later, McKell knocked on the door frame and came in.

"Manitoba Rail is moving the wreck," he said without preamble.

"So I hear." She looked up from the records. He looked fit and fresh this morning, like a man who'd had a good night's sleep. Must be nice.

"Kowalski must be pissed."

Kate shrugged. Alexandra Kowalski's career ambitions were the least of her problems.

"I got Daisy's phone record from the hospital."

Kate set the sheaf of papers down and pulled her glasses off to look at him. The man would never cease to amaze her.

He pulled out a slip of paper from his inside coat pocket and pushed it toward her. "One call only, a cell phone number. Winnipeg, I think."

Of course it would be a cell phone number. There was no reverse directory for cell phone numbers. "Did she make the call, or receive it?"

"Received it."

Kate studied the number, frowning.

"What is it?" asked McKell.

"It looks familiar," she muttered, flipping through the phone records in front of her until she found what she was looking for. Yes, there it was. She looked up at McKell. "Frank Washburn called this number daily on his cell phone, and received almost as many calls from the same number."

McKell's expression tightened and his nostrils flared, as if he had just caught a scent on the air.

"You don't talk to someone twice a day, every day, unless you have an intimate relationship with them," he said.

Washburn was an only child, so it wasn't family.

"It's probably a lover," said McKell flatly.

Reluctantly, Kate nodded. Yes, that was the likely explanation.

But McKell wasn't finished. "Which puts Daisy Washburn right up there as a suspect in her husband's death."

Kate sighed. "Let's not hang her quite yet." Before McKell could speak, she pushed her pad toward him. "Do you recognize any of these names?"

McKell turned the pad around and studied the names. "Balsilie, Chaylikoff, Atli..." He looked up at her. "They're the Mendenhall Hawks," he said. "The men's hockey team."

Huh. Beverington, the Winnipeg firefighter, knew Washburn through hockey.

She pulled the pad back and stared at the names.

"What is it?" asked McKell.

"I don't know yet," she said. "Give me a few minutes."

"*Now* can I put out a BOLO for Daisy?"

The Be On the Look Out alert would go to every police agency in the province. Whether or not she was guilty, she would now be the subject of rumors, even if it was proven she'd had nothing to do with her husband's death. Would an ambitious young woman with political aspirations ever be able to rise above that kind of suspicion?

"Not yet," she said finally.

She met McKell's gaze unflinchingly and he finally shook his head at her. "If it was anyone else," he said bitterly, "you'd have said yes." He turned on his heel and left.

She stared at the empty doorway for long seconds. What exactly did he mean? That if it had been anyone but Daisy, or that if anyone but McKell had asked, she would have agreed to the BOLO?

It didn't matter, she finally decided. The end result was the same: a pissed off McKell.

She pulled out her notebook, flipping through the pages to see if she had jotted down the name of Beverington's hockey team. It wasn't there. Cursing herself for her sloppiness, she pulled out her Winnipeg phone book and looked up Beverington's number.

"Hello?" said a woman's voice.

"Mrs. Beverington? This is Chief Williams in Mendenhall. We met yesterday?"

"Of course, Chief Williams. How can I help you?"

"Ma'am, is your son home?"

"I'm afraid not," replied the old woman. "He's at work and won't be back until tonight. Would you like his number there?"

Kate hesitated. She didn't really want to call him at work, but she didn't want to wait until he was off shift to talk to him. "Yes, please."

Mrs. Beverington rattled off a phone number and Kate wrote it down. Then she thought of something. "Do you happen to know the name of your son's hockey team?"

"Why, yes." The surprise in her voice was clear. "Are you planning to attend one of his games?"

"You never know."

"It's the Winnipeg Wolverines," said Mrs. Beverington.

"Do you know who is on the team with your son?"

"That, I do not," said the woman. "I'm afraid they usually play too late for me."

Kate laughed. "Thank you for your help, ma'am."

"A pleasure, Chief Williams."

Just as she hung up, the phone rang, startling her.

"Williams."

"Hi Kate. It's Bert."

Kate automatically smiled. "Hello, Bert. Are you in town?"

"Afraid not," he said regretfully. "I'm chained to this desk until the chief gets back from Hawaii."

She wondered who John Stendel had taken with him. No doubt another Sweet Young Thing who wasn't old enough to know better.

Before she could ask Bert why he had called, he continued. "I came across some information you might find interesting, since you were asking about her."

"About who?"

"Alexandra Kowalski."

Kate blinked. She had asked him about Kowalski?

"What about her?"

"I was talking to a guy in the EMO office and it turns out he went to school with Daisy, too."

Oh yes. Bert had mentioned that Daisy and Alexandra went to school together in Mendenhall. Interesting, but hardly germane to her investigation.

"With Kowalski, too?" she asked.

"Yes. He was a grade behind them in high school, but apparently, Kowalski and Daisy were rivals all throughout high school."

Kate's eyebrows rose and she stopped fiddling with her pen. "For boys?"

"And sports, and grades. You name it, they competed."

Really. "Thanks, Bert." She didn't know if it meant anything, but maybe it explained Kowalski's cryptic remarks on Monday night when she showed up at her door. What had she said? Something about Daisy standing to gain if her husband died.

"No problem," he said. "How's it going?"

He was asking about the investigation. She sighed. "Isn't there some scientific principle that says no matter how close you get to your goal, you'll never quite reach it?"

Bert stayed silent for a moment. "You mean an event horizon?"

"Yes," agreed Kate, although she really wouldn't know. "That's how the investigation is going." She gave him a brief rundown of what she had learned since she last spoke to him.

"Well, I'm on a hockey team," he said when she finished. "And each one of us has the contact list for the other players."

Kate looked up at the ceiling. Of course there would be a contact list.

"Thanks, Bert," she said. "I have to go."

"All right," he said equably. "But I'm still holding you to that dinner invitation."

He wanted to meet Amanda. "Of course," she said. "I'll call you when this is over."

They hung up and she stared down at her pad. A contact list would include cell phones and land lines. She picked up the phone again and called the number Mrs. Beverington had given her. Moments later, Beverington was called to the phone and she thanked her lucky stars that he wasn't out on a call.

"Hello, Chief Williams," he said. "How can I help you?"

"Mr. Beverington, do you have a contact list for your teammates?"

He hesitated, obviously not expecting her question.

"You mean, for my hockey team?"

Belatedly, it occurred to her that the man might be on more than one sports team.

"That's right," she said.

"Yes, I do. Why?"

It was Kate's turn to hesitate. She didn't want to tell him why, but she didn't want to alienate him, either. He had been very cooperative to date.

"I need to interview the other members of your team about Mr. Washburn," she said. That was true, but vague enough.

"All right," he said, obviously reassured.

"Can you go home now and get it?" she asked. "Or maybe your mother could—"

"It's all right," he interrupted. "I can access it from my cell phone. What's your email address?"

From his phone? Oh. He had one of those fancy ones. She gave him her email address just as a siren went off in the background at the other end of the line.

"Gotta go!" he said.

"Can you—?" But he had already hung up.

Damn. There was no telling now when the man would get a chance to retrieve the list and send it to her. Maybe she should try contacting one of the other team members. But she didn't want to tip her hand. What if the man she picked was the man whose cell phone number she was investigating? No, better to wait.

She leaned back in her chair. Her back was stiff. She hadn't been getting enough exercise lately.

Whoever had called Daisy at the hospital was the same person Frank Washburn had been talking to a couple of times a day, every day, for a month. That was as far back as the MTS records went.

That didn't necessarily mean that the woman who accompanied Daisy out of the hospital was the woman at the other end of that cell phone.

But the chances were good that she was.

A smell that had been tickling her awareness for the last few minutes finally registered. Was that cinnamon?

She pushed away from her desk, grabbed her cup of cold coffee and stepped into the duty room. Charlotte looked up from her computer and Tourmeline glanced over his shoulder at her.

"Is that what I think it is?" asked Kate.

Charlotte nodded. "Cinnamon buns," she said. Her eyes were guarded but there was a smile on her lips.

Tourmeline nodded, too. "Yes, ma'am." He leaned away so she could see the desk in front of him, where a huge, glistening cinnamon bun rested on a plate. It was still steaming. "Your niece just brought them in. She's still in the lunch room."

Kate sighed and headed for the lunch room, where she could hear voices.

Amanda sat at the head of the long table. She was chatting with Trepalli, who was dressed in jeans and a heavy blue wool sweater that brought out the color of his eyes. Johnson was at the coffee pot, pouring coffee into a thermos cup.

"Hi, Aunt Kate," said Amanda as Kate walked in. A platter of cinnamon buns sat on the table, covered in tin foil. Next to it were dessert plates, paper napkins and cutlery. Trepalli looked around at her.

"Good morning, chief," he said cheerfully.

"Constable," said Kate. "Shouldn't you be sleeping?"

He grinned unrepentantly at her. "I'll take a nap this afternoon."

Johnson turned around and looked at Kate. "Cinnamon buns trump sleep," he said, screwing on the lid to the thermos cup. His raised eyebrow told Kate that he was thinking the same thing she was: Trepalli wasn't here for the cinnamon buns.

"How did you know they were here?" she asked Trepalli.

Trepalli hesitated and glanced at Amanda.

"I promised him I'd make him cinnamon buns this morning," said Amanda, shrugging.

Oh lord.

"What's this?" said McKell, coming up behind her. She stepped aside to let him by. "Cinnamon buns?" The incredulity and delight in his voice told Kate all she needed to know about McKell's leanings.

"Have you met my niece?" she asked resignedly.

"Not yet," said McKell, his gaze still fixed on the treats. The promise of cinnamon buns had apparently made him forget he was mad at her.

Amanda stood up. She was wearing jeans and a hoodie with a scarf draped around her neck. Kate hoped that she had a coat somewhere.

"Rob McKell," he said, sticking his hand out.

"Amanda Coburn," she shook his hand. "Please, help yourself." She waved at the plate of cinnamon buns.

Kate watched Trepalli through the whole exchange. He watched first McKell, then Amanda, then McKell. Johnson caught her eye and shook his head slightly. He'd seen it, too.

Kate swallowed a sigh. It had taken her months to get the team working together after a very rocky beginning. She really didn't need Amanda stirring up jealousies.

Something buzzed and Trepalli reached into his jean pocket for his cell phone. He read something, then keyed in an answer and put the phone away.

Kate sighed softly. How much time would they waste now, waiting for the text records to arrive from MTS?

Amanda and Trepalli left together. Kate bit her tongue to keep from reminding Trepalli that he had to work that night—and to keep from warning him away from Amanda.

She went back to her desk to work on her report for EMO. She might as well do something useful while waiting for the text records to come in. McKell had gone to check on the progress of the train and bus removal and Johnson went back on patrol.

She stared at her blank screen for long minutes. This was

always the part of an investigation that drove her crazy. She was so close to a breakthrough that she could almost taste it. There was a key piece missing, and once she had it, she would have enough of the puzzle put together to make out a picture.

The part that drove her crazy was the waiting.

The hell with it. The report would have to wait. She would drive out to the mock accident site herself and see if anyone had found Washburn's cell phone.

She was just getting up when the computer dinged to announce a new email. She hesitated but finally switched screens to see who had written her. She didn't recognize the address and there was an attachment, but no subject line. Damn spam. She was just about to delete it when she read the title of the attachment. It said: WW Contacts. She reread the address: hbev23@gmail.com.

Beverington!

Her heart beating faster, she clicked on the attachment. She could just imagine the man hanging off the back of the clanging fire truck like some Norse god, feverishly sending her the attachment from his cell phone. Bless him.

The file opened to reveal a chart with a list of roughly twenty names, with the position played in the box next to the name and a list of phone numbers in the last box.

She quickly scanned the list of names but none of them looked familiar to her, except for one.

Ash Mann.

"Chief?"

Kate jumped and looked up. Charlotte was standing in her doorway.

"The Washburns are here."

Kate closed her eyes for a moment. Damn. She wasn't ready to release Frank's body yet. For one thing, she was still waiting on the tox results from the Winnipeg lab. For a moment, she toyed with the idea of getting Charlotte to tell them so. Finally she nodded and stood up.

"Send them in." She wanted to call McKell back to fill him in on this latest development, but it could wait another few minutes.

A moment later, Albert and Evelyn Washburn stood in her office. They looked older today. More tired. Kate couldn't even begin to imagine how they were feeling.

"I'm sorry," she began before they could speak. "I should have called you but I still can't release..." She hesitated, wishing she knew what to say in these situations. "I'm still waiting—"

"That's not why we're here," said Albert Washburn, cutting her off with a wave of his hand. Kate fell silent more out of surprise than anything else. She didn't think he had decisiveness in him.

"We remembered something," said Evelyn Washburn, taking a step forward in her intensity. "About what you asked."

What had she asked? Then she caught her breath. "About someone wanting to hurt your son?" she asked softly.

Frank Washburn nodded jerkily. "Someone was stalking him."

Stalking. That was a serious word. And they only remember *now*? "Do you know who it was?"

Evelyn Washburn shook her head. She was wearing her wool overcoat, with a dark scarf intricately knotted at her throat. A whiff of expensive perfume wafted from her every time she moved, reminding Kate suddenly of her mother and the Chanel No. 5 that was her signature scent.

"We never saw her." Evelyn had taken her black leather gloves off and now twisted them in her fists. Her husband reached over and placed a big hand over hers. She immediately calmed down. Albert Washburn looked at Kate. His overcoat was a green and brown tweed, with a dark green plaid scarf still wrapped around his neck.

"Frank came home to visit, about a month ago," he said calmly. "It was just for the weekend, but his cell phone was constantly vibrating. He would look at it, and nine times out of ten, ignore it. Since he did speak to Daisy several times, I was curious and asked who he was avoiding." He shook his head, anger carving deep lines around his mouth. "He just laughed and told us it was his stalker. He didn't know who she was."

"Why didn't he block her number?" she asked.

Evelyn Washburn took up the story. "Because it was a blocked number. She had his number but he didn't know hers."

Kate suddenly flashed back to the cell phone records she had just been studying. There had been an inordinate number of "unknown callers" listed. She wondered if "unknown caller" had also texted Frank.

"Thank you," she said gravely. They were all still standing but Kate didn't invite them to sit. They clearly had only come to tell her this.

"Does it help?" asked Evelyn Washburn. Her gaze bore into Kate's as if she were trying to read her mind.

"Yes, it does," said Kate, even though she wasn't sure if it did or not. She examined the couple, noting the red eyes, the grim set to their mouths. She wanted to tell them to go home, that she would have Frank's body shipped to them as soon as she could, but it wasn't up to her.

It was up to Daisy.

* * *

As soon as they left, Kate pulled up the file Beverington had sent her and ran down the list. Her finger stopped near the end. She hadn't imagined it. Ash Mann was on Beverington's hockey team. He must be the friend Washburn stayed with when he taught at the college. She searched through the papers on her desk, looking for the piece of paper McKell had given her with the phone number. She finally found it tucked between two pages of the MTS listings. She clenched her teeth as she brought the slip of paper up to the screen and compared the number on it with the cell phone number in the contact box for Ash Mann.

They matched.

Holy...

She dropped the slip of paper and feverishly called up the web page for the Winnipeg Wolverines. She scrolled down the list of players until she found Mann's name and then she clicked on it. At once, the screen changed to a photo with statistical information next to it.

Kate stared Ash Mann's image. He was a good-looking man with short, wavy, dark hair and light green eyes. Very handsome, with fine features, high cheekbones and mouth with a full lower lip. With a mouthful of white, even teeth, he either wore dentures or a face guard when he played. She glanced at his stats. He was a goalie. Yep, he'd be protected.

She sat back and glanced at her watch. It wasn't even ten o'clock.

* * *

"You shouldn't go alone," objected McKell.

Kate had driven to the exercise site on her way out of town. She had wanted to fill McKell in and ask him to press MTS for those text records.

"We're short-handed with Fallon in court today," said Kate. "I'm just going to go talk to the guy. He's probably covering for Washburn's affair." It wouldn't be the first time a buddy covered by providing an alibi for a married man's whereabouts. "I want to know who Washburn was having an affair with. Judging by the constant calling back and forth, these two guys were tight."

McKell frowned, still unhappy.

They were standing by her Explorer, which she'd parked behind McKell's patrol car on the shoulder. Paterson and O'Hara were down by the railway crossing, blocking the non-existent traffic. Half a dozen people worked near the wreck of the bus, hooking chains from a locomotive to the destroyed bus. The locomotive would haul the bus to the crossroad, where the tow truck waited. The rest of the train was already being hauled back to the Winnipeg railyards.

"It's Policing 101," argued McKell. "You should take a back up." He looked frustrated. Kate knew he wanted to go with her, but she didn't want them both gone from Mendenhall. Not for an interview.

"I'll call Fallon when I get to Winnipeg," she said. "If he's done with court, he can come with me."

"And if he's not?"

She had already turned away, anxious to get in the car and go. Now she turned back to her DC.

"Then I'm sure I can handle it," she said patiently.

He shook his head, scowling. "You know damned well that you wouldn't allow anyone else to do this alone."

Oh, for Pete's *sake*! She took a deep, calming breath. The guy could be such a pain in the butt.

"The constables do lots of interviews on their own," she pointed out.

"Not in a murder investigation."

Enough. "DC McKell, I *have* done this before."

He nodded stiffly. "I'm sure you have. Give me the guy's particulars, so we know where to start looking for your body."

Kate didn't know whether to laugh or swear, but she scribbled Ash Mann's phone numbers and address from Beverington's contact list in McKell's notebook.

The sun shone brightly in the clear blue sky, deceptive in its promise of warmth. Although temperatures might actually rise above minus twenty today. Still, that breeze brought the wind chill factor down closer to minus thirty, making Kate glad of her down mittens and warm fur hat.

Wood smoke wafted on the breeze coming from the small cluster of houses beyond the turn in the road. Suddenly, the locomotive started moving and the chains linking it to the bus grew taut. All the workers had scurried well out range of a possible snapping chain. With a screech of metal on metal, the bus began to move behind the locomotive, heading for the crossing and the tow truck.

McKell winced at the horrible noise and Kate gritted her teeth. Time to go. She opened the door to the Explorer. Then McKell said something she didn't catch.

"What was that?" she yelled over the sound of the bus scraping along the railroad. She knew it was on a specially made frame with wheels, but it still sounded like a giant was tearing strips off of it.

"I said," shouted McKell, "Avramson was here earlier."

Kate closed the door of the Explorer to prevent the heat from escaping and turned to face him. "What did he want?"

The locomotive stopped with a loud clang and in the relative silence, McKell shrugged. He nodded in the direction of the two officers blocking the road. "Paterson told me he was here. He was gone by the time I got here." His gaze swung back to the giant mess of boot tracks that was the site of the mock accident. "Paterson says he spent most of his time walking around the site."

Huh. Why had the fire chief come? Kate studied the site. It looked forlorn, like the remnants of a battle. With the wrecked train already gone and the bus on the move, she couldn't be sure where Frank Washburn's body had been found anymore. But she could see clearly the path leading from the stand of trees to the general trampled area. That was the trail left from dragging Frank Washburn's body to the site. And the parallel tracks were from where Alexandra Kowalski had dragged DC McKell in an effort to prove a woman could do it.

"What is it?" said McKell just as the locomotive started up again.

Kate leaned in close and McKell obligingly leaned down.

"Find out what Avramson was doing here," she said. "And find out if Kowalski is still in Mendenhall. If she is, bring her in for questioning. But first, find out if Frank Washburn had a will and what it said."

McKell turned his head to look at her directly. They were so close she could smell his aftershave. "What do you want me to ask Kowalski?"

Kate thought for a moment. "Ask her about Frank and Daisy's relationship."

Alexandra Kowalski had a lot of history with Daisy Pitcairn-Washburn. It was time Kate found out more of that history.

* * *

Mann lived in a three-story condo downtown, on Abernathy. The area had been recently gentrified, with dilapidated buildings being snapped up and renovated for yuppies who wanted to live where all the action was. She found a place to park about three blocks from the building and walked back. What had been a breeze in Mendenhall was a steady wind here, and she pulled her scarf up to cover her nose and pulled her hood closer to her face.

Snow mounded in gray heaps along walkways as she passed

a dry cleaner, a fruit vendor, and an office building before finally reaching Mann's address. The building had clearly undergone a recent renovation, but the developer had left the original brick facade, which had mellowed to an old rose color. The vestibule floor was covered in gray tile, with smaller, matching tiles marching up the walls and meeting overhead. A small chandelier hung from the ceiling. The mail boxes were black and stood out sharply against the gray-tiled wall. Kate peered at the names on the boxes and found one listed simply as Mann. She pressed on the buzzer and waited. After a moment, she pressed again.

Still nothing.

Crap. He was at work. She'd been too impatient to wait in Mendenhall, so now she would have to wait in Winnipeg.

Pulling out her cell phone, she stood in the vestibule and punched in Mann's land line. It rang and rang and rang, and she had just about resigned herself to trying to find out where he worked when the phone was picked up and promptly dropped.

"Hello?" she said. She heard scrabbling at the other end of the line and a sound like something dragging on a wooden floor. Had a dog or cat knocked the phone off its cradle? "Hello?" She glanced at the list of contacts. Mann was in apartment 3B.

A middle-aged woman in a long fur coat entered the vestibule, bringing the cold air with her. She carried a small dog in one arm and several plastic bags with handles in her other hand. Kate thought she recognized the name of a high-end store on one lime green bag. The woman glanced suspiciously at Kate before heading to the inner door. She blocked the keypad with her back, but had to set the dog—a Pekingese?—down before she could punch in the code.

The dog growled at Kate and then started yapping, so that she could hear nothing at the other end of the line. She bared her teeth at the animal and it immediately cowered back, whimpering. The woman looked around at Kate, frowning, just as the inner door unlocked. Kate grabbed the door and held it open for her.

"Thank you," said the woman stiffly and made to pull the door closed behind her. Kate smiled and held onto the door. "I can't allow you in," said the woman sternly.

Kate stuck her foot in the door to prevent the woman from closing it and fished through her inner pocket for her identification. The woman studied the identification card long enough to memorize Kate's name and rank, then reluctantly stepped back.

Kate felt the woman's eyes on her as she hurried down the marble hallway toward the wide staircase at the back. She passed a door on the left that read "CARETAKER" on a discreet brass plate and an elevator on the right. She didn't want to wait for the elevator. She still had the cell phone pressed to her ear, but could only make out the occasional moan or faint grunt. She ran up the stairs, finally taking them two at a time until she reached the top floor. The landing split into two hallways and, taking a chance, she headed down the right. Within twenty feet, the hallway ended at a door with another brass plate on it that read, "3A".

She turned around, still breathing hard, and ran to the other end of the hallway, to the only other door on this floor. It was a paneled door made of a dark wood—oak, she thought—with a spy hole just above the brass plate and one of those ornate, black metal door knobs. She was about to knock when she paused uncertainly. She didn't know what was going on on the other side of that heavy door.

Only then did she remember that she was supposed to have called Fallon to see if he was through with court. It would have been awfully nice to have him with her right now.

She gently tried the door handle and to her surprise, it wasn't locked. It hadn't even been latched. She closed the call on her cell phone and slipped it inside her outer pocket. She itched to draw her handgun but this wasn't her jurisdiction. She hadn't even called ahead to tell Bert she was coming.

Protocol dictated that she announce her presence before entering a domicile, but as the door eased silently open on well-oiled hinges, light flooded in from floor-length windows on her right, revealing a wide entryway with a large mirror directly in front of the door and a narrow console table below it. A telephone dangled from its cord, trapped half on, half off the table by the cord wedged behind the table. The receiver was on the floor, next to a blonde woman who was bound hand and foot and had a piece of duct tape covering her mouth.

Blood seeped out from beneath the duct tape and there was a nasty cut on her right cheekbone. By the swelling of her right eye, Kate judged that she would have a hell of a shiner in a few hours.

The woman looked frantically at Kate out of one beautiful, light green eye as she struggled with the duct tape binding her hands behind her back. Her struggles had knocked her wig askew, revealing short, wavy dark hair underneath.

CHAPTER 16

Kate placed a finger against her lips to indicate silence, then pointed questioningly at the back of the apartment. The woman shook her head. There was no one else here.

Not willing to trust someone who had obviously suffered a blow to the head, Kate quickly went through the apartment to make sure. Huge kitchen with a pantry, two bedrooms, one with an en-suite, another bathroom, a linen closet, a bigger storage closet... the woman was right. There was no one else here.

Kate hurried back to the front entrance, knelt on one knee next to the woman and warned, "This is going to hurt." Without giving her a chance to object, she pulled the duct tape away from the woman's mouth in one smooth, swift motion.

"Ouch!" The woman's face contorted with momentary pain, and red welts immediately appeared where the tape had been. The tape had ripped open her split lip and Kate winced in sympathy.

"Who did this to you?" she asked as she worked at the duct tape around the woman's wrists.

"I don't know her name," said the woman. "She took Daisy!"

Kate froze. "Daisy Washburn?"

"Yes," nodded the woman. "That crazy bitch pushed her way in here. She has a gun!"

"The intruder?" asked Kate, just to be sure.

"Yes!" cried the woman. "She pulled a gun on us. She hit me with it. I must have passed out. When I came to, the phone was ringing and Daisy was gone!" She had a deep voice for a woman, but not unusually so.

First things first. The duct tape was wound so tightly Kate was afraid of causing more damage. The woman's hands looked swollen. "Scissors?" she asked.

"Top drawer next to the fridge," said the woman. "Daisy..." she began, but Kate shook her head.

"Give me a minute."

She pushed herself up and went into the kitchen. She paused briefly, blinking at all the stainless steel gleaming back at her. She located the right drawer and found a pair of scissors.

Back in the entranceway, she cut away the rest of the duct tape and helped the woman up. She was taller than Kate by almost six inches. Kate led her to the nearest chair, a plush thing in dark wood and white velvet. The woman sank into it as if her knees could no longer support her. She was dressed in dark green chinos with a paler green silk shirt that had become untucked.

Her feet were bare. They were large feet, with a deep burgundy nail polish.

Kate stood in front of the woman. "I'm going to call an ambulance and the local police in a minute," said Kate. "But first I need you to tell me who took Daisy and why."

The woman looked at Kate as though seeing her for the first time.

"Who are you?" she asked.

"Kate Williams, chief of police in Mendenhall. I came here to speak to Ash Mann." She hesitated a moment. "Would that be you?" she asked softly.

The woman's hand rose hesitantly to her head, as if she had suddenly grown aware that her wig was askew. She tugged it into place, took a deep breath, and said, "I prefer Ashley."

Kate nodded. It was uncanny. The face was clearly the same as the one she had seen on the Winnipeg Wolverines web site, but the features were rounder, softer. There was even a hint of breasts under the silk shirt.

"All right, Ms. Mann," she said crisply. "Who was the woman? How did she get into your building? Why did she take Daisy?"

"I don't know!" Ashley Mann's voice rose on the last word and Kate realized she was more rattled than she had let on. "I don't know her," she said more calmly, "but she was always at the hockey games when we played Mendenhall here. Frank said she was at most of the Mendenhall games, too. He said she was just a crazy woman who didn't know how to take no for an answer."

Frank's stalker. Kate pulled out her notebook and sat down in the matching chair next to Ashley Mann's. "Describe her to me."

"Tall and thin," said Ashley promptly. "About my height. Brown eyes, long light brown hair pulled back in a braid. No bangs." She took a deep breath. "She had on jeans and Sorels, and a red parka with some kind of emblem on the arm. I never got a good look at it. She was very strong." Her hand rose to her cheekbone but stopped short.

Kate wrote blindly, her mind in shock. Ashley Mann had just described Alexandra Kowalski.

"I'm sorry," continued Ashley. "It all happened so fast. I thought it was my neighbor knocking at my door, but when I opened it, she hit me in the face with the butt of her pistol." She shook her head in helpless anger. "That's all I remember until the phone rang." She took a deep breath. "Was that you? On the phone?"

Kate nodded and swallowed hard. Holy cow.

"Why take Daisy?" she asked out loud.

"I don't know." All the fight seemed to seep out of Mann and she sat there looking wrung out.

Kate pulled her Blackberry out and dialed 911. When the operator came on, she gave her the address and requested ambulance and police. After answering a few more questions, she cut the connection then punched in Bert Langdon's cell phone number. He answered on the third ring.

"I need your help," she said, once he picked up.

"Tell me," he said at once and she immediately felt better hearing his calm voice.

She outlined what had happened in a few terse words and told him she had already called 911. When she finished, he asked a few questions.

"Did you see Kowalski yourself?"

"No."

"Do you have any reason to believe Mann might be lying?"

Kate glanced at Ashley Mann, who sat quietly, hands clasped in her lap, eyes fixed on the window. Her face was so pale Kate worried she might faint. Her eye was already starting to bruise and her lower lip was swollen.

"No," she said.

"I'll get a BOLO out on Kowalski," said Bert grimly. "I'll keep you posted." He hung up.

"They're going to be here in a few minutes," said Kate, putting her phone away. For the first time, she took a good look at the room she was in. Hardwood floors. The ceiling was at least twelve feet tall, with great moldings. It opened onto a large dining room with a huge chandelier over the table. There seemed to be a balcony running the width of the apartment. Whatever Ashley Mann did for a living, it brought in some serious money. She walked over to the French doors and peered out onto the balcony. No one was hiding there. No sign of the ambulance.

"Did you take Daisy out of the hospital?" she asked, turning to look at the other woman.

The exhaustion on Ashley's face turned to puzzlement. That wasn't what she had expected. "Daisy asked me to come get her," she said. "I offered to let her stay with me for a few days. She couldn't stay at that hospital any more."

"Why not?"

"Because Frank was in there somewhere, dead."

Kate looked away from the raw grief in the woman's eyes. The facts were rearranging themselves in her head again. She cleared her throat. "How did you meet Frank?"

Ashley Mann looked away. A small, bitter smile stretched her lip, causing it to bleed again. She didn't seem to notice. Her hands clamped on the wooden arms of the chair. They were big hands. No amount of hormone treatment would ever change that.

"We met through hockey," she said. "Funny, isn't it?" She looked at Kate then looked away again. Her voice softened. "He was kind, and funny. He was interested in everything." Tears ran down her cheeks but she didn't seem aware of them.

In the distance, Kate could hear the wail of sirens approaching. Finally.

"We fell in love," continued Ashley, oblivious. "He encouraged me to go for the sex change."

"He stayed here when he played Winnipeg, didn't he? And on Thursdays, when he taught at the college."

Ashley nodded. "Yes."

"But you knew he was married," Kate prodded. If Daisy had learned of the affair, would she have been angry enough to kill her husband?

Ashley looked directly at Kate. "We never hid anything from Daisy. She was happy that Frank had found someone." At Kate's expression, she added, "Frank was gay. Daisy knew that. She always knew."

Huh. "Then why...?"

"Why the charade of the marriage?" Ashley shrugged. "Small town. It's hard enough to fit in when you're an outsider, even harder if you're gay." Her smile was bitter. "Frank was a wonderful man, but not particularly courageous. At least not in this." There was blood on her teeth.

Frank Washburn was gay but he had managed to fall in love with a man who wanted to become a woman. Twice the rejection for Daisy.

The ambulance pulled up outside the building and Kate went down to meet it. As she was holding the door open, a police car pulled up and two unis peeled out, running toward her.

It was going to be a long afternoon.

* * *

She called McKell on her hands-free while driving to WPD headquarters. She had promised Bert she would make her statement to him.

"She drives a white, 2010 CRV," she read from her notebook, then flipped it to the passenger seat and concentrated on the traffic.

"I know," said McKell. "Winnipeg's already put a BOLO out on her and her vehicle, for all of southern Manitoba."

She kept expecting him to say something about interviewing the witness alone, but to her surprise, he didn't. He was probably stocking up ammunition against her.

Oh stop it, she told herself. You were wrong and he was right. Admit it.

But she couldn't.

"Cottage?" he asked, and Kate almost smiled. Their last major case together had involved not one, but two summer cottages.

"Not that I know of, but you should check." The light turned red and she came to a stop. She was on Portage, one of the main arteries running through Winnipeg. It would get her to WPD and Bert, although she could probably get there faster if she took the shortcut the uni had told her about. But she wouldn't. Taking Portage might take her longer, but at least she wouldn't get lost.

"Fallon's back," said McKell. "I'll get everyone out looking for her." He paused and she could hear him breathe. "I doubt she would come here, though."

Kate had to agree. If Kowalski hadn't made a run for it, she was probably still in Winnipeg, where it would be easier to stay hidden. Not that she was behaving logically.

The light turned green and she pulled ahead. Traffic was fairly light for downtown Winnipeg. Still, when she spotted an empty parking spot in front of a billiard hall, she tucked into it and set the hand brake.

They both remained silent for long seconds. Kowalski had kidnapped Daisy. There was no going back to normal life for her. That would make her desperate.

Kate still couldn't get over it. Kowalski was erratic, sure, but Kate had never thought her capable of violence.

Kowalski hadn't gone to work, hadn't called in sick. There was no one at her condo. Kate was growing increasingly certain that the woman had killed Frank Washburn. Why she had killed him was a mystery, but Alexandra Kowalski was probably Frank Washburn's stalker. Had Daisy known about the stalking?

"Does she own a weapon?" asked McKell finally.

"No registered weapon," said Kate. Which meant nothing. She'd used a handgun to kidnap Daisy. "And according to Bert, she has no family in the area." Her parents had retired to Victoria and her only sibling, a brother, was working in the States.

She glanced at her watch. Almost two. According to Mann, Kowalski had attacked them somewhere around eleven. The woman had a three-hour head start.

"She went to school with Daisy in Mendenhall," said Kate. "Find out if any of their classmates are still around. It's a long shot, but one of them might have seen her, or know something about her that would help." She took off her mitten to scratch under her hat. "I want on-site interviews," she continued. "And they are to go in pairs."

"Yes, ma'am." His voice was completely neutral and she wanted to smack him. After a moment, he continued softly. "Daisy could still be involved, you know."

The spike of irritation turned into anger. "How the hell do you figure that?" she demanded. "She was kidnapped!"

McKell's voice grew cool. "Nobody saw a kidnapping," he pointed out. "None of the neighbors heard anything. Yes, Mann was knocked out but he didn't see Daisy getting kidnapped. Daisy might have gone with Kowalski willingly."

Kate struggled with her temper. McKell might be inclined to believe Daisy guilty, but she was just as bad, since she was inclined to believe her innocent. Just because Daisy had secrets didn't make her a murderer.

But wasn't she allowing her feelings to color her judgment just as much as McKell was?

"All right, DC McKell," she said stiffly. "It wouldn't hurt to put a BOLO out on Daisy, too."

"We should have done it sooner," said McKell.

Jerk.

"By the way," he continued, "I checked into the will. Nothing special. Property goes to Daisy. Some sentimental stuff for his parents."

"Insurance?"

"A small policy worth fifty thousand, and another one through work. All in all, it came to something like eighty thousand dollars. Oh, and mortgage insurance that pays off the mortgage in the event of his death."

A respectable sum, but not worth killing over. Kowalski had either thought the insurance was worth much more or it was a red herring.

"And I spoke to Avramson," continued McKell. "Turns out he was looking for his wedding ring at the exercise site."

Avramson was *married*?

"Did he find it?"

McKell snorted.

* * *

Four hours later, McKell called her back.

"There were only fourteen in the graduating class," McKell reported. "Of those, five moved out of province, one's in Winnipeg, and one's on vacation in Hawaii. One died in an accident five years ago. We tracked down the other four and they all say the same thing. Kowalski hated Daisy in high school."

Kate stood in the middle of Bert's office, arms wrapped around herself. Bert had left her alone to take the call and she'd put the Blackberry on speaker so she didn't have to hold it.

"Did they say why?" Headlights flashed by below, the tail end of the evening rush hour.

"It was all on Kowalski's side," said McKell. "According to the classmates, Kowalski competed against Daisy for everything. Boys, sports, roles in school plays. You name it, Kowalski wanted to do better than Daisy and never managed it. They called her Screw-Up Kowalski."

"What about Daisy?" asked Kate, rubbing her arms. She couldn't seem to warm up. "How did she react?" The petty rivalries of high school hardly seemed relevant, especially eight years after graduation. Who kept a grudge that long?

"She barely noticed," replied McKell. "According to the ones we spoke to, Daisy was the most popular girl in school and she treated Kowalski the same as she treated everyone else. Nice." He said the last word as if it dripped with venom.

Kate glanced at the phone on Bert's round table and frowned. It was the words that struck her more than McKell's tone. "I don't understand," she confessed. "Why would Kowalski hate Daisy if Daisy treated her well?"

He made a small sound at the other end and she heard papers rustling. "Beats me," he said. "But one of them... here it is... Barb Molloy. She said she thought Kowalski was being treated for some kind of mental condition while she was at school. She didn't know what."

Great, thought Kate. Just great.

* * *

By seven o'clock, Kate's stomach felt like it was lined with lead. She paced up and down in front of Bert's desk, trying to tune him out as he talked on his desk phone. He had tried to convince her to eat something, but the thought of food just made her feel worse.

There was no sign of Kowalski or her SUV in Winnipeg or in Mendenhall. Or anywhere else in southern Manitoba.

Should she have seen it? There had been clues. Kowalski's insistence on holding the exercise despite the brutal cold. Her increasing tension. Her obvious hatred of Daisy, which had started as far back as high school, apparently.

When had she first noticed Kowalski at the exercise? They'd been given the all clear by the HazMat guys. She'd been just about to head down to the site when Bert called her to say he was still in Winnipeg and was going to be late. Then she saw Kowalski walking toward her.

In her mind's eye, she saw Kowalski approach from the west. Not from the EMO tent. From the west.

In the dark, it would have been easy enough for the woman to slip away from the confusion and excitement. Maybe she didn't arrive with the other organizers. She must have driven Frank's car to where it had been found, half-hidden in the woods. Frank certainly hadn't been capable of driving. Then all she had to do was wait until it was almost time for the "victims" to arrive. She could have dragged Frank's unconscious body to the perimeter of the exercise and hurried back to the blocked-off highway to establish her presence and to wait.

And wait.

When she realized that no one had seen Frank, she snuck back down and mingled, hiding her identity, disguising her voice, and maneuvering Avramson and his men into stumbling across Frank. She was the one who volunteered to go find a medic. Kate had counted six people when she responded to Avramson's call, which meant that Kowalski had snuck back, sticking around long enough to learn that Frank was dead.

Then Avramson called Kate to inform her they had an extra victim. Kowalski was still there at first, which was why Kate had counted six people, but slipped away in the ensuing confusion.

Kowalski had waited too long to make sure Frank was found. Screw-up Kowalski.

Why had Kowalski drugged Frank? *How* had she drugged him? While he might have known her, Kate couldn't imagine Frank sharing a drink with Kowalski.

The transcripts of the text messages had come in, finally, but they didn't tell her anything they didn't already know. According to MTS, Frank had changed his phone number in the last couple of months. He wasn't much of a texter. Most of his messages had to do with confirming arrival or meeting times with friends, especially Ashley Mann. No, Frank didn't send many texts, but in the four-week period covered by the transcripts, he had received over sixty text messages from the same unknown caller. The texts had become more frequent in the last few days of Frank's life.

And nastier.

U can change ur # but ill always find u.
Ur wife is a whore and ur a fag.
I no where ur faggot lover lives.

That last one had been sent the night Frank Washburn died.

There was no way of finding out who had sent the texts, but Kate knew it was Kowalski. That last text had been calculated to send Frank running to Ashley Mann. At the time it was sent, Frank was at Assiniboine College's reception. Kowalski could have been at the same reception. It would be easy enough to check once they got the invitation list from the dean.

The Washburns had said Frank didn't know who his stalker was but that wasn't true. Frank might not have known Kowalski by name, but he'd known her by sight. He'd pointed her out to Mann.

Had Daisy known about the stalking? Had she known who the stalker was?

Why hadn't Frank gone to the police? They could have put a stop to the stalking—but she knew why. Kowalski would have made Frank's homosexuality public.

And Frank didn't want that. He was afraid of what the revelation would do to his career in small-town Mendenhall. Ashley Mann had said it: Frank was courageous, but not in this matter.

How had Kowalski slipped him the drug? Frank would have recognized her if he'd seen her.

Kate sighed. She knew how easy it was. She'd participated in awareness-raising campaigns where plain clothes cops walked into a bar and by the time they walked out, they'd placed coasters over a dozen drinks. The coasters were a warning that they could easily have slipped a drug in the unattended drink. Kowalski had found a way, obviously.

And then, before the drug took effect, she could have texted him that nasty last message, threatening Ashley Mann.

Kate went to the chair where she had flung her parka and pulled out her notebook from the inside pocket. She checked her notes of the interview with Dean Deverell. It worked out. The dean had overheard Frank talking on his cell, promising he'd be home soon. Frank had called Ashley Mann, not Daisy. He had called to make sure his lover was safe and to tell her he was on his way.

Kate jotted down a reminder to confirm if Alex Kowalski had been at the reception on Saturday night, but she knew she was right.

"All right," said Bert behind her. "Keep me posted."

She turned around, but the look on his face told her everything she needed to know. Still nothing. Bert looked grim as he walked toward her. "It's only a matter of time," he said.

He didn't try to touch her and she was grateful. She didn't say it, but they both knew that the more time went by, the less chance they had of finding Daisy alive.

She reached for her parka. "I have to get back to my people."

Bert put a hand on her arm. "Are you sure?" he said. "We're going to find her." His expression was grim and Kate suddenly remembered that he and Daisy were friends. She put a hand on his cheek and tried to smile, but it wouldn't come.

"I have to go," she said. Right now she couldn't afford to accept comfort from him. Right now she was the chief of police, not Katie Williams.

He saw it in her eyes and nodded. Without a word, he took the coat from her and held it while she slipped into it.

There was no telling where Kowalski had taken Daisy, but Kate's instincts were driving her now.

She had to get home.

CHAPTER 17

THE NUMBERS on the Explorer's thermometer dropped steadily the closer Kate got to Mendenhall. It was only eight o'clock and already minus twenty-seven. The car's heater blew hot air against her windshield and onto her feet, but she couldn't get warm.

As she left Winnipeg and its outskirts behind, she passed fewer and fewer cars, and more and more stars emerged. The moon hung in the sky like a crown jewel among diamond chips. The snow would squeak like styrofoam if you walked on it.

Her mittened hands clenched on the steering wheel. A few nights ago, Frank Washburn had been alive and well, hobnobbing with VIPs at a college function. Hours later, he was dead in the snow. She was presuming that Alex Kowalski was responsible for his death, but what if she was wrong? What if, in spite of Ashley Mann's statement, Daisy was not the understanding wife in a sham marriage? What if Daisy doped her husband, and when he was unable to defend himself, dragged him out the exercise site?

Daisy had been involved in all the tabletop exercises leading up to the real thing. She knew exactly when the volunteer victims were supposed to arrive. She knew how much time she had. And since Daisy wasn't participating in the actual exercise, no one would miss her if she didn't show up.

But Kate couldn't see it. For one thing, Daisy was too ambitious. She would never have risked her career, and political plans, by murdering her husband, even if she had been inclined to. And while Daisy was young and fit, Kate didn't think she had the strength to haul a hundred-and-eighty-five-pound man from his car, through the woods, and across the field.

Alexandra Kowalski did. And passion ran deep in Kowalski. Rage, resentment... Still, why now? What would have made her suddenly snap?

Her phone rang, startling her out of her troubled thoughts. She pulled over to the side of the highway to answer.

"Williams."

"It's McKell." He sounded far away and she turned the fan down to hear him better. Before she could say anything else, he continued. "We found Kowalski's CRV."

Her heart jumped and she leaned forward. "Was Daisy—?"

"Chief," he interrupted. Kate sat back. He never addressed her by her title if he could help it. "The CRV is parked in your driveway."

She forgot to breathe. Her foot twitched on the accelerator, revving the engine.

"Are you still there?" asked McKell.

"Tell me," she said shortly.

"Trepalli just drove by your house," said McKell. "He saw Kowalski's car and called it in."

Jesus. "Amanda..."

She heard him swallow at the other end. "According to Trepalli, her car is gone and the house is dark." He paused, then ploughed through. "Can you think of anywhere she might be?"

Kate shook her head. Amanda only knew Kate, and Kate's staff. "You have to search my house," she said grimly. She had a spare key in her desk drawer, but the office was fifteen minutes away from her house. "Break down the door if you have to."

"Yes, ma'am," said McKell.

"I'm half an hour outside Mendenhall," she said, her tone matching his. "Call me as soon as you've searched the house. And change the BOLO to Amanda's car," she said. "It's a green Tercel with Quebec plates."

"Already on it," said McKell.

* * *

The moment Kate walked in the door, Tattersall put up a hand to stop her. She stopped in front of the duty desk and waited for him to finish his phone call. McKell emerged from his office and came to stand next to her.

"There was a residential break-in on Stromberg Street," he said in a low voice. "Neighbor called it in. Said the owners are visiting their kids in Vancouver. I sent a patrol to check it out."

Kate nodded but couldn't say anything. She stared at Tattersall, willing him to finish his call.

"All right," said Tattersall finally. "Yes." He hung up and looked at Kate. "That was Paterson. The back door was jimmied open but there's no one there now." He took a deep breath. "They found blood on a dishcloth," he said softly.

Someone gasped and only then did Kate notice Charlotte at her desk. McKell had called everyone in. Half of them were patrolling in their private vehicles, looking for Amanda's Tercel.

Oh God, Amanda.

Don't go there, she warned herself. Not yet.

"That doesn't mean anything," said McKell crisply. He looked directly at Kate. "We get break-ins all the time."

Not all the time. Not on the same night two women were kidnapped, one of them her niece.

"My house?" she asked McKell.

"Nothing," he said grimly. "It looks like Amanda opened the door to her."

Kate closed her eyes tightly.

Don't think about what she would say to Rose if something happened to Amanda.

Then she opened her eyes. "Get your cold weather gear on," she told McKell. She brushed past Charlotte on her way to her office. "And bring the rifle."

"Where are we going?" he asked, turning to follow her progress.

"We're going to find that crazy bitch," she said. She glanced over her shoulder when Tattersall made a noise. "Get Trepalli and Friesen, Holmes and Martins to come in," she said grimly. "I'm not taking any chances."

She wouldn't put it past Kowalski to be monitoring the police radio. The woman had access to digital hand-helds and knew which bands they used.

She gave Tattersall a look and he immediately picked up the land line telephone.

* * *

The last time Kate had worn a vest, she had been shot. She gripped the steering wheel in an effort to control her trembling hands. The Explorer was parked off Burndale Road, not far from where they had found Frank's car. Now as she sat waiting for word, the ticking of the cooling engine was the only sound she heard— that, and her labored breathing.

The last time she had worn a vest, it had pinched her waist. Now it floated on her, but wouldn't for much longer thanks to Amanda's cooking.

Amanda, who, if Kate had anything to do with it, would live a long, happy life.

Clouds had rolled in, making the night even darker, but there was still enough light reflecting off the snow to show tracks in the snow.

She glanced at the clock. Everybody should be in position now.

As if called up by the thought, her cell phone rumbled on the seat. She picked it up and glanced at the screen. "TEAM 1 IN POSITION." That was Trepalli and Friesen.

Another rumble and she read, "DITTO TEAM 2." Martins and Holmes.

She waited another few minutes before McKell texted her. "IN POSITION."

Good. Martins and Friesen would approach the mock accident site from the east. There was cover of a sort in that direction: scrub brush, the occasional tree. Trepalli and Friesen had the trickier approach, from the Burndale Road to the west of the accident site. They had parked on the highway, well out of sight, and had approached on foot. They would keep to the trees until they saw her emerge from the forest.

McKell's position was a fir tree on the other side of the highway. He needed height. He had the department's only set of night goggles, to allow him to find Kowalski quickly.

He was a sharpshooter. He would shoot the bitch if necessary.

She worked her jaw to loosen the muscles. She had to stop clenching her teeth. She took a deep breath to calm the pounding of her heart.

Please be there.

She'd seen the doubt in McKell's eyes when she told him where they were going, but there had been no doubt in Kate's mind, then. This place was the beginning of the end for Kowalski. Everything had begun to unravel here. Her attempt to save her career had failed here. Her hatred for Daisy had led directly to Frank's death, here. Back at the station, Kate had been sure Kowalski would return here.

But now she wasn't so sure.

She flicked the ceiling light switch off so the light wouldn't automatically come on when she opened the Explorer's door. Then she eased the latch open and slid out, pushing the door closed silently behind her.

The wind snatched her breath away and she shuddered. Was Amanda dressed for this? Daisy? No, of course not. Daisy had been pulled from Mann's apartment. Kowalski hadn't stopped to let her fetch a coat. And Amanda?

Was Amanda still alive?

She pushed away from the car, refusing to consider the unthinkable. She had taken the long way around to approach the spot, knowing that Kowalski wouldn't be able to see her unless she was still in the trees. Kate had been so sure she would find Amanda's Tercel parked in the same spot as Washburn's car had been, just off the side road. But it wasn't there.

The moon gave enough light for her to see the mishmash of tracks left when the tow truck had pulled Washburn's car out. There was no telling if any of the tracks were the Tercel's.

There was no ditch to speak of. Kate followed a well-packed path toward the trees, peering into the darkness, hoping to catch sight of Amanda's car. She had left her hat in the car and the wind bit her ears, but she wasn't going back for it. She wanted to be able to hear clearly.

Her boots squeaked in the snow, despite her efforts to remain quiet. Then she saw a set of tire tracks that led away from the others and into the trees, and her stomach dropped. She automatically pulled her mitten off and reached under her parka, unhooking the cover of her holster and pulling the Glock out.

The metal immediately froze her hand and she dropped the gun into her parka pocket. She could reach it faster there.

The wind ruffled icy fingers through her hair and found the gaps at her neck and wrists. The wind was even more dangerous than the cold. It would hasten hypothermia.

She pushed deeper into the trees and there it was. The green Tercel. She glanced down but it was hard to tell how many sets of tracks were around the car. She approached it carefully, mindful that Kowalski was unpredictable, but there was no one inside.

That left the trunk. She pulled on the driver's door handle, half expecting it to be locked, but it opened, immediately flooding the interior with light. Kate located the trunk release button and pushed on it then quietly closed the door.

She waited, listening intently, but heard nothing but the wind. At last she forced her feet to carry her to the back of the car. Without giving herself a chance to hesitate, she pulled up the trunk lid.

The relief almost robbed her of strength. She had half expected to find Amanda's body in the car. But it was empty. It wasn't Amanda that Kowalski hated. Amanda was just collateral. Or maybe Kowalski wanted to hurt Amanda to punish Kate, like she wanted to hurt Frank to punish Daisy.

Stop it!

She wouldn't know what Kowalski's motivation was until she questioned her.

She took off her mitten again and placed her palm on the hood. Warm. Or at least, not frigid.

She pulled out her cell phone and fumblingly texted all three teams that she had found the car and was following the tracks into the woods. She slipped her freezing hand back into its mitten and followed the tracks toward the field, moving as quickly and silently as she could. It would be even slower going for Kowalski, punching through the snow, forcing two women ahead of her at gunpoint.

Why hadn't they jumped her? They were two strong young women, against one. Daisy was still recovering from the car accident, but her *life* was at stake. And Amanda... Amanda wasn't used to violence but surely she was capable of fighting for her life?

But Kowalski had drugged Frank. She'd used a drug that made a person act drunk. Made them unable to resist. Had she forced Amanda and Daisy to take the drug? Were they now unable to defend themselves?

Wait... was that voices?

She stopped moving, turning her head to pinpoint the sound. There! She strained to hear better, but the wind snatched the words away. It was definitely female voices.

She began moving again, heading for the voices, moving quickly, although she doubted she would be heard over the wind. She wanted to tell the others to get ready but there was no time.

Then a woman's voice rose high pitched and shrill above the soughing of the wind in the trees.

"No-o-o-o...!"

Kate jerked into a stumbling run just as a shot rang out. She broke through the trees to find two struggling figures silhouetted against the snow less than thirty feet away. Next to them, a third figure lay crumpled and unmoving in the snow.

Afterward, she would always revisit the scene like a series of black and white snapshots. The short figure fighting one-handed with the taller one to keep her gun hand away. The two figures paused on the Burndale Road, as if caught in mid-step, and the still, still figure lying in the snow.

She became aware that someone was screaming like a banshee.

She must have stopped screaming then because, between

one blink and the next, she was moving. She thought nothing, felt nothing. She was drive incarnate: drive to reach Kowalski; drive to stop Kowalski; drive to kill Kowalski.

Neither woman saw her coming. Later she would wonder how they hadn't heard her scream. Perhaps she had imagined that she had screamed. Kate caught a glimpse of Daisy's teeth-bared grimace as she twisted and turned in her effort to hang on to Kowalski's gun hand. She struggled to free her cast from its sling but they were moving too fast. Then the moonlight fell directly on Kowalski's hate-filled face, her clenched teeth, her raised fist.

The fist landed on Daisy's head and she dropped to the ground as if felled by a mallet. Still unaware of Kate's approach, Alexandra Kowalski raised the gun and pointed it at Daisy. She was growling, a sound that profoundly shocked Kate and brought her to her senses.

She wasn't going to make it in time. She was going to be too late. Even as she thought it, she launched herself at Kowalski and let loose with a blood-curdling yell filled with all the rage in her.

Kowalski jumped and turned, raising the gun toward Kate.

But she kept turning, spinning around in a graceful pirouette, her arms curling in towards her body, her head flung back as if in ecstasy. Then her knees buckled and she began to fall.

Only then did Kate hear the rifle shot and realize that she had seen a flash of light out of the corner of her eye. Her momentum carried her forward and she tripped over Kowalski's legs, sprawling face first in the frozen snow.

She struggled to her feet just as Friesen arrived, followed by Trepalli. Friesen bent over Kowalski and pulled the gun out of her grip. He put the safety on and then pushed away her scarf to feel for her pulse. But Kate could see it was too late. Kowalski's eyes were open, staring unseeingly up at the moon and the stars.

She turned toward the two other women just as Martins and Holmes arrived, breathing hard from running through unbroken, knee-deep snow.

Trepalli took his parka off and wrapped it around Amanda, and Friesen was already on the phone, calling for an ambulance.

Trepalli looked up at Kate, and even bleached by the moonlight, his face looked pale.

"She's been shot, Chief."

* * *

Kowalski wasn't dead.

The paramedic found a pulse and closed her eyes, even as he was calling out her blood pressure. Kate knelt in the snow next to Amanda, covering her hands with her own gloves, while Trepalli and Friesen wrapped her bare feet with their scarves.

Bare feet. Kowalski had taken her from the house and forced her into the killing cold in her bare feet.

Martins had wrapped Daisy in his own parka and she had sent him and Trepalli back to the patrol car while Friesen and Holmes helped the paramedics load first Kowalski then Amanda into the first ambulance.

Moments later, McKell came running down the embankment and across the open field to stumble to a stop next to her. He was breathing hard but the expression on his face told her what he wanted to know.

"They're all alive," she said.

He nodded in relief and although she felt numb, she remembered to put a hand on his arm and squeeze.

"Good job," she said. "Good job."

* * *

McKell's bullet had shattered Kowalski's right shoulder blade. It was an amazing shot, from that distance, at night. While it was a serious wound, it wasn't life-threatening. And yet, Kowalski didn't regain consciousness. When Kate saw her in the hospital emergency room, her eyes were open again but even so, Kate could tell she wasn't in there.

Daisy had a concussion from the blow and mild hypothermia but would recover.

The bullet had only grazed Amanda's scalp, but it had been enough to knock her out. What worried Kate most was the frostbite on her toes, even though the doctors assured her that there likely wouldn't be any permanent damage. Certainly she wasn't going to lose any of them.

How was she ever going to explain this to Rose?

* * *

"Mom, I'm fine," repeated Amanda patiently from her hospital bed. A pristine white bandage circled her head, making her bloodshot eyes stand out even more. "I just have a headache and they tell me that's going to go away soon." She glanced up at Kate. "No, it's my fault," she said firmly. "I didn't want Aunt Kate to call you until I was ready to talk to you myself." She pushed the breakfast tray away and sat up straighter in the bed. She hadn't touched her food, and her hands were shaking.

And there were still tracks on her face from all the crying she had done during the night. She hadn't smiled at Kate since coming to in the hospital.

Kate sighed softly and stood up, gathering her parka and her mittens from the second guest chair by Amanda's bed. The room had two beds but the other one was empty.

Rose was going to be very angry at her for putting her daughter in harm's way. And rightly so.

Last night, Amanda hadn't been so calm. Last night had been shock, followed by tears and rage, especially when she found out she had frostbite on her toes. Kate had held her and let her cry it out. Finally she had fallen asleep and Kate had gone back to the station.

She and McKell had debriefed the searchers and sent everyone home who wasn't on duty. Then Bert had called and she had retreated to her office.

"Hey," she said, absurdly happy to see his number on the display. "You're up late." It was past three in the morning.

"I've been waiting up," he said. "You're all right?"

"Yes," she said firmly. "It's been a long night and it's not over. How did you know…?"

"Charlotte. I keep her on retainer."

Kate laughed, but there was an odd note in his voice.

"Is everything all right at your end?"

"Oh sure," he said and now there was no disguising the

sarcasm. "I'm fine. I just love knowing that you were almost killed tonight, while I sat here, not able to do a damn thing about it."

Kate stayed silent for a long moment. All the pleasure had gone out of the conversation. This was exactly what she had been worried about. And the worse thing was, she knew she would have felt exactly the same way if he'd been in danger.

"I'm sorry you were worried, Bert," she said finally. She tried not to let sadness creep into her voice. "That's the job. It's part of me. You can't have one without the other." Suddenly, she felt sadder than she'd felt in many, many years and she had the horrible feeling that she might start crying herself. "Gotta go," she whispered. "They're calling me."

Without giving him a chance to reply, she ended the call. She sat there for a long time, finally allowing the tears to trickle down her cheeks. She didn't know what she was crying over—Amanda almost getting killed, the death of a good man, or the loss of a relationship that never got a chance.

Finally she had wiped her cheeks and turned her computer on to get started on her report. Bert tried calling a few times but she ignored his calls, knowing it was pointless to discuss it anymore.

Now she listened as Amanda tried to reassure her mother. Her niece glanced up and gave her a small wave. "Actually, Mom, I kind of like it here. I think there's a market for a good caterer..."

Kate closed the door and leaned back against it, fighting a sudden sense of alarm. Catering? Amanda was thinking of staying? In spite of everything?

That would be the end of her peaceful life, judging by the way she'd had to chase Trepalli and Friesen out of here a little while ago. If Amanda stayed, Kate was going to have a talk with those boys. And with Amanda.

With a sigh, she crossed the hallway—making way for a nurse's aide hauling the breakfast cart—and knocked on Daisy's door before pushing it open. To her surprise, McKell was there, standing awkwardly at the foot of Daisy's bed. The other bed in this room was empty, too.

"Chief," he nodded formally. He glanced at Daisy, who was

dressed in a pretty, flowered nightgown that Kate was sure was not standard issue.

Kate nodded an acknowledgement and turned back to Daisy. "How are you feeling?"

Daisy considered for a moment. "I've had better weeks."

She did look a little ragged around the edges, but considering she'd survived a two-vehicle collision, been kidnapped at gunpoint, and then been knocked out, that wasn't so surprising.

Not to mention the fact that her husband had been murdered.

All right. There would be time for sympathy later.

"Do you feel up to answering a few questions?" she asked.

Daisy started to nod, then clearly thought better of it. "Have a seat." She indicated the chairs next to her bed.

Kate dropped her parka and mittens on the empty bed before appropriating one of the chairs. "I don't know if you heard," she began as McKell took the chair next to hers, "but Alexandra Kowalski isn't dead." Contrary to what she had thought at first.

A series of emotions flitted over Daisy's face. Then she looked down at her hands clasped over her belly. "I did hear. They tell me she's not really conscious."

The shot seemed to send Kowalski into a catatonic state, which led the doctors to believe that Kowalski was schizophrenic.

Which would explain quite a bit, actually.

"She's catatonic," said Kate. "Which means I don't know when, if ever, we'll be able to interview her."

McKell stretched out his legs and took a deep breath. He must be as tired as she was.

The cart rattled outside their door and the nurse's aide came in to remove Daisy's tray. She frowned at Kate's coat on the empty bed but said nothing. She picked up the tray and asked Daisy if she was comfortable.

"Yes, thank you," said Daisy, smiling politely.

Kate glanced at her watch. Just past seven-thirty. She expected she had a few hours before the mayor and his wife showed. She wanted some answers before then.

"Miss, could you close the door behind you?" she asked. The

aide looked uncertainly at Daisy, who nodded, then winced in pain.

"And we'd appreciate no visitors for the next little while," added McKell. He smiled and the girl blushed.

"Yes, sir," she murmured and left the room, closing the door.

"Maybe you could start with where you were going on Sunday morning," said Kate.

Daisy looked blankly at her, then she closed her eyes. "I was going to Winnipeg," she said softly. "To tell Ashley."

McKell glanced at Kate. She had told him about the relationship between Mann and Frank Washburn.

Daisy opened her eyes to look at Kate. "I'd just heard about Frank," she said. Her eyes filled with tears. "I didn't want Ashley to be alone when she found out."

"She?" said McKell softly.

Daisy bristled. "Yes, 'she'," she said sharply.

"And it didn't bother you that "she" was having an affair with your husband?" There was the faintest trace of contempt in his voice, and Kate wasn't at all sure if it was part of his role as bad cop, or if it came out his true feelings.

Either way, Daisy didn't bite. She sighed. "Frank and I loved each other very much," she said. "We had everything in common. We loved spending time together. Unfortunately, we were the wrong gender for each other."

Kate blinked a few times, letting that sink in. Next to her, McKell grew very still.

"Are you saying you're a lesbian?" he finally asked. His voice sounded choked and Kate suddenly remembered that he blamed Daisy for the end of his marriage.

"Yes, Rob, I'm a big old mean lesbian," said Daisy mockingly. "And Frank was gay."

"So the marriage...?" said Kate, stepping in before McKell's shock turned to accusation.

"That's right," said Daisy. "We both wanted the 'respectability' "—she did air quotes around the word—"that marriage would bring for our careers, but we both knew it could end. Neither one of us was all that happy about lying to our friends and colleagues."

Something clicked inside Kate's mind. "The mayor knows," she said. She looked at Daisy. "He knows, doesn't he?"

Daisy looked surprised and went to nod but stopped herself in time. "Yes, he knows. It never bothered him, but he agreed to keep our secret."

Well, that explained why the man was so reticent.

"So you find out that Frank is dead and you get into an accident on your way to tell Ashley. Why did you leave the hospital against your doctor's wishes? Why go with Ashley?"

Daisy gave a small laugh. "Funny, isn't it? I got hurt trying to rescue her, but when she found out what happened, she ended up rescuing me. We spoke as soon as I was out of the coma and I begged her to come get me." Tears filled her eyes again and spilled over. "I knew Frank was here. In the building. I knew they had cut him open. I couldn't bear the thought of staying here, or going back home." She took a long, shuddering breath. "So Ashley came to get me and take me back with her."

McKell was fidgeting in his chair and Kate wished he'd stop. Then she thought of something.

"Wait," said Kate, putting a hand up. "How did you find out about Frank?" Kate learned that the dead man was Frank Washburn *after* Daisy's accident. How did Daisy know before she did?

Daisy's face grew somber. "A drama student from Brandon was one of your 'victims'," she said. "He saw Frank being loaded into the ambulance. He recognized him from a course Frank taught there last year and called to offer his condolences."

"Why didn't you tell anyone, or check for yourself?" asked Kate.

Daisy shook her head. Her eyes filled with tears. "I knew it was true. Ashley and I had been calling each other all night. We both knew something was wrong. And I thought you already knew."

They remained silent for a while, letting their thoughts settle.

Finally Daisy continued. "That was Tuesday," she said. "I spent the night at Ashley's. The next morning—was that yesterday?" At Kate's nod, she swallowed and continued. "I was in the kitchen getting myself a cup of coffee when someone knocked at Ash's door.

She told me she was expecting one of her neighbors to return a tray, but the next thing I knew there was a horrible sound and then Alex was in the kitchen. She had a gun." She gulped and clenched her hands into fists.

"She grabbed me and told me she'd shoot me if I yelled. Then I saw Ashley lying there, all bloody..." She trailed off in a whisper and Kate gave McKell a warning look. *Give her time to compose herself.* Finally, Daisy continued.

"She made me tape Ashley up. Then she took me by the back way and into the alley. She'd parked her car by the back door." She looked from Kate to McKell and back again. "She must have been there before. How else could she have figured out a way in past the security door? And she knew exactly where to go."

"She'd been stalking Frank," said Kate.

"What?" Dismay bloomed on Daisy's face. "Why didn't he tell me?"

Kate shrugged. There was no way of knowing now.

"Because that's exactly what she wanted him to do," said McKell unexpectedly.

They both turned to look at him.

"It wasn't Frank she was after," said McKell. He stared at Daisy as if she were thick headed. "Don't you get it? Kowalski was in love with you. As near as I can tell, she'd been obsessed with you since high school."

Daisy's mouth dropped open in astonishment and Kate's eyebrows tried to crawl off her forehead.

Finally Daisy closed her mouth. "She's not gay. I know gay and she's not gay."

McKell shrugged. "The woman was sick. And maybe she wasn't gay, but she had strong feelings for you. She swallowed them, and swallowed them until they ate her up."

At their blank looks, McKell leaned forward, resting his elbows on his knees. "All that stuff in high school—the competing against you. That was all an effort to attract your attention. She wanted you to notice her. And you never did."

Daisy looked horrified. "But why now? It's been eight years

since high school!"

Kate looked at McKell. He seemed to be doing well on his own. He shrugged again. "She was under a lot of stress at work. Her job was on the line with this exercise. I think it was seeing you at the tabletop exercises that brought it all back for her. What better way for her to finally get you to notice her than by going after Frank?"

Daisy put up a hand. "That doesn't make any sense."

"Think about it," said McKell. "You turn up at her tabletop exercise, successful in your career, happily married, clearly on your way up in the world. You were everything she wasn't. Everything she'd never be."

He stood up and began pacing. "I'm just guessing here, but she must have seen you with Frank and it was too much for her. She loved you and she hated you. I think drugging Frank was an impulse move, but once she'd done it, she was stuck. She had to get from the reception in Winnipeg to the exercise site, but what to do with Frank? So she brought him along, and dragged him close to the exercise site, believing we'd find him."

It made sense, in a weird, twisted way. As near as Kate could figure out, the harassing texts started soon after the first tabletop exercise. It was the trigger.

"But Frank didn't tell me about the stalking," said Daisy.

Kate nodded. "He didn't want you to worry," she said. "Him staying quiet must have enraged Kowalski. So she upped the ante by threatening Mann." Kowalski must have followed Frank for a while to find out about his affair with Ashley Mann.

A search of Kowalski's condo had found Ativan in her bathroom cabinet. It was prescribed to her, to relieve anxiety, according to her doctor.

They might never know just how Kowalski managed to slip Frank the drug. But she did.

"Why did she leave him there to die?" whispered Daisy.

McKell stopped pacing and faced Daisy. "She thought he'd be found in time," he said gently. "He'd be saved and wouldn't remember what had happened and she'd be safe."

"Oh God," whispered Daisy. "Frank." Then she looked up at

Kate in horror. "All because of me? Because she hated me...?"

"Worse," said McKell. "Because she loved you."

Kate snapped a frown at him. "Because she was sick," she said firmly. "You are not responsible for what she did."

"I could have been kinder to her," said Daisy softly. She shook her head again and groaned.

"Want me to call for a painkiller?" asked McKell. In spite of himself, he seemed to feel sympathy for her.

"No," said Daisy. "I'm fine as long as I don't move." She looked at Kate. "She wasn't making much sense, you know. She shot Amanda when she tried to fight and then broke into a house to find some bandages. All she ended up doing was mop up the blood and then we left again. She *carried* Amanda over her shoulder. I tried to convince her to leave Amanda at the house."

McKell looked at Kate.

"What I don't understand is why she came after your niece."

"I don't think she planned to take Amanda," said Daisy. "She knew that hiding her car at your house would buy her a few hours." She laughed mirthlessly. "Finding Amanda there was too good an opportunity. She made her drive. By then, nothing she was saying made sense. She was talking about stuff that happened in class, at her work... She seemed confused."

Kate looked down at her knees, trying to control the sudden surge of rage. It was over and done with. Amanda was safe. So was Daisy. And Alex Kowalski wouldn't hurt anyone ever again.

"Maybe I will take that painkiller now," said Daisy.

Kate stood up. She had what she needed for now.

* * *

The meal cart was gone when they emerged from Daisy's room. Kate looked up and down the hallway. This ward wasn't the same one Daisy had been on a few days ago. The nurses here were more relaxed and cheerful, so clearly, the patients on this ward didn't need constant attention. Which was a relief.

"Well, unless you need me," said McKell, looking down at her, "I'll go finish up my report."

Kate glanced at her watch. It was going on eight o'clock. She was bone tired, not to mention starving. "I think reports can wait until tomorrow," she said firmly. "Go home."

McKell grinned. He really *was* a handsome man sometimes. "I'll go home if you go home," he said.

Smart ass. "I'm just going to pop in and see Amanda, then I'll leave."

"Of course," he agreed, poker-faced.

What a jackass. But she found herself reluctantly grinning back. She knew she'd find him back at the station after she checked in on Amanda.

He turned and left, and Kate knocked at Amanda's door before pushing it open. Only then did she hear the deep rumble of a man's voice, but she couldn't see past the curtain drawn partway across the room.

"Come in," said Amanda cheerfully. Kate took a few steps in and stopped in surprise.

"Hello, Katie," said Bert with a smile. "I've just met your niece."

"Bert," she said. Squawked. "What are you doing here?"

He stood up and came toward her. He was dressed in jeans and a green sweater that brought out the copper in his eyes. The look he gave her quickened her breath and weakened her knees. Her lips parted and she took a small step back. He grinned rakishly. Then he had his hands on her shoulders and was drawing her to him so that she could feel his warm breath on her lips. He gazed at her, eye to eye, then he deliberately took her face in his hands and gave her a long, sensuous kiss that left her with no illusions as to what he was doing here.

When he pulled away, she just stared at him and something in her face made him smile with satisfaction.

"Aunt Kate, you didn't tell me you had a boyfriend!" said Amanda with delight from her bed. "Wait 'til I tell Mom!"

Dear God. Kate felt her face flame, but for the life of her, couldn't think of a single thing to say.

THE END

MENDENHALL MYSTERIES SERIES

The Shoeless Kid
The Tuxedoed Man
The Weeping Woman

About the Author

Marcelle Dubé grew up near Montreal. After trying out a number of different provinces—not to mention Belgium—she settled in the Yukon, where people still outnumber carnivores, but not by much. Her short fiction has appeared in a number of magazines and anthologies. Learn more about her at www.marcellemdube.com.

Made in the USA
Charleston, SC
07 August 2013